WHEN WE FALL

WHEN WE FALL

AOIFE CLIFFORD

Published in 2022 by Ultimo Press,
an imprint of Hardie Grant Publishing

Ultimo Press   Ultimo Press (London)
Gadigal Country   5th & 6th Floors
7, 45 Jones Street   52–54 Southwark Street
Ultimo, NSW 2007   London SE1 1UN
ultimopress.com.au

 A catalogue record for this
book is available from the
National Library of Australia

When We Fall
ISBN 978 1 76115 019 7 (paperback)

Cover design Design by Committee
Cover photograph John Gaffen / Alamy Stock Photo
Author photograph Courtesy of Nicholas Purcell
Text design Simon Paterson, Bookhouse
Typesetting Bookhouse, Sydney | 12/18.25 pt Simoncini Garamond
Copyeditor Ali Lavau
Proofreader Pamela Dunne

10 9 8 7 6 5 4 3 2 1

Printed in Australia by Griffin Press, part of Ovato, an Accredited ISO AS/NZS 14001 Environmental
Management System printer.

 The paper this book is printed on is certified against the
Forest Stewardship Council® Standards. Griffin Press holds
chain of custody certification SGSHK-COC-005088. FSC®
promotes environmentally responsible, socially beneficial and
economically viable management of the world's forests.

Ultimo Press acknowledges the Traditional Owners of the country on which we work,
the Gadigal people of the Eora nation and the Wurundjeri people of the Kulin nation,
and recognises their continuing connection to the land, waters and culture.
We pay our respects to their Elders past and present.

For the girl with raven hair, and the bearded king.
In memory of Lia Clifford and Ronan Lynch.

'I think he gets everything from novels,'
Taryn explained to Berger.
Berger was exasperated.
'Everyone gets everything from novels.'

The *Absolute Book* by Elizabeth Knox

Chapter 1

At the edge of the car park the path turned from compacted dirt to soft sand, ribbed with tufts of beach grass. Seagulls swooped overhead, wings outstretched, feathered angels. The old lighthouse stood proud further along the coast at Eden Point, a white scar in the granite sky. Alex experienced a curious sensation, as if it was watching her. She looked for her mother to ask if she felt it too, but Denny was already walking towards the dunes.

'Wait for me,' Alex called, but her mother just marched away.

Swapping her jacket for a hoodie in the back of the car, and then taking off her shoes, Alex Tillerson followed Denny down the hill to the beach, praying that no one would drive ten kilometres out of Merritt looking for a second-hand Toyota to steal, because she hadn't renewed the insurance yet.

The sand was cold beneath her feet as her mother receded into the distance, making her way towards the slate-black rocks at the headland. Denny's short grey hair was being pushed upwards by the wind into a spinnaker-shaped sail. Denny was shrinking in real life as well, diminished like a bird losing feathers. Her bones were as thin as a violin bow. At just over five feet, she could have curled up on her daughter's lap, childlike, tucking her head beneath Alex's chin, but theirs was a relationship best suited to carefully written emails that kept each other safely at arm's length.

Clumps of seaweed lined the high-tide mark. Alex rolled up her trousers and waded ankle-deep into the water, feeling the saltwater sting of the ocean. Part of her wanted to just keep walking. There were seventeen jars of Cottee's raspberry jam sitting in her mother's pantry. This morning Alex had lined them all up on the kitchen table and then explained she had made an appointment for an inspection at the assisted living facility in the next town. Denny had snuffled, pretending neither the appointment nor the jam was anything to do with her.

When Alex could no longer feel her toes, she hopped on the spot, stamping her mottled feet to get the blood circulating again. The phone in her pocket vibrated. Alex checked it, hoping it would be her clerk, Glenys MacCarthy, ringing about a new case, but the message was from Tom, her almost ex-husband.

We need to talk.

Not now, thought Alex. Perhaps not ever.

The wind picked up. She looked back at the lighthouse. Years ago, when she was small, her grandfather had promised to climb to the top of it with her. He said he knew the last keeper and could get the key from his son, but Denny had been infuriated and chucked Alex and their luggage into the car, driving away right before lunch was about to be served. Sunday roast dinner morphed into a Filet-o-Fish and strawberry thickshake, with Denny sitting opposite, swearing she would never, ever go back to Merritt again. Since then her mother had changed her mind about the town but not about the lighthouse. When Alex suggested driving up to it, Denny had insisted on a walk along Beacon Beach instead.

Turning to gaze in the other direction, Alex saw a stranger jogging along the sand towards her. Tall, broad-shouldered, dark-skinned, he skirted the shore, running along the crumbling edge of the sand's crust. Getting closer, he put up a hand in greeting, pulled out earbuds and slowed to a walk. Alex expected him to move past her, but he stopped, stretched and said hello in a way that was too cheery for this weather. She smiled in reply.

The man looked over his shoulder, pointing back the way he had come. 'You here with Denny?'

'Yes,' Alex said, surprised. 'I'm her daughter.'

'Just wanted to be sure. I know she doesn't drive anymore.' He smiled broadly, revealing a row of straight white teeth.

Tom had straight white teeth that always looked as if they were trying to sell you something.

'Alex isn't it? You're the barrister?'

She nodded.

'Denny's told me all about you. I'm Kiran Seth, your mum's doctor.'

Her mother actually liked him, which was nothing short of a miracle. As the daughter of a doctor, and being an ex-nurse herself, Denny had a lot of opinions about medics – most of them negative.

'You here visiting?'

'Just for a few days,' Alex explained. 'A trial settled so I had some free time.'

That was the euphemism she had come up with in the middle of the night. Kiran seemed to accept this, or had enough manners to pretend to believe it, at any rate.

'Denny suggested running out here,' he said. 'She told me it was relatively isolated so I could have a break from patients wanting a free consult.' Dark eyes crinkled as his smile widened into another grin.

Alex, who had opened her mouth to ask for advice about how to convince her mother that she really needed to sell her house and move into assisted living, choked down the question and instead muttered something about her mother understanding the perils of being a country doctor.

'Once a nurse, always a nurse, I guess,' he said, turning away from the wind to face the direction he had come from.

Once a pain, always a pain, thought Alex, but she managed to keep that to herself as well.

Kiran looked into the distance and frowned. He pointed behind her. 'She seemed fine when I passed her before, but . . .'

At the far end of the beach, Denny had reappeared, arms flailing, looking like she was screaming, though thankfully the wind had tossed the sound away.

Blinking, Alex pushed the hair out of her eyes. 'Just trying to get my attention!' She hoped that was true, and she raised a reluctant hand in reply. Denny kept beckoning with extravagant sweeps. 'I'd better go see what she wants.'

'Should I come?' Kiran asked. 'She seems a little agitated.'

Denny had found a stick now and was jabbing it into the air as if to declare battle.

'I'm sure she's fine,' said Alex, starting to walk up the beach. A shout from behind her.

'Sorry,' she called, turning. 'I missed that.'

'Nice to meet you,' said Kiran.

'Oh, you too.'

Alex followed the trail of footsteps Denny had made. 'So, where's the fire?' she asked when she got within her mother's hearing.

Denny's thin mouth betrayed her impatience. 'You should have run.'

Her mother's cross expression was so familiar, so uniquely her, that Alex felt a bubble of hope that perhaps the diagnosis was just a terrible mistake. A diagnosis she was still coming to terms with; a diagnosis her mother had known about for much longer.

'I was talking to your doctor. You gave him advice about running as well.'

'I found something,' her mother interrupted, and a look of childish delight flitted across her face. 'Over here.'

Denny seized Alex's wrist and darted forward, dragging her daughter with her. She was still physically fit.

They stopped at a nearby rock pool. Thick brown ribbons of bull kelp lay across the sand dragged in by the last tide.

'Look at this.' Denny stretched out a hand, pointing to a nest of it.

Alex expected to see a shell or a jellyfish but instead she saw a sneaker among the sinewy leaves.

Poking out of the sneaker was a severed leg.

Shocked, Alex looked away, her gaze immediately sliding back down to the safety of the shoe. It was so normal – blue, Adidas, wet and sand-encrusted – as if the owner had misplaced it on the beach and would be cursing themselves when they got home.

Blinking, she tried again.

The leg had large bruises visible under the light covering of sand, but it was the fact that the flesh ended mid-thigh that froze her brain. She couldn't think of what to do or say until Denny put an arm out to move the seaweed. Alex grabbed her wrist. 'Don't touch anything.'

Leaning over the leg, she unzipped her pocket to get out her phone.

'What are you doing?' Denny was annoyed now.

'Calling the police, of course.' Alex tried to remain calm, but her hand shook so much that she accidentally hit the camera first before she dialled triple zero. Tears welled in her eyes as she tried to describe what was in front of her to the matter-of-fact voice on the other end of the line. The emergency operator sounded like a bored telemarketer reading through a standard list of questions.

'Any identifying marks?' As if she got calls about severed legs most days of the week.

Alex forced herself to stare down at the leg. There was a mole under the kneecap and, just at the side of the anklebone, about half the size of her little finger, she caught sight of a tattoo. She crouched down to get a better look.

It was an exquisitely drawn black feather.

Prue drove out to take home a protesting Denny, who was furious at missing out on the excitement. Technically a cousin of Denny's, Prue had the kind of personality that meant half the town claimed her as their aunt, so Alex did as well. It was Prue who had been keeping an eye on Denny for her and had rung to say she needed to come visit her mother, that Denny was beginning to struggle.

Alex stayed behind to wait for the police. At first she did her best to avoid looking at the leg, to ignore it altogether. If there had been a nearby towel she would have carefully draped it over the pile of seaweed as a sign of respect. Perhaps she could use her hoodie? But she knew that the first rule of any investigation was to preserve any potential crime scene, so she left it alone.

No matter how hard she tried, over the next half-hour, her eyes kept darting towards it again and again. Alex had once been a junior on a murder case, had heard witness testimony about torture and seen the after-effects of violence, but this was the first time she had ever seen human remains in real life. It seemed so mundane and yet completely wrong at the same time. There was a woman on her netball team, Mattie, who worked at the state mortuary and cut up bodies for a living. Alex had always been curious about Mattie's job, but now, sitting beside human remains, all she could feel was revulsion, and she had to try to keep at bay the sort of irrational panic usually reserved for enormous hairy spiders. To distract herself, she googled what to do at a crime scene and was advised to shoot a video and write down her observations. That kept her busy for another twenty minutes.

By midday, with still no sign of the police, she was starting to get impatient and resentful. Thursday mornings must have more going on in Merritt than she realised. Still, she was a busy person who should be spending her time writing encouraging emails to her clerk, reminding her that she had capacity available for any new matters, or trying to convince her mother that assisted living centres were not gulags.

The sky changed from an indifferent grey to an effortless blue, empty of everything except the large golden coin of a sun. Alex moved upwind of the leg, worried it was going to start smelling. Her stomach wouldn't handle that.

Finally, the police siren's rising wail billowed on the air. Alex appreciated the suggestion it was still an emergency two hours after she had called it in, but even so, that seemed like overkill. A four-wheel drive, flashing lights and all, came barrelling across the sand between the waterline and high-tide mark, heading towards her.

'Hey,' she yelled, putting up her hands. Alex hadn't interfered with the crime scene for the last two hours; she wasn't about to watch someone else destroy it in a matter of seconds. She had heard of cases where the site was trampled on by off-duty police officers coming to have a gawk while their on-duty colleagues hadn't blinked an eye.

Running down the slope, almost floundering through the loose sand, she gestured wildly for the car to stop.

The four-wheel drive skidded to a halt about ten metres away.

'What do you think you're doing?' she shouted, all the morning's frustrations coming to the boil.

The driver was older, at least sixty, powerfully built, as substantial as a slab of beef. He had probably started life as a redhead but now his hair was as white as a cloth napkin at an expensive restaurant. This wasn't some rookie cop.

Alex found herself on the end of a hard stare as the man clambered out and stood there, taking in the crumpled hoodie, bare feet and dark wavy hair escaping from her disintegrating ponytail.

'I'm Senior Sergeant Kelly of Merritt Police Station.' The raspy voice demanded attention. 'And who exactly might you be?'

'Alex Tillerson,' she answered, even though she was contemplating returning that surname to Tom along with the divorce papers currently sitting on her kitchen table in the city.

Kelly shifted position, crossed his arms and stared at her. 'What are you doing here in Merritt, Ms Tillerson?'

Was he about to interrogate her? Surely, he couldn't think she'd dismembered someone, phoned the police to tell them about it and then waited around half the morning for them to turn up? Still, Alex had expected questions. In her experience, boss cops were like wolves: always territorial, always suspicious.

'I'm here visiting relatives.'

'You on holidays?'

'Working remotely.'

Which was possible, if there was any work.

Kelly gave a snort of derision, as if he had full knowledge of her bank statements and fee slips, but all he said was, 'Who are the relatives?'

'Denny Walker, my mother.'

Unexpectedly, the man chuckled. 'You're Denny's girl?'

'That's right.'

'Well, you've certainly inherited her temper.'

Alex tried to keep her inherited temper under control. 'Look, I've shot a video of the . . .' What was the best way to refer to it? 'Leg' seemed too blunt. 'Of the remains in situ, and I've recorded my observations. Tell me where to send them to and I'll let you get on with doing your job.'

The man ignored this and kept on talking. 'You should have said. Known your mother for a long time.'

'Actually, she's the one who found it. If you require her to make a statement, I can bring her into the station tomorrow.'

'A statement from you should be fine. You know, the last time I saw you . . .' And he held a hand to somewhere near his knee before hitching up his pants around a thickening belly. 'Oh well, better take a look.'

Kelly stood over the leg and stared at it for a long time, like he expected it to get up and start hopping down the beach of its own accord.

'Had the odd body before,' he said. 'Mostly drowned fishermen. Amazing how many of them can't swim.'

'It probably washed ashore last high tide,' said Alex. 'From the shape, size and the fact that the leg looks to be shaved, I'd suggest it's female.' She was doing her best to keep this interaction professional, but now that Kelly had taken charge she could feel the facade begin to slip and her mind raced to imagine the state of the rest of the body. Her stomach lurched in response. 'It must have been in the water for a little while,' she concluded.

'Bit messy round the thigh,' said Kelly. 'We have had a few shark sightings in the last couple of weeks. Might need to head out on a fishing trip.'

Had the poor woman been attacked by a shark? Forensics would determine what had happened to it and hopefully they'd be more thorough than Kelly.

'Anyone been reported missing in the last few days?' she asked.

'I'll get that checked.'

There was something dismissive about the way he said this, and all at once Alex wanted to push this man to give her answers, to fill in the blanks, to do this properly. The morning had been tipped off its axis, and she needed to right it again. 'There's a mole on the knee and a tattoo on the ankle,' she informed him. 'A black feather. That should help in identification.'

There was no discernible change to his expression, but an alertness appeared that wasn't there before, like a dog pricking up its ears, body all aquiver. Something she'd said had snagged his attention. Kelly squatted down on the sand and took a look. He stared at it wordlessly for a long time and then got up.

'Any ideas?' Alex asked.

He blinked and gave a quick nod but didn't volunteer any information.

In that moment, Alex changed her mind and decided not to press him. Right now this was still a random limb, but give it a name and it would transform into someone real.

Kelly looked at his phone. 'You can head off now. Nathan's on his way. Forensics shouldn't be far behind.'

'All right,' said Alex, relieved. 'Good luck . . .' She stumbled. Was that what you said in a situation like this, where good luck seemed to be missing? 'Um, with the investigation, I mean.'

'Good to see you, Alex,' he said. 'You tell your mother King Kelly said hello.'

King Kelly. That was a name you were unlikely to forget. Fingers crossed, Denny hadn't.

Another police car had arrived by the time Alex walked up the hill from the beach. A constable, male, mid-twenties, sandy hair in sweaty tufts, was running towards her and slowed down to talk. This must be the Nathan that Kelly had referred to.

'Don't know if you should be here, miss,' he called. 'This beach has been closed to the public.'

At least he was being more vigilant about keeping the crime scene uncontaminated.

'I'm the person who phoned it in,' Alex explained. 'Not what you expect to find on a morning walk.'

'Doesn't happen much around here, that's for sure.' Nathan gave an animated smile. 'Farm accidents, brawls at the pub, nicked farm equipment, stolen cows, you get plenty of those.'

'But no disembodied limbs,' said Alex.

Nathan shook his head. 'In my very first week here we had a murder, local girl found up at the Wyld, and I thought a rotation in Merritt might actually be exciting, but then nothing . . . until now.' It seemed like Nathan was relishing the prospect of looking for body parts. 'Anyway, sorry we're late. A bad crash between a truck and a couple of cars on the road to Durrell. Could barely work out the make of the car it was that badly wedged. Needed to wait for the crane and lifting equipment.'

Back when she was a solicitor, Alex had been involved in enough insurance cases concerning car accidents to imagine the metallic wrench of car roofs being peeled back to retrieve bodies and to smell the hot mixture of petrol, blood and flesh.

'Not a scratch on the truckie,' Nathan continued. 'High as a kite. Probably still doesn't realise what's happened. The people in the car weren't so lucky. Four dead, the youngest in nappies. Forensics are still up there.'

'That's awful,' said Alex.

'Carnage,' said Nathan, and he grinned.

Driving out of the car park a few minutes later, Alex decided on a whim to take the track that ran parallel to the beach. Trundling along, she could see the younger policeman sprinting across the sand in great determined strides. Kelly was still huddled next to the leg, head bowed. It was possible that he was studying the scene, but from her vantage point, it looked almost like he was praying.

Chapter 2

The breeze had picked up and clouds were emerging by the time Alex arrived at Prue's house. It would probably rain again later that afternoon and then on and off for the rest of the week. In a continent known for sun and desert, Merritt was a little wet patch of perpetual grey. Her narrow window of sunshine had been taken up with babysitting a body part.

The house, with whitewashed walls, narrow windows and a tiered corrugated-iron roof, was surrounded by a well-kept garden of established trees and flowerbeds. Alex didn't bother knocking on the front door; that was strictly for strangers, spruikers and proselytisers.

Tayla, nineteen years old, Prue's youngest child, was sitting in the back garden, painting her fingernails a fluorescent yellow. There were small jars of candy-coloured polish lined up on the tiles next to her like miniature spirit bottles in a hotel minibar.

Denny was lying in a hammock strung between two large apple trees, alone at the end of the garden. Alex waved to get her attention and was pretty sure Denny saw her. There was an adjustment of her head, a jutting of the chin, but then her mother turned in the other direction. She must still be annoyed about not being allowed to stay at the beach. Alex decided to postpone dealing with her until she had at least drunk a cup of tea. She'd catch her breath in a world where limbs stay attached to their owners and even got their nails painted.

'Need a spruce up?' asked Tayla. 'I've got time before my rehearsal, if you like.'

Alex suspected this was a pretext for gleaning information about what had happened with the police and declined.

'What's the rehearsal?'

'My band, Hatpin Panic.'

'Hatpin what?'

'Panic. It was a real thing. Suffragettes used hatpins to defend themselves. Men panicked about the hatpins.'

'And probably the suffragettes,' Alex said.

Tayla stretched out her arms like a cat unfurling. 'Anyway, we're playing at the climate change protest on Friday week. Only got two songs but we figure that should be enough.'

'You'll need a permit and marshals. It's official, right?'

That received the kind of late-teenage eye roll it probably deserved. 'There's a committee and everything.'

'Talked to the local police station about your route?'

'You really like rules, don't you? Don't worry, we know what we're doing.'

'There you are, Alex.' Prue Walker stood at the back door, her round face pensive. She was almost sixty, the same age as Denny. 'Did you get it all sorted?'

'Yeah, found out whose leg it is yet?' Tayla asked.

Alex glared at Prue, who had been sworn to secrecy.

'Don't blame Mum. Aunty Den told me about it in way too much detail. Besides, I reckon half the town will know by now. It's almost impossible to keep a secret in Merritt.'

'How do they work out who it is?' asked Prue. 'I don't suppose you can fingerprint toes?'

Tayla gave another withering look. She had quite the array of them. One for almost every sentence. 'God, Mum, it's DNA.'

'I wonder if there are any missing persons locally?' Prue asked.

'More like missing bits of person,' said Tayla. She fanned out the fingers of her left hand for them to admire her artwork.

'Eye-catching,' said Alex.

'It's very bright,' murmured her mother.

'DNA is so interesting,' said Tayla. 'At work, I had this idea that we could take people's saliva samples during check-ups and send it off for genetic testing. For a fee, of course.'

Tayla was the world's most reluctant dental hygienist.

'That's very entrepreneurial,' said Alex.

Prue gave a snort, muttered something about being busy in the kitchen, and headed back inside the house.

'Work didn't agree.' Tayla sighed. 'They said it would cause World War Three in town when men realised they'd been paying child support for someone else's kid, and the dental clinic would get in trouble for bringing the bad news.'

'That's a fair point.'

'Reckon I'll quit there anyway. Might go get an admin job at the Quirke Salmon Farm. They pay more.'

Here was another person having a career crisis.

Alex had heard the name Quirke before. He was some tech billionaire who had bought into Merritt in a big way, purchasing great swathes of land just outside town, as well as the salmon farm. Perhaps he might also have a need for underemployed barristers?

Tayla frowned with concentration as she assessed her left hand. 'Have you ever done one?' she asked Alex.

'My nails?'

'No, a DNA test.'

Instinctively, Alex's eyes flickered towards her mother, but there was no movement from the hammock. Prue saved her by yelling from inside, telling her to come in for some lunch.

The kitchen was large, built in the days when servants were assumed to be essential. Haphazardly cluttered with chairs, fruit bowls and drying laundry, at its centre was an ancient wooden table that could seat twelve people easily. Alex preferred this much happier place to her grandparents' house, which Denny had inherited.

A bowl of thick red soup and homemade bread sat out on the table, spoon alongside.

'You must be starving,' said Prue.

It was hours since she had eaten but Alex had lost her appetite.

'Sorry about the DNA stuff. Tayla always lets her imagination run away with her.'

'Don't worry about it,' said Alex, sitting down.

'Wouldn't blame you for being a bit curious,' Prue said. 'Perhaps you should try talking to Denny about it again, while she can still remember.'

The horrible inevitability of Denny's diagnosis. Alex had been devastated when her mother had eventually told her about it, no doubt prompted by Prue in the background. Still, it had helped to explain her mother's behaviour over the last couple of years. The fact that she had forgotten birthdays and other important events, hadn't been at all supportive when Alex had broken up with Tom. Her communication in general, which had never been great, had become even more sporadic and one-sided. At the time Alex had found her behaviour very upsetting, but now she felt guilty for not realising something was seriously wrong. The problem was that Denny had always been difficult; it was only now that she had a reason for it.

'You never know,' Prue said. 'Maybe she's waiting for you to bring up the subject.'

Alex shook her head. When she was younger, she had begged Denny to talk about it, but her mother had remained tight-lipped, saying it was just the two of them and that should be enough for her. The matter was not to be discussed. As she got older, Alex realised that pregnancies could be the result of violence and fear as well as the work of strangers and decided that perhaps it was better to remain ignorant.

She tried the soup. It was hot and burnt her mouth. She stirred it with her spoon and suddenly the colour reminded her of blood and she had to look away. 'Delicious, thanks.'

She was rewarded with a wide crooked smile from Prue. 'Tried to feed two bowlfuls to Denny. She's lost a lot of weight, you know.'

Alex nodded in agreement as Prue started fussing about in the kitchen. 'And trust your mother to go on a lovely beach walk and find something horrible.'

'I don't know if we can blame that on her,' replied Alex, though part of her was tempted.

'I'm glad you were there,' Prue said. 'It was right to call you, wasn't it? To tell you that you needed to come visit. I mean, Denny's always been so independent, hates to have to rely on anyone – even family – and I know how busy you are, and you've had your own troubles–'

'I'm glad you let me know,' Alex interrupted.

'Anyway, here you are. How are you?' Prue asked the words lightly but Alex knew what she was getting at.

'Fine,' Alex said. 'Everything is fine.'

'I was sorry to hear about Tom. Must have been hard for you.'

'It's had its moments.'

'Denny's delighted, of course; she never liked him. But, then, no one would be good enough for you in her eyes.'

Alex gave a thin smile. The whole relationship had been a whirlwind courtship. Sensible, practical, follow-the-rules Alex had decided to throw caution to the wind and be spontaneous, and look where it had got her. The fact her mother had warned her from the start only made it more mortifying.

'How long will you be in town?' Prue asked.

'A couple of weeks. Maybe longer, if that's what's needed.'

Prue smiled as if this was the answer she'd wanted. 'Merritt's really moving ahead, getting quite cosmopolitan. New cafes, investment coming into town. There's a commercial art gallery as well.'

'That sounds fancy.'

'Not my cup of tea.' Prue opened the fridge, removed a glass bowl of snow-peaked cream and put it next to a pavlova, the indented centre hazed with cracks. 'But my boss, Robyn, thinks it's wonderful.' Prue was a volunteer guide at the regional museum next to the library and took her responsibilities very seriously.

'Robyn's invited Maxine – that's the owner – to curate our next exhibition. Hopefully it's more popular than our current one. Hardly anyone's been through. I tried to take Denny to it after the beach, just to get an extra visitor number, and she refused point-blank to come in. Robyn even came out to the car to try and talk her round. Your mother wouldn't have a bar of it.'

Alex wasn't surprised. She had heard Denny's views about Robyn Edgeley. The grudges were longstanding. Incidents from childhood were starting to be regularly relitigated in her mother's mind.

Looking out the window, she noticed that her mother hadn't shifted at all. It was like she had sent herself into quarantine.

'I hope Mum has been behaving.'

'Tayla's pestering was getting on her nerves, so I sent her off for a rest. But Denny did mention something about a trip to the assisted living place up at Durrell.'

Alex caught a trace of accusation in her tone.

'We're checking it out tomorrow.'

'Durrell, of all places.' Prue clicked her tongue, half admonishing, as she brandished a spatula in one hand and began attacking the pavlova, layering the cream on thick.

Small-town rivalry ran deep.

'Now, you know I helped out with your grandmother, and I can help out with Den too. She was by herself for so long in some sort of self-exile from Merritt that I can't bear for her to be sent away again. There's no need for strangers – not yet.'

This was kind but not realistic. Alex pretended to be absorbed in the soup, which now only resembled itself, in order not to answer. She took a mouthful and then another.

Prue must have realised that she wasn't convincing Alex because she pivoted with her next sentence. 'We are all so proud of you – your mum as well, though she would never say it. I'm always telling people about my clever niece, the barrister.'

'I wish I was a lawyer in the city,' said Tayla, coming in from outside. 'Nothing exciting ever happens in Merritt. If it wasn't for Theo, I'd leave this dump tomorrow.'

'Merritt has its moments,' said Alex. 'Nathan seemed quite excited about today's discovery. Kelly not so much.'

'That Nathan!' Prue made a face. 'And Kingsley should be thinking about retirement. He's aged badly these last few years. Now he's married to Cath. She couldn't have children, so no grandchildren either, which is sad.'

Prue's conversations were like shopping trolleys, always taking unexpected detours.

'Not everyone wants to have children,' said Tayla. 'I wouldn't want to have King Kelly's babies. He's a sleaze.'

'And I'm sure Kingsley doesn't want to have children with you either.'

'I don't know about that. He fancied Bella Greggs. Kept coming to our basketball games, asking Bella if she needed a ride home.'

'Now, really,' said Prue. 'Leave that poor girl to rest in peace.'

Tayla sidled up next to her mother and ran her finger around the rim of the mostly empty bowl of cream. 'I saw it with my own eyes. He was always hanging around. It was gross.'

'For pity's sake, at least get a spoon,' Prue said, distracted. 'Bella Greggs died a few years back,' she explained to Alex. 'She was quite the miss, I don't mind saying. Always a great one for telling you her opinions and not that good about listening to others, but of course what happened was dreadful.'

'What Mum is trying to say is Bella was murdered,' Tayla interjected. 'They still haven't solved it.'

'I think Nathan mentioned that case to me,' Alex said. 'Was she the one found in the Wyld?'

The Wyld was the local nickname given to an area of wilderness a few kilometres outside of Merritt that included Jackson Falls and the river. Alex had a vague memory of seeing reports of a death online.

'It was terrible,' said Tayla. 'I mean, Bella could drive you crazy. Never shutting up about logging and old-growth forests. You'd buy a new top and get this lecture about working conditions in the third world. She was obsessed with global warming.'

'And here you are about to play at a climate change rally,' retorted Prue. 'Do you have any principles at all?'

'It's our first gig,' said Tayla, outraged. 'I wasn't going to turn it down. Anyway' – she turned back to Alex – 'Kelly was the one who found her.'

'Really?'

'He was part of the search party,' Prue pointed out. 'There's nothing suspicious about that.'

'Well, Silver heard at the pub that–'

'Tayla!' Her mother's mouth had drawn itself tight with disapproval. 'In fact, I was just hearing from Robyn, who got it from Maxine, that the police are putting in an application to try to get a reward to encourage people to come forward with information about the case. They're asking for a million dollars.'

'A million dollars!' Tayla squealed. Her face took on a calculating look, like she was trying to work out how she would spend it. 'I wish I knew what happened to Bella.'

'It is a shame that we need a reward system at all,' continued Prue firmly. 'People who know something should just tell the police, not expect to make a profit out of it.' She gave her daughter a hard look. 'The truth is never anything to hide from.'

'Exactly what I was saying about people's genetic history,' said Tayla.

'Well, that's different,' said Prue.

'I don't see why,' countered Tayla. She glanced down at her hand. 'Damn it, I smudged my nail.'

'You should have stayed still and let them dry,' said her mother. 'Patience is its own reward.'

Tayla turned and flounced back outside.

'Bring in the washing while you're out there,' her mother yelled after her.

Prue cleaned as Alex finished her soup. 'I should probably go out and check on Denny,' Alex said.

'See if she's ready for a big slice of afternoon tea.'

Alex walked outside to find Tayla lying on the sun lounge, out of sight of her mother. Tayla looked up at the sound of the banging door as Alex interlocked her fingers and stretched her arms over her head.

'I *do* know something about Bella's murder.' Tayla glanced at the back door as if checking that her mother wasn't nearby. 'Silver heard it from Dylan, who was part of the search party. He was with Kelly when they found the body. They were on the other side of the river, so Kelly had to swim across to her. He told Dylan to radio in the location but the radios and phones weren't working.'

'Reception is terrible around here,' said Alex.

Tayla ignored the interruption. 'Kelly was acting strange. He told Dylan to walk back up the river until he got a signal.'

'That doesn't seem odd.'

'Dylan reckoned that Kelly wanted to get rid of him, so he only pretended to head into the bush. He saw Kelly take something off her body!' Tayla made a superior sort of face, as if she knew that Alex couldn't just dismiss that out of hand.

'What was it?' asked Alex.

'A set of black wings.'

Instantly, Alex's mind was drawn back to the feathered tattoo on the leg. 'What?'

Tayla waved a set of yellow fluorescent-tipped fingers impatiently. 'They belonged to Bella. She made them out of chicken wire and feathers. Used to wear them at protests.'

'And they were black?' Alex wanted to make sure she'd heard correctly.

'Yeah.'

'And then what happened?'

'Dylan kept walking until he got a signal. By the time he returned, and the rescue party arrived, there were no black wings. No one ever mentioned them. You're a lawyer – that's dodgy, right?'

'That would be interfering with a criminal investigation and police misconduct,' said Alex.

'If I told the police about it, would I get some of that reward?'

Alex shook her head. 'I think you'd need a bit more evidence than just a conversation at the pub.'

Tayla gave an exasperated sigh and returned to examining her nails.

Denny was lying on the hammock, covered with a towel that Alex presumed had come from the nearby washing line. She looked like a small child tucked up in bed.

'Are you cold?' she asked. 'Come on, Prue wants you to have some pav. It looks delicious.'

She lifted the towel and held out a hand to assist her mother to stand. There was a wet patch on Denny's dress at crotch level, a faint smell of urine. Her mother was shivering and had the look of an animal that expected to be hit.

'Couldn't find the toilet,' she whispered. 'Couldn't find it anywhere.'

Today was one long line of problems, each of them being washed towards Alex on successive waves, impossible for her to ignore.

'Oh, Den.' Alex should have checked her when she arrived.

Using the towel, she attempted to pat Denny down and then, taking off her hoodie, she put it on her mother, who stood hunched and shrunken. The size difference between them meant it hung down far enough to cover the wet patch and would at least enable them to leave without the others guessing what had happened. She waved through the window at Prue, shouted goodbye and thanks, and got Denny into the car as quickly as she could.

Chapter 3

Alex dressed under the watchful eyes of the dead. She had packed only one set of lawyer clothes: a favourite red silk shirt and her lucky blue tailored suit. The stern faces of the yellowed photographs of forebears looked on with disapproval from their moulded wooden frames, as though her grandparents knew exactly what she was up to. If she was going to stay in this house another night, she needed to hide the pictures at the back of the wardrobe in the other room.

She had slept badly. An unknown thing had kept scampering across the tin roof. Alex had worried it was her conscience, and later in the night dreamt it was the severed leg, but then she always slept badly when she was worried. Kept awake by the anxious beating of her heart, waiting for the solace of dawn. Tom sleeping beside her, oblivious. Except this time she was utterly on her own and Tom was probably sleeping obliviously beside someone else.

The favourite red shirt was creased but she wouldn't bother trying to find the iron. She would just keep the jacket on.

It was for the best. Denny would come round to the idea eventually.

'Leaving in ten minutes,' she called, as she pinned her bun into place and then expertly slicked back the strands of stray flyaway hair.

No answer.

'Mum. Ten minutes.'

Alex looked at herself in the mirror. This was an outfit designed to convince Kathleen at the assisted living facility that she was a barrister with a lucrative practice, thank you very much, and therefore well able to afford the eye-watering amount of money required to have her mother properly looked after. This was the suit that would hide the reality of her threadbare bank account and non-existent cases and the fact that they would be rushing to sell her grandparents' house the moment her mother left in order to pay for Denny's care.

Out of habit, she checked her phone again for the third time that morning. No messages from her clerk.

She had heard other lawyers talk of inevitable career slumps, just part of the highs and lows of barrister life, when the phone stops ringing and the work dries up for no real reason, but it seemed less a coincidence and far more personal when it was directed at you. Sometimes, when she couldn't sleep, Alex wondered if it had to do with Tom. Whether she was losing her career in the divorce along with her confidence and sense of humour.

Walking out to the kitchen, she grabbed her handbag and reached for the car keys on the peg near the fridge.

They weren't there.

'Mum, do you know where the car keys are?'

Silence.

Denny had been on an unofficial campaign of non-cooperation, dressing herself under supervision only to deliberately spill breakfast down her top. Surely she had changed by now. Alex walked into the living room to see her mother sitting upright on the sofa, hands on knees. Denny had dressed for the occasion as well, wearing an old faded blue scarf, a worn brown corduroy jacket, teal dress with full skirt, black leggings and red ankle boots.

Alex sensed trouble.

'Have you seen the car keys?'

Denny gave Alex a blank stare. Her eyes were a startling green, all the better for looking like a wide-eyed innocent who had no idea what the problem was.

'We have to leave now or we're going to be late.'

Silence.

The next twenty minutes was spent frantically checking pockets and shaking out her handbag contents onto the kitchen table, opening drawers and slamming them shut, and then doing it all again, convinced that her eyes must be slipping past them. But the truth was some things got lost in this house (so far this visit a bank card, vegetable peeler, the remote for the stereo), never to be found again, whereas the jars of jam kept multiplying.

After another quarter of an hour had ticked by, Alex was reduced to checking the fridge and the microwave. Eventually she grabbed her phone and clicked through to the maps app to see exactly how late they would be if she smashed the side car window with a hammer, hot-wired the engine (how hard could it be?) and drove like the clappers.

The preferred route of the morning had turned from a benign blue to a deep pulsing red. The entire highway between the small town of Merritt and the larger town of Durrell was bleeding in both directions. It must be another bad car crash.

Alex wanted to scream with frustration, but that wasn't what responsible daughters did, so instead she rang Kathleen and apologised. Kathleen, brisk and businesslike, said that Fridays were never a good day to visit anyway and promised to get in contact with a new time. Then, because Alex couldn't face talking to her mother just yet, she sat outside on the front doorstep. Looking for a distraction, she googled 'feather tattoos'. Something about that severed leg bothered her. Probably the fact that it was severed. Still, what did a tattoo of a black feather mean? She was directed to an online tattoo encyclopedia that claimed some cultures believed a feather tattoo offered spiritual protection.

It hadn't done much for that poor person who'd lost their leg, Alex thought.

The post ended with: *See also 'bird', 'Icarus', 'wings'.*

There was nothing about human remains on the web – since the local paper had shut down, Merritt didn't seem to rate a mention anywhere – so she checked her emails instead. Glenys had sent her through the weekly payment summary. Taking a deep breath, she opened the attachment. A payment had come in: preparation for court documents for a trial that had been scheduled to last two weeks but instead had settled the day before it was supposed to begin. It would cover her chambers' rent this month but little else. Alex's last eighteen cases had all been settled. Could you even call yourself a barrister if you never get into court?

Payments by date, work billed, aged debt – all of them looked so dire that Alex closed her phone. Tayla wasn't the only one who could do with a financial injection of a million dollars.

She put the phone away and just sat there taking deep breaths. A memory came back to her of sitting in the exact same spot as a child, crying. It must have been the very last time they visited, a few years after the abandoned lunch. She would have been around eight. Denny had gone off somewhere with Prue, and Alex had been left alone with her grandparents. It was the only time she could remember that happening. Something had broken – a cup or a bowl, Alex couldn't remember now – and her grandfather had shouted at her. He called her a word she had heard in the playground but which she didn't quite understand the meaning of, only that it applied to her and was shameful. Alex had fled outside to wait for her mother. Denny had dark hair then; it didn't start going grey until her early fifties, and then it seemed to happen dramatically overnight. She could still picture the younger version of her mother opening the gate and walking up the path, sitting down next to her on the step and listening without interruption as Alex sniffled her way through the tale of woe. Denny was never one for hugs, kisses or comforting platitudes. There was nothing soft about her. When she finished, her mother said nothing but walked inside, packed up their belongings, and they had left again, never to come back.

'We don't need them,' Denny told Alex. 'You're all the family I need.' In the years that followed, Alex had chafed at the responsibility implicit in those words and then had eventually escaped by heading to university in the city.

The frustration that she felt towards the present-day Denny dissolved into sadness. Alex walked inside and found her mother still sitting on the couch, one fist clenched around hidden treasure.

'You win,' said Alex. 'We've missed the appointment. You can give them up now.' She held out her hand.

Denny let go of the car keys like dropping a pebble into a still lake.

Next time she would tell Denny they were going to the Durrell Botanical Gardens to look at the flowers and sleep with the keys under her pillow. She tried to think of something nice to say, wondered if she should reference that old memory to see what Denny would make of it.

'Let's go for a walk along Beacon Beach this morning,' her mother said.

'What?'

'Beacon Beach. You've been saying we could go on a walk ever since you arrived.'

If Denny couldn't remember yesterday, how could they talk about memories from thirty years ago? It was impossible and Alex decided against trying.

Luckily, they were both distracted by a text from Prue offering to take Denny out. While it was diplomatically phrased, Alex thought that the reason for yesterday's quick exit with her hoodie wrapped around Denny might not have been as well concealed as she'd hoped.

'I don't need babysitting,' Denny snapped. 'And it better not be going to Robyn's bloody exhibition.'

She remembered that much at least.

'Prue wants to take you out to a nice cafe.'

'So many cafes. Merritt is getting too fancy. New people keep arriving all the time.'

'Like me?' asked Alex.

'Not you,' huffed Denny. 'You belong here.'

Alex didn't see the point in arguing. 'I'm going to go and get changed for a run.' She could drop in at the police station to hand in the statement that she had written up last night and ask if they had identified the victim yet. Denny didn't need to know that.

'Running?' Denny looked at her suspiciously.

'I need to get fit in case you want me to run along the beach again.' It was meant as a half-joking reference to yesterday but Denny didn't react, as if that memory had been wiped clean.

Alex thought about reaching over and giving her mother a hug. They had never been a physically demonstrative family, but there were articles about how important physical contact was for dementia sufferers. Now that Denny seemed to be getting smaller and more helpless, Alex felt increasingly desperate about trying to tether her to the present.

Getting changed, she tucked her statement into the waistband of her leggings. Mercifully, the house keys were in the right spot and, yelling goodbye, she headed out the door. Standing on the front porch, stretching, Alex noticed one of the verandah posts was rotting. She pressed a finger against it. The wood felt soft and pulpy beneath the paint, like a warm Easter egg under shiny foil. The whole place was falling apart. Denny couldn't stay here.

Alex had never liked this house and still remembered how she would peep nervously around the doorframe at her grandfather sitting in the front room in his special chair (it was still there and Alex refused to sit in it) before running down the hall to the kitchen, where her grandmother would be worrying about what to cook for them while her mother glowered in the corner. The effort of pretending to be a happy family on those rare occasions they were together was so heavy that Alex could still feel the weight of it all these years later.

Alex jogged up the street, turned the corner and kept on moving until Fish Hook Bay came into view, the jutting headland dominating the vista. Running on the spot, she watched a rainbow shimmer and dance far out at sea before disappearing, the sea turning from blue to grey. She picked the dirt path that hugged the caravan park rather than heading onto the sand. Already her hamstrings disapproved and her breathing was laboured. It always felt like this at the start, Alex told herself.

Heart thumping loud enough to cover the white noise of the ocean, she headed up the hill towards the new playground. The treacherous metal affair she remembered from childhood (it could blister bare skin on contact during summer) had long ago disappeared, and instead there was an elaborate wooden structure in the shape of an old-fashioned schooner and a large lighthouse with ropes and a climbing frame.

Past the playground, along the boardwalk, getting into a rhythm now. People were fishing along the pier. A group of solemn-looking kayakers with black bands tied around their arms, sleek as seals, were in the water. Stopping to tie a shoelace, she watched as they headed out past the breakers, moving towards the mouth of the bay, skimming over the dark surface.

Turning inland, Alex manoeuvred her way through keen coffee drinkers milling around a shop called Rosie's. There were more cafes than Alex remembered. Denny was right about that, at least. In fact, the entire town centre was looking more upmarket, as Prue had described. She paused at the real estate agency, large photos of houses and blocks of land rotating in its double window. The prices made Alex stand still. They all seemed to have gained an extra zero. Denny would make some serious money if she could be convinced to sell.

Around the corner was the library and the local museum. A woman was out the front, briskly sweeping near the sandwich board that said OPEN one side and WHEN WE FALL on the other. Across the road, Alex saw the police station, a square concrete bunker with the familiar blue and white chequerboard trim, lurking on the far side of the supermarket car park. Tall Norfolk pines shaded one side of the building and birds had decorated the nearest wall in a splattered white paint impressionistic homage. Yesterday, Kelly hadn't been interested in her photos or statement, but Alex felt it was important to do things correctly. There was something about finding the remains that made her feel strangely involved. It was as if she shared some of the responsibility for reuniting the leg with its owner, even if the woman was dead.

'First I've heard of you.' The woman behind the reinforced glass looked suspicious, as if Alex had just asked to borrow a large amount of money. There was a name tag, identifying her as Julie O'Farrell, on her chest. Short, in her fifties, she must be an unsworn officer attached to the station, Alex figured.

'I spoke with Senior Sergeant Kelly yesterday,' Alex tried to explain. 'I was the first person on the scene.'

'I'll need to see some ID.' This was imparted through pursed lips.

'I only want to drop off a statement.'

'I still need to see a driver's licence,' Julie said tartly.

'I don't have it with me. I'm out for a run.'

The woman gave her a look that said, *Pull the other one, it's got bells on it.*

'Can I just speak to Senior Sergeant Kelly?'

A shake of the head as the woman shuffled some papers in front of her, not even looking at Alex now. 'He's not here.'

Alex cleared her throat, uncertain what to do next. From the corner of her eye, she could see an old guy sitting on a chair in the waiting room, the size of one jockey, the weight of two. He straightened up, like he was enjoying the exchange. His dress sense had more than a touch of racing identity about it, with a paisley tie, loud check jacket and a large gold signet ring on his pinkie.

'Could you phone him, please?' she asked Julie.

'Senior Sergeant Kelly is a very busy man.'

'I am also very busy and I insist you phone him,' said Alex, holding the other woman's gaze until Julie was uncomfortable enough to break it by looking away. It was the type of look that judges gave bumbling advocates, something Alex had experienced enough in her lifetime to reproduce.

'Sit over there then.' Julie waved a hand in the direction of the chairs.

A teenage boy was slumped on one chair, staring at his phone screen. His dirty blond hair hung over his face like he didn't want to be identified. Alex chose the seat nearer the flashily dressed man, who dropped the form guide he was reading onto his lap with a rustle. Up close, she could see his bald head was made up of patched skin grafts and a map of scars. Untidy chunks had been cut out of his nose and ears. Skin cancers, Alex guessed.

'Door bitch didn't let you pass go?'

Alex had to smother a smile. 'Not yet.'

'Me neither.' He leant back in the chair, a big grin on his face.

'What are you here for?' Alex asked.

'Mower's been nicked. John Deere, fifteen horsepower, almost brand-new. Some cheeky bugger took it straight out of my shed. I'll show you a picture.' The man got out his phone, clicked through and then presented her with a snapshot of him with a garden hose in his hand, standing next to a sparklingly clean mower.

'That's no good.'

'You're telling me. Not the first one to go missing in town. Been waiting here for over an hour.'

'Can't you just leave the details with . . . Julie?'

'And hear diddly-squat? No, thank you. I'm taking this straight to the boss man, whenever he decides to turn up. You see, I've got an idea who did it.' He was relishing having a captive audience. 'I'll say no names at this stage, but there are a few young fellas in this town who want a good kicking, if you ask me.'

The teenager glanced over, dark eyes lost in the hair like a tiger in the grass, and then returned to his screen.

'It's called mud-mowing, isn't that right, Curtis?' He addressed the boy opposite. 'Curtis knows all about it. Hot them up, put on dualies, and race each other out in the bush.'

Curtis shifted uncomfortably in his seat.

'Curtis here is waiting for Kelly to come back to give him some unofficial community service. Been running with the wrong crowd again, haven't you? Johnny Ewart and the rest. Only get you into trouble, mate.'

There was a rap on the glass. All three of them glanced up. Julie beckoned to Alex to come over.

'Special treatment,' said the old man, but not unpleasantly.

'Sorry about jumping the queue,' replied Alex.

The man picked up his form guide. 'Prepared to wait. Kingsley Kelly has been playing favourites in this town for far too long. I'm not letting it happen this time.'

Julie radiated disapproval as Alex approached the counter. 'Boss says to meet him at Rosie's coffee shop,' she said, her expression sour. 'Know where that is?'

'Yes,' said Alex. 'Thanks for all your help, Julie. I really appreciate it.'

Julie sniffed at the sarcasm.

Rosie's occupied the ground floor of an old gold rush–era building that had once been a bank. Generous arched windows had *Rosie's* written in an elegant font, soft pink outlined in black. The grand panelled front door was propped open.

Kelly sat in the corner booth near the window, back to the wall as he watched everyone come walking in the door. It was such a cop kind of move that Alex wanted to laugh. She waited in the middle of the cafe as he finished chatting to an older gentleman with round glasses and stooped shoulders, feeling like she was being ordered to come and pay public homage. It was tempting to drop the statement on the table and just walk off.

The old man nodded his head and said something about it being good to be back in Merritt as Kelly grinned broadly, reaching out to shake his hand. Platitudes about catching up soon were exchanged and then the old man began to move away.

'Take a seat,' called Kelly, using his foot to push out a chair for her.

Alex sat. From here, she could see through to a courtyard out the back, tables dotted around, set with mismatched plates and jumbled cutlery, which stood to attention in small wooden boxes. Large pots of herbs provided the greenery.

'I should have introduced you to Alby – Alby Sadler,' Kelly said, gesturing to the man making his way to a table outside. 'Your grandfather's old partner. One of the best doctors this district has ever seen. Just got home from working in Timor. You should let your mother know he's back in Merritt.'

Alex gave a noncommittal smile, hoping that Kelly would get to the point. She presumed he'd summoned her here for a reason.

'Grub's pretty good.' His wide smile stretched across his face but didn't get as far as his calculating grey eyes, underlined by bloodhound bags of skin. 'Bring us the food menus, love,' he called to a passing waitress wearing a black t-shirt and denim apron. 'I'm sure my friend here is hungry.'

'I'll just have a flat white,' Alex told her.

Kelly gave an if-you-insist type of shrug as a fat slice of Victoria sponge and another coffee arrived for him.

Briny air breezed in as her coffee arrived on the double.

'You'll find it's as good as any place in the city,' said Kelly.

Alex wouldn't have picked him for a coffee snob. She played along and took a sip. Better than she expected.

'Nice.'

Kelly looked so pleased he might as well have planted and roasted the beans himself. He speared a piece of the cake with his fork and gobbled it. A dribble of cream curdled at the corner of his mouth and was quickly wiped away.

'So, Alex,' he said, 'I hear you're a lawyer.'

This was hardly the work of a super sleuth. Like every barrister in the state, there was a photo of her on her clerk's website, perched on an expensive leather chair, in her best suit with a very carefully curated inventory of her achievements underneath.

Alex had met police who hated lawyers on principle. Lawyers were to blame for getting the crooks off, clogging up the system with appeals, being pedantic and not understanding the real world. She suspected Kelly might be one of these cops.

'We identified that leg,' he said.

She waited as he took another bite of the cake.

'A local girl, Maxine McFarlane. Taught art at the high school. She also started up that picture place on Hope Street.'

Maxine? Shocked, Alex realised that was the person Prue had mentioned yesterday. On her way to the cafe she had walked past her gallery, large modern artworks in the window.

'That poor woman. Any idea how it happened?' she asked.

'Won't have the autopsy for another couple of days, but Maxine was a keen sea kayaker, often went out by herself. Her boat's still missing. Probably got hit by a rogue wave. Dirk Gardiner found the rest of her body when he was out fishing.'

Alex felt a weird mixture of relief and sadness. She rested her elbow on the table and cupped her chin with her hand.

'Did no one notice she was missing?'

'Maxine had told people she was heading off down the coast to Kinsale for a few days. She'd been working pretty hard and wanted a break. Unfortunately, she must have gone out for a paddle before she left.'

'When was that?' Alex asked.

Kelly ignored the question. 'We've got a homicide detective from the city coming here to tell us how to do our jobs. He'll find it's an accident and then leave. A bloke called Karl Vandenburg. Heard of him?'

'I haven't been doing much criminal work lately.' She tried to say this in a manner that implied she was far too busy working on other matters.

Kelly stretched back in his seat. 'So, what sort of work do you do, Alex?'

'Bit of this, bit of that.' She took another sip of her coffee.

'You'll find Merritt a dull place after living in the city so long. Nothing much to interest a lawyer here.'

The friendliness of yesterday had disappeared. Kelly was trying to size her up, to work out if she was going to be a problem. Well, interrogation could work both ways. 'I wouldn't know about that,' she said. 'I've been hearing a bit about the Greggs murder. That sounded interesting. I understand you're applying for a million-dollar reward in the case.'

The reward did intrigue her. Not the amount, necessarily – quite a few unsolved murders had a million dollars attached – but the fact that the police were asking for a reward at all in a relatively recent case. The large rewards were mostly reserved for cold cases old enough to be considered frozen.

'One million dollars.' Kelly's jowls made it hard to distinguish chin from neck, gravity dragging them both down. 'The price we put on a murder these days. Not my idea.'

Alex had looked up the case last night after Denny had gone to bed. The lead detective had been Charlie Farinacci, a name she recognised. He was a poker buddy of Tom's. Initially, the case seemed unremarkable. Bella had gone out for the day but when she failed to return that night, her mother raised the alarm. An informal search party made up of locals assembled at first light to walk through the bushland near where Bella lived. The girl's body was found at the bottom of a ravine next to the Jackson River. As Tayla had told her, there was no mention of black wings, but there were references to Kingsley Kelly. He was the designated overseeing officer, which Alex understood was normally an operational role, not one that involved actually taking part in the search. As far as Alex could tell, no one had called in Bush Search and Rescue, park rangers, mounted police or helicopters. Instead, Kelly had just got the locals together. She'd already witnessed Kelly's unorthodox approach to the preservation of crime scenes. Perhaps he was just a cowboy.

Kelly took another forkful of cake and shoved it in. 'A reward, especially one of that size,' he said thickly, 'will just bring out the crazies and those stupid enough to think they'll make a quick buck out of it. It gets in the way of the investigation. Besides, those big rewards never even get paid out.' Agitated, he pointed his fork at her. 'The average one is a thousand bucks from Crime Stoppers for someone dobbing in their neighbour.'

'It could make the difference,' Alex countered. 'Even the act of publicising the reward could bring attention to the case. Someone might be prompted to tell the truth because of it.'

'The truth!' Kelly dropped his fork on the plate with a ringing clatter. At the till, the young waitress's head spun in their direction. 'All people want is someone to blame. Someone they can punish. An eye for an eye, that's what people want.'

'Surely it's more than that. People need the truth so they can move on with their lives.'

'Not families. The only people that move on are the detectives. They can finally close the file and move on to the next poor murdered soul or retire to play some golf. And don't give me that "the truth can set you free" bullshit. The truth sends you to jail and those psychos, if they are smart enough, know it. All a million dollars will do is encourage the con men and liars, and they tie up resources.'

Kelly was almost shouting now. Eyes in the room flickered in their direction and then turned away, as if they were used to Kelly pontificating.

'Anyway,' he continued in a lower rumble. 'Maxine's death was an accident. Thought you'd want to know that.'

'That's up to the homicide detective to decide,' said Alex, trying to keep her anger checked. 'Please let him know I expect to be contacted about my statement.' There was no point giving the statement to Kelly now, and she wasn't going to sit by and watch as the outcome of a case was determined before it had even been investigated. The dead woman deserved more attention than that.

Kelly pointed a finger at her. 'Merritt's not a place for the pedantic following of rules. You need to know when it's better to have a quiet word with someone than throw the rulebook.'

'This isn't some shoplifting charge we are talking about,' Alex argued. 'This is a possible murder. Rules need to be followed.'

Kelly shook his head in disgust. 'Country policing is a little different from working as a smart-arse lawyer in the city. Requires another level of judgement when you're part of the community, not separate from it. It isn't strangers you need to worry about here. Blood lines run deep and in unexpected places. Every victim, every accused, we'll know. Blink and the roles are swapped. The past runs alongside us all the time. Some days it spills right open.'

It was the speech he had probably delivered to every young cop who had to work with him. Alex had no idea why he thought he needed to give it to her.

Kelly stood up. 'Now, make sure you give Denny my regards. Tell her I remember the old times and I hope she does as well.'

There was something swimming underneath those words but Alex couldn't catch what it was.

Kelly caught the eye of the girl behind the counter. 'See you, Erin. The cake was excellent.'

'Bye, Mr Kelly,' said Erin. 'See you tomorrow.'

Alex took her time finishing her coffee. The other customers went back to their own conversations. She heard Maxine's name being mentioned again and again. The people at a nearby table were talking about organising a memorial for her down on the beach for late on Sunday.

At the counter she decided to take some Anzac biscuits home for her mother. It was the first biscuit Alex had learnt to cook in high school cooking classes and she had made them for Mother's Day about five years in a row during her teens. Would Denny remember?

Erin opened the jar and extracted the biscuits one by one with a pair of tongs, popping them in a brown paper bag and folding it neatly. Alex pulled out her phone to pay.

'And don't forget the flat white.'

'Oh no,' said Erin, pink-cheeked. 'You were with Mr Kelly. That's all been taken care of.'

Alex hesitated. 'There must be a mistake. He doesn't pay for me.'

Erin looked flustered and Alex realised a beat too late that Kelly didn't pay for anything in this shop. Perhaps Kelly didn't pay for much in this town. She put her phone down on the counter.

'I'll wait for a receipt.'

Chapter 4

The kayakers stood in a line on Merritt Beach with their paddles raised as the late afternoon sun turned the sky red. People gathered in tight knots around the boatshed. A group of teenagers were closer to the water, writing messages in the sand that would be washed away at high tide. A lone bird circled in the sky overhead calling mournfully. Alex threaded her way through the crowd to look at the large photograph of Maxine McFarlane on an art easel under the trees on the foreshore. A face to add to the leg. The fact that she could imagine this woman into pieces did not feel good.

The picture was a professional headshot, artfully lit, black background, black clothes, all to make Maxine's face stand out more. Plum lipstick covered a gentle smile. A slight touch of rouge emphasised her cheekbones. Her head was tilted slightly. A dark fringe had been gently swept in the same direction. Slight crow's feet radiated from the corner of each green eye. She was looking straight into the camera as if wanting to be engaged in conversation. It was an image of a woman who looked like nothing bad had ever happened to her and yet something awful had.

Prue had insisted that Alex should come to the memorial, that it was the right thing to do. To Alex's surprise, Denny and Tayla had agreed with her. Tayla walked barefoot at the water's edge, studying the love hearts and R.I.P.s etched in the sand, as she chatted to a serious-looking boy in a wetsuit who ambled beside her.

'We meet again,' said a voice behind Alex. The old guy from the police station. A wetsuit was peeled off to his waist, making him look like a leathery banana. 'I didn't introduce myself last time. Lou – Lou Buckley. I heard you were the one who found Maxine. That must have been rough.'

'Who told you?'

'Half the town is talking about your run-in with his nibs at Rosie's.' He waved his hand up the hill, towards the playground.

Glancing in that direction, Alex saw Kelly in his police uniform standing up there, arms folded. A tall man in a suit was next to him.

'That's the detective who's come to investigate. I've got to meet him at the boatshed in the morning, tell him what I think happened with Maxine. I'm president of the Sea Kayak Club, you see.'

'Kelly says it was an accident.'

'He also says my mower will magically turn up of its own accord. Doesn't mean it's true.'

Up on the foreshore, Kelly said something to the detective, who laughed and then pulled out his phone.

'If that detective seems all right, I might just mention my mower to him as well. See if he can put the boot up Kelly.'

'Any progress on that?'

'A solid lead,' Lou said, tapping the side of his nose. 'It's do-it-yourself policing around here. Catch you later for a chat after the ceremony? I've got a proposition to put to you.'

Alex wasn't sure she wanted to hear it, but she nodded all the same.

Denny and Prue sat on a large picnic blanket halfway along the beach. Prue was busy acknowledging friends and neighbours walking past. Denny was huddled against the cool sea breeze, her thoughts unknowable. Did she even remember finding poor Maxine's remains?

Alex looked up at the detective again – Karl Vandenburg, Kelly had said. He was still on the phone, pacing back and forth. She had been expecting a call from him to run through her statement. She considered introducing herself to him now to sort out a time, but Kelly seemed to be standing guard beside him and she didn't fancy another run-in.

There was the sound of singing.

'It's starting,' Prue said. 'We'll need to get a bit closer. Help your mother, Alex.'

Alex held out a hand, which Denny ignored as she clambered to her feet.

A lectern and microphone decorated with flowers had been set up at the front of the surf club. People held up phones to record the singer. She was a slim girl with lovely long red hair, accompanied only by an acoustic guitar and the sound of the ocean. Even the birds overhead, hidden in the Norfolk pines, hushed to listen to her. Alex caught sight of Lou standing at the roller door into the shed, wetsuit now fully on and a paddle in his hand.

The ceremony was short, heartfelt but odd all the same. There seemed to be no family present. No spouse or partner spoke. It became clear that Maxine didn't have kids. Instead, students from the high school talked about her being their favourite teacher, saying that Maxine was the sort of person that changed the way you looked at the world. That she always believed in her students and thought the best of people. One of the speakers dissolved into such hard crying that a woman standing nearby – another teacher, perhaps – put an arm around her shoulders and led her away as someone else finished the speech. Prue gave an audible sniffle and dabbed her eyes with a tissue.

Next, a solid older woman with a pixie cut and salon silver hair, a silk scarf with a geometric pattern knotted around her neck, approached the microphone with a look of grim determination. The pieces of paper in her hand fluttered in the breeze.

'That's Robyn, my supervisor at the museum,' Prue whispered to Alex.

Denny turned to look at Prue, eyes narrowed. She was a head shorter than those who surrounded them and had to stand on tiptoe to even glimpse the speakers. 'Robyn's talking? We'll be here all night.'

Alex gave her mother a sharp nudge to shut her up as a low chuckle came from behind them.

Robyn seemed like she'd be the last person to dissolve into tears over anything. Instead, she took people through a very detailed timeline of Maxine's artistic career. Apparently, Maxine had been very successful and selected pieces of hers had been sold to different collectors internationally. There was a murmur in the crowd at this and Alex sensed that people seemed genuinely surprised that their art teacher had made it big. Robyn finished on a rather curt note of hoping that the police investigated the death thoroughly.

A sense of pessimism seemed to linger as she finished her speech and took a step back. Alex looked up the hill: had Kelly heard? But he and the detective had now disappeared.

The final speaker was Lou, who talked about Maxine and the Sea Kayak Club like he was giving her a job reference. 'Dependable,' he told the crowd. 'Give her something to do and she'd see it through to the end. You could count on her.'

A local minister gave a blessing and most of the crowd mumbled Amen at the end.

'Thank goodness that's over with,' said Denny. 'I'm freezing.'

'Where was her family?' wondered Alex.

'Apparently, she had fallen out with them.' Prue picked up her handbag and the folded picnic rug. 'They didn't approve of her lifestyle. Robyn tells me that they're planning a private funeral back in Maxine's home town in Western Australia. That's why she organised this. I don't know if Maxine would have appreciated it. She was a shy person and only really had a few close friends in town. That girl who sang at the start, she worked for her at the gallery. Maxine was close to Sasha Greggs as well. Poor Sasha – another loss for her.' Prue gave a watery sigh.

'There's Tayla,' interrupted Denny.

Reluctantly, Tayla detached herself from a group of girls and came over. 'Silver's cancelled tonight's rehearsal. I'll probably go to Theo's instead.'

'Where is Theo?' asked Prue. 'I didn't get a chance to say hello to him.'

'He didn't want to stay,' said Tayla. 'This sort of thing is hard for him.'

'Understandable,' said her mother.

'Prue!' came a loud call.

Tayla groaned. 'It's Robyn. Let's pretend we didn't hear her.'

'Make a run for it,' said Denny, who clearly agreed, but Prue was already turning towards the voice.

'That was a lovely speech you gave,' she said to the woman who surged through the crowd like the prow of a ship through water.

Robyn acknowledged the praise with a nod of her head. Her sharply cut hair stood as an angular contrast to the roundness of the rest of her. 'I wanted to catch you.'

'Actually,' said Tayla, 'we were just leaving.'

'This won't take long,' said Robyn.

Prue fumbled through her bag and handed Tayla the car keys. 'Take Denny to the car and go order some fish and chips for tea. Hang on, I'll find my wallet for you.'

'I'll pay,' said Alex. She hadn't quite maxed out her credit cards.

'Actually,' said Robyn, turning to Alex, 'it was you that I wanted to talk to.'

A furtive expression crossed Prue's face, and her cheeks flushed red.

'Come on,' Tayla said to Denny, clearly delighted to escape. Denny needed no encouragement to abandon her daughter.

Robyn waited until they were out of earshot. 'Perhaps we should sit down over at the picnic tables.'

'Good idea,' agreed Prue, not catching Alex's eye.

The sun was setting. Families were heading home for dinner as Merritt dipped into shadows. One mother shouted to her kids to get out of the water, right now, if they knew what was good for them! Streetlights blinked on and Alex could just make out the silhouettes of Tayla and Denny heading into the takeaway on the other side of the Promenade. The Chinese restaurant next door was doing a roaring trade and loud music came cranking out from the pub. Informal memorials were good for business.

A group of teenagers sat at the first picnic table talking loudly, their faces illuminated by the blue light from the small screens in their hands. Alex thought she recognised the boy from the police station among the group. Nearby, a girl, all long legs and arms, was rotating on a swing in the playground, twisting the metal chain around and around and then spinning back the other way, both she and the swing squealing loudly.

The teenage version of Denny must have found Merritt a hard place to grow up in. Alex wasn't convinced it had improved that much in the years since.

Robyn gave the group a sour look and chose the table furthest away from them.

Alex sat across from her. Women like Robyn made her nervous, with their strong opinions and a generous disposition when it came to sharing them. From the serious looks on both the women's faces, Alex was getting the impression that this was some sort of interview for a job she probably didn't want.

'I understand you are a lawyer.'

'Not just a lawyer,' said Prue. 'A barrister.'

Perhaps Robyn was only after a quick bit of legal advice for free, an occupational hazard. Alex relaxed ever so slightly. What would it be? A dispute with a neighbour over a fence? Someone in the family getting a divorce? A young relative in trouble?

'Yes.'

'It's about Maxine,' said Robyn.

'Oh,' said Alex, taken aback. 'Well, that's really a police matter.'

'Unfortunately, they're part of the problem,' said Robyn. 'Kelly in particular.'

That wasn't surprising, but warning signs about being entangled in small-town politics flashed before her eyes. 'I'm not quite sure . . .' she began.

'You see . . .' murmured Prue.

'Maxine was murdered,' said Robyn, 'and it's connected to Bella Greggs's death.'

A small black feather tattoo and a pair of black wings floated into Alex's mind. Even though she had realised right from the beginning that murder was a possibility, it was still a shock to have someone state it as a bald fact. The discovery of Maxine's leg had affected her more than she had been prepared to admit. For one moment Alex just needed silence, so she could let Robyn's declaration sink in. Putting her elbows on the table, she rested her forehead on her hand. Then, swallowing hard, she composed herself and raised her head to look at Robyn. 'The police seem certain that it was an accident.'

'Kelly might genuinely think that, but he's wrong.'

'Then it definitely is a police matter.'

'Merritt doesn't work like that,' said Robyn. 'People here are a bit like trees, with roots deep in the earth, far more tangled than what's visible on the surface. We're connected, for better or worse. Saying that her death is an accident is much easier than investigating it properly and digging up things people would prefer to keep buried.'

The burbling from the nearby table got louder. One of the girls told a boy to get stuffed and marched away stiff-legged, arms swinging. A friend ran after her. Robyn kept her focus on Alex. 'You've met Kelly, you've seen what he's like. If we don't get that detective to listen, then it's going to be like Bella's case all over again.'

'Kelly isn't a bad man,' chided Prue. 'He really should have retired.'

'Stop making excuses, Prue,' snapped Robyn. 'He should have been sacked.'

'Then you should get whatever *evidence* you have and give it to Detective Vandenburg.' Alex hoped Robyn had noted her emphasis.

'The world doesn't listen to older women like Prue and me,' said Robyn.

The world didn't often listen to underemployed younger women either, Alex wanted to assure her.

'I don't understand what you think I can do about any of this.'

'All Robyn wants,' said Prue, 'is for you to listen to what she has to say. If you deem it important enough–'

'–then you take it to that detective,' interrupted Robyn. 'You're a professional, a barrister, he'll have to pay attention to you.

You'll know how to present it in a way to make him sit up and take notice.'

'Please, Alex, we need your help.' Her aunt reached across the table and patted Alex's hand. 'Maxine was a good person. She deserves a proper investigation.'

A nagging voice in Alex's mind reminded her that she already intended to talk to Vandenburg over her concerns about Kelly's attitude towards the case.

'You understand the legal system far better than we do,' finished Robyn, like it had already been decided.

That bit was definitely true. Alex could feel the mental cogs turning, thinking through options in her head as if this were a legal case being presented to her. The first thing was to find out what the autopsy report said. If that found it to be an accidental drowning, then no matter what Robyn thought it was case closed. If it found otherwise, then Vandenburg might even be grateful for information.

'And if I don't think it's evidence of anything criminal, that's where this will end.' Alex directed this at her aunt. It was important that Prue understood the limits of what could be done.

'Of course.' Prue smiled. Robyn gave a dubious half-nod.

There was the sound of smashing glass, followed by a chorus of swearing and hoots of laughter from the nearby table.

'Good,' said Robyn, standing up. 'I'll let you know when you can come to the museum and see the evidence for yourself.'

Alex waited until Robyn had walked all the way back to the clubhouse before addressing her aunt.

'Do you know what this evidence is supposed to be?'

Prue shook her head.

'But you believe that Maxine has been murdered?'

'I don't know,' said Prue. 'Robyn seems so sure.'

Alex suspected Robyn specialised in seeming sure.

'You could at least have warned me.'

'You might have refused.'

'Is it a good idea to get involved in this?'

'Alex, you found a bit of poor Maxine's body. You already are involved, whether you like it or not.'

It was impossible to say no to Prue.

'All right,' Alex said. 'I've got a friend who works at the state mortuary. I'll call her in the morning and ask about the post-mortem.'

Chapter 5

Different coughs filled the air, at times drowning out the endlessly excitable voice crackling from the radio debating whether a shark cull was needed. There was a deep-chested baritone, rich in mucus, from the elderly man in the corner. It competed with the tight-throated wheeze from the woman sitting across from Denny. A gummy-eyed toddler crawled around on the floor, ignored by his exhausted mother.

Alex wouldn't say she was fond of dead bodies – or body parts, for that matter – but they were infinitely preferable to sick people. There was no way she would ever have chosen to be a doctor like her grandfather or a nurse like her mother.

Denny sat next to her unperturbed, as if immune to other people's ailments. Today she wore a pair of blue-and-white-striped overalls and her hair stood on end. She looked like an electrocuted hedgehog.

This place had been her grandfather's surgery. Alex had never been inside before, even though Denny had worked here as a teenager, doing the cleaning, and then later on as the receptionist. That was to be her job for life, or at least until she got married to a nice local boy, but Denny had bolted instead.

Another woman, mid-sixties, faded blonde poodle-like hair, came in the door with an apologetic hello to the glum-looking receptionist sitting behind the high wooden counter.

'Oh, hello, Denise,' the lady said as she sat down across from Alex and her mother.

Denny gave the woman the sort of cool blank look that meant she hated her, or perhaps hadn't a clue who she was. No one called her mother by her full name. Alex, almost feeling sorry for the woman, introduced herself.

'Curl,' the woman said in reply. 'Carol, really, but with my hair . . .' This was accompanied by a nervous laugh as she pointed a finger at her head. 'I did Girl Guides with Denise.'

'Girl Guides?' Alex repeated.

'Oh, she wasn't there that long. Robyn Edgeley – she was our unit leader – caught her and some other girls smoking, so Denise was kicked out. Dr Walker, your grandfather, wasn't happy. You got a good hiding, didn't you, Denise?'

So that was why Denny hated Robyn. Alex shot a sideways look at her mother, who clicked her tongue in irritation.

'Pretty quiet for a Monday morning,' Curl said. 'Some days you come in here and you can't even find a chair.'

'Really?' murmured Alex. Curl seemed a determined talker who didn't need encouragement.

'You're a lawyer, aren't you, love?' Curl asked.

Alex could feel eyes around the room turn towards her. Even the consumptive child stared.

'That's right.'

'Criminal matters?'

'Sometimes,' Alex answered.

Curl stood up and moved to the seat next to Alex. Alex prayed she didn't have a cough as well. 'My Bernie's disappeared. Been gone this last week. Put up posters everywhere but no one's seen anything.'

Another missing person. 'Have you reported it?' asked Alex.

'Kingsley Kelly wouldn't be interested. He'd tell me to look for Bernie myself. Had him seven years.'

Denny muttered something derisively under her breath and Alex understood.

'Bernie is . . . ?' she prompted.

'A cockatiel,' explained Curl. 'Grey with cheddar cheeks. Such excellent company.' She pressed her lips together, her eyes suddenly shiny with tears.

Denny leant across, tapping Curl on the knee. 'She's a barrister, Carol. Only reason she'd be interested in Bernie was if he hopped out of his cage and pecked you to death. She'd probably want to defend him.'

Curl retreated into her chair at speed. 'What a terrible thing to say,' she exclaimed, wide-eyed. 'My poor Bernie.' Flustered, she turned her attention to the noticeboard and started pretending to read a poster about sexually transmitted diseases, recoiled again and picked up a pamphlet about government-subsidised annual immunisation shots.

'Was that necessary?' Alex murmured.

Denny ignored her.

Alex's phone buzzed. She glanced down at the screen and saw that it was Mattie Crannock. Alex had left a message for her first thing that morning.

The receptionist made a show of pointing to the sign saying, TURN YOUR MOBILE OFF.

'It's for work,' Alex assured her.

The receptionist gave her a sceptical look.

'Hang on, Mattie.' Turning to Denny she said, 'Won't be long,' then rose and crossed the room. As she opened the door to outside, she could hear the receptionist remarking on the hypocrisy of people who like to enforce the rules but couldn't be bothered to obey them, Denny loudly agreeing with her.

Alex walked up the path and sat on the low brick wall out the front of the surgery.

'Where have you been?' asked Mattie. 'Haven't seen you in ages.'

'I'm down the coast at the moment. Mum hasn't been well.'

'Sorry to hear that. I saw Tom the other day. Met his new girlfriend.' Mattie had the sort of tact that suited a job working with dead people.

'New girlfriend?' She shouldn't be surprised. Poor woman, whoever she was.

'You know – the one from morning telly.'

'From *television*?'

She knew Tom had been trying to build a practice in entertainment law as well as styling himself as a media commentator on legal matters, but this seemed an escalation.

'The blonde one who said some racist stuff on her socials and then cried so everyone would be nice to her.'

'Oh, her.' Alex could think of at least three women this could be. She'd have to create a fake identity and check out his Instagram account. Maybe she didn't feel that sorry for the new girlfriend after all.

'Anyway, which part of the coast?'

'Merritt,' said Alex. 'I was calling to–'

'That's a coincidence! I've just finished working on a body from there. It arrived a couple of days ago.'

'Um . . . yeah. I found it . . . well, part of it.'

There was silence on the other end of the phone and then, 'Should we be talking?' asked Mattie.

'Consider it off the record,' said Alex. 'C'mon, I had to babysit it for hours until the police showed up.'

'Cry me a river, Alex. I spend my day surrounded by dead bodies.'

Just the thought of that made Alex start to feel a little queasy.

'Look,' Mattie continued, 'I've finished the preliminary report. Still waiting on toxicology, but it's a possible homicide.'

Alex's breath caught in her throat. 'Not an accidental drowning?'

'It's not a drowning. There was no salt water in her lungs.'

Alex let this information tick over in her mind. 'Shark?'

'It's not a shark attack, despite the frenzied media speculation. Apparently, some local cop fed them that line and now talkback radio is yelling for the coroner to recommend a cull.'

'I just heard something about that,' said Alex.

'All the tried and noted fishermen from the villages near and far sort of thing,' said Mattie. 'I'm sorry to disappoint them. Fish might have had a nibble, but she was already dead.'

'How come the body was in pieces?' The idea that Maxine might have been tortured and dismembered made Alex feel even worse.

'It could be as simple as the body decomposing in the water. The buoyancy from the shoe would be enough to bring the leg up to the surface.'

That was something, at least, thought Alex. 'What killed her then?'

'She took a nasty blow to the head – fractured skull.'

The sick feeling came back in a rush. 'The body of a young woman called Bella Greggs was found near the Jackson River two years ago. Don't suppose you did that one?'

'Not mine,' said Mattie, 'but we all knew about it. One of those weird ones that gets discussed over lunch. Found in the middle of a national park but turned out she had drowned in the ocean. Not run of the mill, that's for sure.'

Drowned in the ocean? No one had said anything about that. Bella was found miles away from the ocean. She knew that the police often held back crucial facts from the public to help them distinguish genuine informers from the crazies and the conspiracy theorists. As Alex had always found it easier to get information from people by pretending that she knew it already, she tried not to react to this revelation.

'That's right. Salt water in her lungs. I mean' – and a thought occurred to her – 'it's like the opposite to the current case. A woman found dead in the ocean but didn't drown. They're the reverse of each other.'

'I guess so.' Mattie was beginning to sound uncomfortable. 'All off the record, remember.'

'How do you know Bella was murdered as opposed to an accidental drowning? Was there something else?'

There was murmuring in the background. 'That one was definitely murder,' Mattie replied. 'Suspicious bruising on her arms and body indicated she was being held down, and of course the body was then moved. Look, I've got to go. Let's catch up when you get back to the city.'

'Sure,' said Alex. 'And thanks.' But Mattie had already hung up.

Alex remained sitting on the wall, trying to think through the implications of what she had been told. It looked like Robyn was probably right about Maxine being murdered, but was she right about it being connected to Bella's death as well?

Her phone rang again. It was a private number so unlikely Mattie was ringing back, but it could be work. Please let it be a solicitor with a big juicy brief, Alex thought. She pressed the green button to accept the call.

'You've been avoiding me.' It was Tom, her almost ex-husband.

'Of course I haven't,' Alex lied, cursing herself for not letting it go to messages. 'I was just talking about you, in fact.'

'Saying nice things.'

Alex looked around. There was no one in hearing distance. 'Apparently your new girlfriend is a bit of a racist.'

There was a strangled cough on the other end of the phone. 'I think you'll find that it was all a terrible misunderstanding. Everyone knows Shantelle was taken out of context.'

Shantelle!

'What did you want to talk to me about?' Alex asked. 'I'm actually walking into a meeting.' She stood up, pretending she was doing exactly that.

'You've got a matter? Good for you. Glenys happened to mention that you'd been pretty quiet.'

This only confirmed her fears that the bar might not be big enough for both of them. She didn't want Tom to know anything about how her career was going unless she was number one on the list of best lawyers.

'What is it, Tom?' He'd better not be wanting to borrow money. His gambling was one of the reasons there had been so few marital assets to divide.

'The divorce papers. You still haven't signed them.'

That was true. It wasn't that Alex wanted to remain married to Tom; she just wasn't quite ready to admit that her marriage had failed so quickly. She had so badly wanted to be different from her mother, to have a lifelong stable relationship. Unfortunately, she'd backed the wrong horse. Something Tom also did on a regular basis.

'I need you to sign them, Alex.'

'Look, I'm away. I'll sign the moment I get home and then courier them around to you.'

'When are you back?'

'There isn't a firm date yet.' Which reminded her: she hadn't heard from Kathleen at the assisted living facility. Alex would have to call her today and make a new time to visit. 'Shouldn't be more than a week.'

'Where exactly are you?'

Alex decided to play the sympathy card. 'Merritt. Mum hasn't been well and I–'

But Tom interrupted her. 'We can meet halfway. I'll work it out and text you. I can't do it tomorrow or the next day, but Thursday could work. It'll have to be early.'

'Can't you just send them to me again?'

'No, let's do it Thursday.' Tom sounded impatient. 'There's something I need to tell you face to face.'

This wouldn't be good news. Alex took the phone away from her ear and pretended to check if she could possibly fit a meeting with Tom into her busy schedule.

'All right,' she said reluctantly, but then a genius idea occurred to her. 'Actually, there's something you can do for me.'

'What?'

An old woman was tottering down the path to the doctor's surgery on a walking frame. Alex felt a few drops of water on her hand and looked up. Fat grey clouds brooded overhead. She clambered over the wall and moved towards the far corner of the garden, sheltering underneath a tree.

'You still play poker with Charlie Farinacci, right?'

'Yeah, I know Charlie.'

'I need to know about a case he was involved in, the Bella Greggs murder. He was lead detective – just put in a reward application.'

'Why do you want to know about that?'

'It's related to a matter I'm working on.'

There were so many lies in this sentence that Alex would need to cross her fingers and toes to cover them.

'Since when do you run murder cases?'

'It's confidential.'

'So are police case notes.'

'Do you want those papers signed on Thursday or not?'

'You are seriously blackmailing me over our divorce.'

'Don't think of it as blackmail,' said Alex. 'More like quid pro quo.'

'A more suspicious person might think you were just making excuses to delay, that you might still have feelings for me.'

If he kept talking like this, Alex's only feelings would be homicidal.

'Send me a text in relation to Thursday,' she said. 'Got to go now, my meeting has started.'

She disconnected before he had the chance to reply.

'Doctor is waiting for you.' The receptionist put an acidic emphasis on each word and pointed to a door up the hall.

Alex knocked and then opened it.

'Sorry, Doctor,' she said. 'Urgent work call.'

'Kiran, please,' he answered. Today he was wearing dark trousers and an open-necked shirt. 'Denny was just telling me that she thinks the Donepezil is helping. Have you had any side effects?' Kiran asked, turning his attention back to her mother. 'Nausea, diarrhoea, weight loss, fatigue?'

Denny smiled brightly and shook her head. She was acting like a different woman in here. Alex couldn't work out if she was just putting on a brave face for the doctor or whether she really believed it.

'Loss of appetite,' Alex said.

'Nonsense,' scoffed Denny, frowning at her.

Kiran's brow furrowed. 'All right, let's keep the dosage as is for the time being and monitor the appetite issue. Now, sit up on the bed, Denny, so I can examine you.'

Blood pressure, heart rate and a chest examination. Kiran smiled and cajoled Denny through it. Denny told him about the leg on the beach.

'You ran straight past it.'

Kiran seemed relieved to have missed all the fuss.

Denny sat back beside the desk. Alex put out a comforting hand to touch her mother's leg, but her mother shied away, like an irritable teenager trying to avoid being comforted.

Kiran ran through a series of mental functioning questions. Denny was having a fair day cognitively and Alex wanted to clap when her mother finished.

'There have been presidents of the United States with allegedly worse scores,' Kiran said with a smile. 'We'll do your immunisation shot next visit, and at some stage we will need to talk about advanced care planning. I thought it would be good to raise that with you now as you might want to talk it over with Alex, so she knows your wishes. It's important for us to document how you would like your late-life care to be managed.'

Alex wasn't quite sure what this entailed, but when Denny didn't open her mouth, she offered, 'We were planning on visiting the assisted living facility up at Durrell to see if that might be an option.'

'That isn't what he's talking about,' snapped Denny, suddenly agitated. Alex could see red spots appearing high on her mother's cheeks. Between that and the hair, she could be mistaken for Bernie the missing cockatiel.

'Okay,' said Alex.

'And I said no to that place!' Denny stood up.

'Mum, I'm just wanting to get some information about it, that's all,' Alex said, attempting to placate her.

Generously, Kiran's gaze moved away from them and towards the window.

'I'll bloody decide where I live, not you or anyone else.' In a blaze of motion and fury, Denny stood and left the room, slamming the door behind her.

Alex sat there, mortified and furious at her mother.

Kiran cleared his throat. 'What I meant was more along the lines of attitude towards resuscitation, feeding tubes, that sort of thing. I just thought, given her professional background, she'd prefer to face it head on.'

'Oh,' said Alex. 'My mistake. Sorry.'

'Was that out of character for her?' the doctor asked. 'With younger onset dementia, heightened anxiety leading to outbursts is not uncommon, I'm afraid.'

Alex gave him a wan smile. 'To be honest, it was more of a signature move.'

'Anyway,' Kiran said, 'this gives me a chance to ask how you're going. It's important to check up on the carers.'

'I'm not really her carer,' Alex admitted. 'Mum's always been so independent.'

Kiran nodded.

'I'm still struggling with the diagnosis. Some days she seems completely fine, but then others aren't as good. I'm in a bit of a lull at work at the moment . . .'

Why was she telling him this?

'. . . and I thought we should use that time to make plans for the future.' And then, worried she sounded callous, 'Of course,

I'm happy for her to live independently as long as she can safely do so, but . . .'

The truth was Alex liked plans and rules and certainty, all things that Denny didn't want a bar of.

'These are difficult conversations,' Kiran acknowledged, 'but it's important to have them. Your mother is a brave woman who faces her situation head on when she talks to me. I know she doesn't want to be a burden on anyone, but there will come a time when she'll need twenty-four-hour care. And you're definitely doing the right thing by enjoying the time you have left with her.'

Enjoying time with Denny wasn't quite how Alex would describe it. There had always been an electric spark to her mother, like foil in a microwave, that meant in recent years it had been easier to keep her at a distance.

'Running your own business must be stressful,' he said.

'Not as stressful as dealing with sick people.'

'It's nice to get to know the patients, like your mother. Some of them have become good friends.'

Alex wanted to linger, to ask this man more questions about the town, her mother, whatever she could think of, but she forced herself to stand.

'I should let you get to the next patient.'

'Just so you know, I work one day a week up at Durrell Hospital, so I've treated some of the residents from the assisted living centre there. They seem well cared for. There's a good ratio of carers and qualified nurses working around the clock.'

'That's reassuring,' said Alex.

'I'm sorry about what happened on the beach,' he said. 'It must have been quite upsetting. Hopefully the rest of your time in Merritt will be more relaxing.'

'I hope so,' said Alex.

'Rosie's makes the best coffee, and counter meals at the Sail are worth checking out. Maybe I'll see you there sometime.'

This sounded genuine rather than just a throwaway remark.

'That would be nice,' said Alex.

Chapter 6

The next day, Lou was standing outside the front of the boatshed when Alex arrived. No wetsuit today, instead he wore a pork-pie hat with a natty purple polka-dot hanky poking out of his jacket pocket.

'Just the girl I wanted to see.' He grinned broadly.

Lou was just the man Alex wanted to talk to. She needed to find out as much as she could about Vandenburg before she met him so had decided to track down Lou to hear how his interview had gone. She had already left several messages for the detective via Julie, but he hadn't bothered to get in touch. Likewise, there had been no reply from Kathleen about a new appointment. She was turning into one of those people whose calls were never returned.

'Why?' Alex asked.

'Word is you're a top-notch barrister.'

Nothing spreads faster in country towns than the inaccurate boasting of relatives.

'You must have some juicy stories to tell,' said Lou.

'Not really.'

'I came up with the idea of having talks once a month, charge a few bob as a fundraiser for the Sea Kayak Club. Locals love them. Last one was a female true-crime author – could have filled the hall twice over. Bloody good books, too. I've read a couple. All about crooked cops and dodgy lawyers.' Lou chuckled, displaying two gold fillings. 'We could do with a legal eagle's perspective. We've had two murders in Merritt now. People want to know more. Understand the psychology of a killer. I reckon we'd get most of the town along and it's for a good cause. We're a great little club. You'd have seen that the other night at Maxine's memorial.'

'I've only been a junior on one murder case,' Alex began, 'and even that ended in a plea.'

'Perfect,' he said. 'You can tell us all about that and any other story you've heard.'

Alex needed to stop this before Lou started handing out flyers and organising the sausage rolls and urns of tea, but she couldn't help noticing that Lou had assumed Maxine's death was a murder.

'You said in your speech that Maxine McFarlane was on the club committee.'

'She was,' he answered. 'Took over from Kingsley Kelly actually. Which means he should know better than to be going around saying that what happened to Maxine was an accident.'

So Kelly was still doing that, despite the autopsy results.

'How do you know it wasn't?'

'Her kayak might have gone out on the water, but I can guarantee she wasn't in it. I've already told that to the detective. Not the sharpest tool in the shed, if you ask me. Told me they haven't found her boat yet and then had the hide to quiz me about our water safety procedures and training! I reckon Kelly put him up to it to get back at me making a fuss about my mower.'

'But how can you be sure she was murdered?'

'Waters round here are dangerous; Maxine knew that as well as anyone else. Wind can come straight out of nowhere, storms come through all the bloody time.'

A couple of women walked past clad in exercise gear and sneakers, arms pumping, chatting loudly. Lou yelled out a hello. They flapped their hands back at him.

'Need rescuing, love?' one of them called to Alex.

'Don't believe a word that comes out of his mouth,' said the other. 'Especially if it's about the greyhounds. Lose your shirt with his tips.'

Lou put his hands on his heart and staggered as if he had been mortally wounded.

Laughing, they power-walked off in the direction of the shops.

'Maxine took her safety seriously,' he continued. 'All clubs have their cowboys who just wing it, but that wasn't her. Now you tell me, where was the float plan? As far as I can make out, she told no one she was going for a kayak and I've checked with every single person in the club.'

Lou had obviously taken Vandenburg's questioning of the club's safety protocols as a personal insult.

'Couldn't she have just forgotten this time? Spur-of-the-moment decision?'

'All right,' conceded Lou, 'but what about the paddle?'

'The paddle?'

'The one that's still missing along with her boat. I'm telling you, it's the wrong one. Maxine kept a paddle down in the shed, a fibreglass one. It's still there. One of our rubbish beginner ones is what was taken. They're kept up close to where her kayak was stored.' Lou pointed into the darkness of the clubhouse behind him. Alex could see kayaks sitting in a metal frame, all in rows like bottles in a wine rack.

'Max would never grab one of those by accident, not when she could use her own. That's why I initially thought Maxine's kayak must have been stolen.'

'Did Maxine own other paddles?'

Lou nodded. 'There's a snazzy carbon fibre one – ridiculously overpriced, they are. Kept that at her house to stop it from being pilfered.'

'Couldn't she have used that? Is that one missing?'

An extravagant gesture involving arms and mouth. 'But then why is a *beginner* paddle missing? I asked the fancy city detective that and got no answer. But just say for argument's sake she did take out her special paddle' – Lou pointed a finger at her – 'then it's not a spur-of-the-moment decision to go out. If she has long enough to go home and get that paddle, then she had enough time to do her plan. All she had to do was text it through. There's a system in place.'

Part of her could understand why Vandenburg might not have paid Lou much heed, but perhaps there was a kernel here that warranted further investigation.

As if on cue, the police four-wheel drive went past. Kelly was at the wheel.

'There he is,' said Lou, 'out on patrol. Doing nothing about Maxine and nothing about my mower. I'll just have to head in tomorrow with a packed lunch and camp out in the waiting room until Senior Sergeant Big Boss Man deigns to see me, because Dylan Ferris is not going to get away with it, not this time. You think about the speech, love. I'll even throw a few bob your way for being the speaker, can't say fairer than that.'

Maybe she should consider it after all.

Kelly was putting his thumb on the scale of this investigation and Vandenburg was listening to him. Why? Alex wasn't naive about delivering justice. Police investigations went wrong all the time, but not right in front of her eyes. She had drawn up a mental list of people she would talk to if she was Vandenburg, and Dirk Gardiner, who had found Maxine's body (minus a leg) was at the top of that list.

Waves darted across Fish Hook Bay like yapping dogs. Swaying boat masts emitted an eerie metallic song. A storm threatened and the chilly air that preceded it grabbed at Alex's t-shirt and hair. Walking down the jetty, she passed a young, broad-shouldered man washing down an expensive-looking boat. There were untidy brown curls poking out from under his beanie. The polar fleece he was wearing had a QI logo on its chest.

'I'm looking for Dirk Gardiner,' Alex said. 'Do you know if he's about?'

'You're in luck,' he said. 'That's Dirk coming in now.'

An old fishing trawler, grey with a faded hull, chugged towards the wharf, a man in the open-air cab guiding the boat in. He was large, in grubby waterproofs, a faded denim cap on his head.

Alex waved to get his attention. She had to call out several times before he even looked in her direction. Frowning, he cut the engine and then started to fasten the mooring line.

'Hello there,' she said again.

He turned away to pull the tarp over large boxes, muttering something. Waves slapped the side and the boat teetered, but the man was nimble in his black gumboots. He began coiling a thick rope.

'Excuse me,' she said, addressing the man's back now. 'Are you Dirk Gardiner?'

He turned around. 'Who wants to know?'

'I'm Alex Tillerson. I was wondering if I could ask you a few questions, Mr Gardiner.'

He leered at her, exposing nicotine-stained teeth, some of which had been worn down to little more than stumps.

'Good job is it, walking around and asking questions? What's the pay like?'

Alex had to laugh despite herself. 'Not as good as fishing.'

'Not a fisherman anymore,' he said. 'I'm retired.'

A pungent smell of oil and fish came up from the grimy slick in the bottom of the boat. 'Are you sure about that?'

Gardiner turned on her. 'You here about my bloody fishing licence? You working for Quirke? Already got the letter from his lawyer. That fucker has everyone in his pocket.' Gardiner jerked an angry thumb in the direction of the first boat she'd stopped at. 'How about checking out the salmon farm? Killing the bay, but no one cares about that.'

'Quirke's Salmon Farm?' she asked, trying to decipher what he was angry about.

'Not just the salmon farm. He poisons everything. Might as well change Merritt's name to Quirkeville. Everyone's falling over themselves to get on Mr Bloody-High-and-Mighty's money teat. That salmon farm is an environmental disaster and he's got the gall to come chasing after me. What's the world coming to when a man can't even fish? It's bloody criminal.'

'I thought you said you'd retired.'

An anxious look scudded across his face but was quickly replaced by one more cunning.

'So I have. Tourist operator now. Could show you the sights. Bit of whale watching in season . . . dolphins . . . Get the bird obsessives, too – especially when the shearwaters are here.'

It was time to come clean. 'I'm not here about your fishing licence. You found Maxine McFarlane's body.'

That pulled Gardiner up short. He stared at her and then rested a stained boot up on the side of the boat.

'Not a pretty sight,' he said. 'Didn't smell good neither. What are you, a cop?'

'No.'

'Then why are you interested?'

'Because I'm the person who found her leg.'

That got a sharp look from his driftwood eyes, and his expression softened.

'She was a pretty young thing,' he said. 'Used to see her kayaking a fair bit out in the bay and beyond.'

'Have you been interviewed by the police? There's a detective called Vandenburg in town.'

Gardiner sneered. 'Why would he want to interview me? I was just the mug who found her. Didn't have anything to do with it.'

'Did you see Maxine kayaking that day?' Alex asked.

He shook his head. 'I was out further than she'd ever go. She was a good kayaker. Must have been a freak wave.'

Here was someone who agreed with Kelly.

'They haven't found her kayak yet,' said Alex.

'Eh?' Gardiner frowned.

There was the sound of footsteps behind them. It was the beanie-wearing man who had pointed Alex in the direction of the fisherman. Now that she saw him up close, she realised he was even younger than she had originally thought – late teens, early twenties at most.

Gardiner's demeanour changed instantly. 'I'm not answering your bloody questions,' he shouted at Alex. 'Didn't see nothing.' And he hawked up some spit for punctuation, before heading back into the cabin.

'Looks like you've been experiencing some of Merritt's famed hospitality,' the young man said to her. He seemed almost apologetic. He pulled his beanie off and shoved it into his pocket, then rubbed a hand through his curly hair.

'Something like that,' said Alex.

'Good day fishing, Dirk?' he called out to Gardiner, now on the far side of the boat. The tone was half friendly, half cheeky.

Gardiner mumbled to himself but didn't bite.

Alex started walking back up the jetty. The man from the boat quickly caught up with her. He was taller than she was, much taller, muscled and tanned.

'I'm Theo,' he said, sticking out a large, callused hand. 'Theo Rushall.'

She had heard the name before but couldn't place it.

Alex stretched out her own hand. His skin was rough but warm. 'Alex,' she said in reply.

Behind them, Gardiner yelled something about thirty pieces of silver. Out of the corner of her eye, Alex saw an annoyed expression cross Theo's face.

'Forgetting your roots, boy,' Dirk yelled, voice clearer now.

Theo picked up his pace and Alex followed his example. They passed more boats jostling in the water.

'I expect Dirk was getting in your ear about Nic Quirke and the salmon farm,' Theo said.

'He doesn't seem to be a fan.'

'And yet chances are Dirk will sit down to a nice plate of tasty salmon tonight.'

'Stolen salmon?'

'Let's just call it "poached".' A dimple appeared in his cheek as he smiled at his own joke.

'Do you work for Mr Quirke?' she asked.

He tapped the logo on his chest. 'As far as Merritt is concerned, I kind of *am* Quirke Industries.' There was more than a touch of ego to this, but he had enough self-awareness to correct it almost immediately. 'At least when Nic isn't around.'

'You run the salmon farm?'

'Oversee management of it, among other things.' Shoulders back, chest pushed out, he stood there proudly.

'Criminal charges could be laid if you make a complaint to the police about the poaching.'

The wooden planks of the jetty shivered underfoot from the combined weight of them.

'Go to the cops over a few fish?' Theo laughed. 'They wouldn't take it seriously. Besides, I reckon Nic Quirke can afford for a few fish to go missing every now and then. Can't have the locals going hungry.' A slow grin warmed his face.

A sign stuck to a nearby pillar detailed upcoming work to improve the facilities. Down the bottom of the notice was the QI logo alongside that of the council. 'Another of our side projects,' Theo said, pointing it out to her.

'Pretty big side project.'

The sign detailed additional vessel berthing and a new scuba and snorkel access platform as well as building a lower landing.

'Keep it to yourself, but Nic's not short of a bob.'

'What's he doing in Merritt?' Alex was genuinely curious as to why someone who had made profits the size of a small nation's GDP would think that this town was a good investment.

'Come on, Merritt's the best place in the world. Why would you want to live anywhere else?'

'The phone reception's bad and internet speeds are awful.'

'I think Nic likes the fact he can go completely offline here. We just finished building on his land up in the hills. The Eyrie.'

'The Eerie? As in spooky?' asked Alex.

'No, Eyrie with a "y". Think eagle's nest. It's close to the cliffs surrounded by trees. The view is spectacular.'

They reached the path that ran along the foreshore. The sun had started to disappear behind the hills, the long dusk rushing into darkness. Alex should head home. Denny would be wondering where she was.

Looking back the way they had come, Alex could just make out Gardiner standing on his boat, watching them. He had seemed happy enough to talk about Maxine initially but had abruptly changed his mind when Theo arrived. Maybe he was worried about the 'poached' fish?

Something about Dirk Gardiner bothered her . . . But, then, there seemed to be a lot about Maxine McFarlane's death that was starting to worry her.

Chapter 7

The trade in Rosie's was steady, the Wednesday lunchtime crowd beginning to trickle in. As Alex sipped her coffee, waiting for her takeaway order, Kiran Seth walked up to the counter. The waitress, Erin, who had served Alex last Friday, handed over an order in a paper bag. Alex noticed that Kiran paid for his food, unlike Kelly.

'Oh, hi,' Kiran said, noticing her and walking over. 'You found the place.'

'And the coffee's as good as you promised.' It had just occurred to Alex that Kiran might be a useful person to talk to about Maxine. Surely the local doctor would know what was going on in town. 'I'm about to order another, if you'd like to join me.'

Kiran grinned but then looked at the clock. 'Can I take a raincheck? There's a waiting room full of patients I've got to get back to.'

'No problem,' said Alex.

'He is so cute,' said Erin, her head popping up from behind the counter as Kiran disappeared out the door.

'How long has he been in town?' asked Alex.

'A couple of years. You should have heard the carry-on. People don't cope well with change around here.'

'I guess they're a bit old fashioned,' said Alex.

'More like a bit racist,' said Erin. She had a red headscarf tied around her light brown hair, a perky knot adorning the top of her head. 'You're Tayla's cousin, aren't you?'

'That's right.'

'I'm in her band.'

'You're playing at the protest,' said Alex. 'Hatpin' – she struggled to remember the rest of the name – 'Fear.'

'Hatpin Panic,' corrected Erin. 'Appropriate, seeing how I'm feeling about our performance. Silver talked us into it. She's the only one with any talent, but don't tell Tayla I said that.'

'Silver?' Alex asked. Tayla had mentioned that name a couple of times.

'She's the other member. Works at the art gallery around the corner.'

Silver must have been the girl who sang at the memorial. Prue had mentioned she was one of Maxine's close friends. Another person that Vandenburg would have interviewed. Maybe Alex should drop in and have a chat.

There was a ding from the back of the cafe.

'That'll be your chicken and bacon roll,' said Erin. 'And probably Silver's lunch as well. We take it around so she doesn't have to close up.'

'The gallery that was owned by Maxine McFarlane?' asked Alex, wanting to be sure.

Erin nodded. 'Poor Max. She taught us all art at school.'

'What was she like?'

'Eccentric, but in a good way. She was always saying kind of hippie things about how art can change the world, but you sort of went along with it because she was so passionate about it all. She really cared, even if you had zero talent, like me. Such a terrible accident.'

'An accident?'

'That's what Mr Kelly said. He was in here earlier with a detective from the city.'

Alex frowned. Vandenburg would have the autopsy results by now.

Two bags came out from the kitchen. Erin handed one to Alex. 'Is that Silver's lunch?' she asked, pointing to the other.

Erin nodded.

'I can take it around to her,' Alex volunteered. 'I've been meaning to drop by and have a look at the art.'

Erin gave her a dubious look. 'Have you seen the prices? They're crazy.'

As Alex pushed open the door to the gallery, she caught sight of her reflection in the glass. Her face seemed to be asking if this was a good idea.

Probably not was the answer, but she was here now.

An electronic buzz sounded and a young woman's head appeared from a doorway in the back wall. Up close, her hair was the sort of red that would have a Pre-Raphaelite painter itching for his brush. Alex smoothed back her own hair in an automatic response.

'Just a minute,' the girl said. 'I'll be right with you.'

'No rush.' Alex's voice echoed slightly off the stark surfaces. With its polished cement floor and matt white walls, this was nothing like the sort of gallery Alex had expected to find on Merritt's main street. She had thought about spinning a story around wanting to choose a nice little piece for her mother's birthday before asking about Maxine, but that wouldn't fly now that she'd seen the paintings. They all looked as expensive as thoroughbreds.

Now the whole of the young woman appeared. Silver wore a black silk singlet over black harem style pants, which meant either she was in mourning or just very artistic. Alex noticed on her forearm a tattoo of a stylised rocket ship, a red-headed girl astronaut inside it.

'Can I help you?' Silver asked.

'Actually, I'm just dropping off your lunch for Erin.' Alex held up the paper bag that matched her own in the other hand.

'And there I was thinking you were about to buy three paintings.'

'Busy morning?'

'Oh yeah, run off my feet,' was the faintly sarcastic reply. 'Thanks for the food, though.'

'No problem. I'm Alex – Tayla's cousin.'

This met with an instant reaction. Silver took a step back and put her hand to her mouth. 'You're the one who found Max . . . Tayla told me.'

'Yes,' answered Alex simply. The need for her to spin a story to start the conversation crumbled.

They stood there looking at each other. The smell of bacon wafted around the room and Alex realised the bag she was holding with her lunch in it had become translucent with grease.

Silver noticed the bag as well. 'This is actually a no-food zone. Come out the back. We can talk while we eat.'

A bunch of Australian natives, spiky and sculptural, in burnt yellow, purple and green, commandeered an enormous smoky glass vase on the windowsill.

'I couldn't leave them out the front. It made the place look like a funeral home.'

Alex recognised Prue's writing on the note.

'Tayla's boyfriend dropped them around yesterday,' Silver explained. 'He minded the store for me while I spoke to the police – not that we had any customers.'

A bunch of white lilies in a large, chipped glass jar next to a worktable nearby wafted a drowsy perfume. Alex looked around as Silver pulled over an office chair for her to sit on and busied herself with getting plates and cutlery from a cupboard in a small kitchenette.

'Tayla told me that you're a lawyer,' she said, 'but your marriage broke up and now you've got no money.'

That was an arrow right to the heart. She might have been able to fool Prue that everything was going fine but Tayla was another matter.

'My career is currently in a rebuild phase.'

'So you can't afford to buy any of the paintings?'

Who said this younger generation were a bunch of snowflakes? Silver would be pretty good at cross-examination.

'Not even close,' said Alex.

'I tried to sell one to that detective who came in yesterday, but he said the only people who could afford our prices were crooks.'

'Detective Vandenburg?'

'He wanted to ask questions about Maxine and the gallery. Pretty surreal, the way you found her.' Silver pulled a Japanese-style metal bento box from her paper bag. 'I mean, just a leg.'

'Yes it was,' said Alex.

An awkward silence followed.

'That's nice.' Alex gestured to the bento box.

'Max bought it for me,' explained Silver. 'Less food waste. This girl called Bella at my school was really into plastic-free living and she got Max involved. I'd drop mine and Max's boxes up to Rosie's each morning for our lunch orders but they always use a paper bag anyway. It used to drive Max nuts.'

She opened the box to reveal a grainy-looking salad, all quinoa and kale. Alex's sandwich slid onto the plate she had been handed, slick in its own grease. Silver gave it an ambiguous look, of jealousy or revulsion, Alex couldn't tell. All of a sudden, she found that she was starving and took a bite.

Silver picked at her salad dispiritedly with a fork.

'Did you mean Bella Greggs?' asked Alex, with a full mouth.

If Tayla had been at school with Bella, then she guessed Silver must have been too.

Silver didn't seem surprised at the mention of Bella. 'Yeah.'

'Did Bella and Maxine know each other well?'

Silver gave her a classic 'duh' look. 'Max was Bella's art teacher and Bella was just about her favourite pupil. That's why Max was organising that retrospective of Bella's work at the local museum.'

Alex remembered that she hadn't caught up with Robyn yet. Perhaps, she should give her a ring.

'The exhibition was meant to open in a fortnight,' continued Silver. 'All for Bella the genius.'

This seemed a sensitive topic. Alex decided to retreat to something more neutral.

'I like your tattoo.'

Silver stopped pretending to eat and held out her arm for Alex to inspect. 'Max designed it for me. We had so much fun scribbling on paper to come up with it and then drawing it on me to work out placement. I thought my back, but she convinced me to put it on my arm.'

'Did you help design her feather together?'

A shake of her head, the mane of hair added a visual exclamation mark.

'She got that done recently. I was pretty surprised because Max had a total phobia about needles. She had done lots of rounds of IVF with her last partner and it didn't work. That was why they broke up and she moved to Merritt to teach.'

Alex felt a wave of sympathy for Max. Trying to reinvent yourself after a break-up was something she could understand.

'Why a feather?'

'Probably a reference to Bella's wings.'

'Tayla mentioned something about those.'

The girl nodded. Alex let the silence hang there, with all its invisible weight, to force Silver to explain herself. Eventually, she buckled.

'Bella made them for an environmental protest against logging when we were in year eleven. Max helped her. She called it "performance art", dressing up as this kind of evil angel thing and pretending to curse anyone who dared cut down a tree. It really freaked people out. She loved the attention. Like, if you did a painting, she had to do one better. If you wanted to go to a protest against logging, she had to chain herself to a tree. Everything was always so dramatic.' Silver poked at her salad. 'Anyway, she used to wear the wings and try to get arrested, but the police would never do it. If anybody else had behaved like that, they'd have been charged for sure.'

This fitted with what Tayla had said about Kelly giving Bella special treatment. Alex took another bite of her sandwich, chewed, swallowed, then said, 'Tayla told me that Bella was wearing those wings when she died.'

'That's what Dylan said.'

'Do you believe him?'

Silver shrugged. 'I don't think he's got enough of an imagination to make up something as weird as that.'

There was silence as Alex ate more of her lunch. Silver kept stirring her salad with a fork like it was a spoon in coffee.

'What did the detective say about Max's death?' Alex prompted eventually.

'Said it was probably a kayaking accident.'

Vandenburg was parroting what Kelly had told him. Alex had to stop herself from shaking her head in disagreement.

'What's going to happen to this gallery now?' she asked Silver.

'I'm hoping Nic keeps it open and I still have a job.'

'Nic?'

'Nic Quirke. He was Maxine's business partner. He owns half of the gallery.' Silver gestured around her.

Nic Quirke again. Maybe Dirk Gardiner had a point about Merritt being addicted to the billionaire's money.

'How does a tech tycoon end up owning somewhere like this?'

'It's a funny story,' Silver said. 'You see, Nic saw one of Maxine's fakes.'

'A fake what?'

'A fake painting. It's like the equivalent of costume jewellery. Rich people do it all the time. Keep their Dutch master in a vault somewhere, get a knock-off up on the wall so they can still show off – or, even worse, pretend that they own it when they don't.'

'Are you serious?' But Alex immediately started to think of some of the pretentious barristers she knew with their architecturally interesting houses.

'Absolutely. Maxine's speciality was the Dutch Golden Age. She was one of the best. Could have had a long list of commissions if she wanted them. The money was excellent.'

Robyn had said that Maxine's work had been bought by serious art collectors. She'd conveniently skipped over the fact that the paintings were fakes.

'Is it that hard to do? To copy a painting?'

'To do it properly? Absolutely. There's a real talent to it. You have to have an eye for the smallest detail and an encyclo-pedic knowledge of historically appropriate methods and paints. Everything is ruined if you put the wrong style of lace on a portrait. The only problem was she absolutely hated it. Thought it was hack work, cynical and money grabbing. Why make a copy when the world already had the original? They were like children, she would say to me. You had to let them be free to be themselves, not just replicas. She said lots of cracked things like that. If there was a person who loved art a bit too much, it was Max.'

Silver sighed, and bent down to pick up some of the fallen flower petals from the floor.

'Most rich people just think of art as a classy way to wave their bank statements in people's faces,' she continued, 'but not Nic. He was kind of like Max's patron and thought if Max wasn't so worried about money, then maybe she would have more time to work on her own art and freedom to do other stuff, like this new exhibition of Bella's works. She was completely obsessed by that.'

'What was so special about the exhibition?'

'At the start, it was just about showcasing Bella's work and raising money for her mother, but then it seemed to get more complicated. Max was really stressed, kept saying that it was going to divide the town and really upset people.'

'I had no idea that Merritt was so into art.'

'It wasn't the art that was the problem; it was Bella.' Silver definitely wasn't a fan.

'But she's dead.'

'Do you know that policeman Kelly?'

Alex nodded.

'Don't tell anyone, but he came round and told Maxine not to have the exhibition. They had an argument about it.'

'What did Kelly say?'

'I was outside in the courtyard having my lunch and only came in when I heard the yelling, but he was saying something about how it would just upset everyone and wouldn't achieve anything. When he saw me, he clammed up right away and then left.'

Alex thought about this. What harm could an exhibition do? 'How did Max respond?'

'It only made her more determined. She was even working on some new pieces to add to the exhibition herself.'

'One of her copies or an original?'

'I don't know. She wouldn't show me.'

'Did she show Nic?'

'Definitely not. I think she was really worried about how he'd interpret it.'

'What do you mean?'

'She said something about how he was going to hate it but that truth in art had to mirror truth in real life. But, then, maybe he did see it and wasn't bothered? She was up at the Eyrie that morning, before she was supposed to go away for the weekend.'

'You mean the morning of the day she died?' Alex felt a tingle in her spine, whether from shock or excitement she couldn't tell. 'Did she have any other appointments that day?'

'Don't know. You could check her diary.'

'Where is it? Online?'

Silver shook her head. 'Max was old school. She carried around a sketchbook with her to draw in. Sometimes she used to write notes in it. I mean, she had a phone, of course, but she mainly used that for texts and social media.'

'Did you give the diary to Detective Vandenburg?'

'He only asked about her phone. He seemed in a bit of a rush yesterday. Didn't ask many questions.'

'Have you got the diary here?'

Silver got up, walked over to a desk and pulled open the drawer. 'It was a kind of visual record of her life.'

The book was a small, black Moleskine fastened with an elastic strap.

Silver handed it to her. 'Maybe I should have told the detective about this.'

'I'm going to see him,' said Alex. 'I can take it, if you like.'

She turned to the front page. Maxine's name was written in blue ink. Opposite was an exquisite hand-drawn picture of the sea in a rainstorm, clouds above, waves below and, right in the middle, a lighthouse, a slim steady oasis of white amid the blue ink.

'Gorgeous.' Alex showed it to Silver. She really should make time to drive up to the lighthouse while she was here. Denny could stay behind if she wasn't interested.

She slowly turned the pages of the diary. Among some scribbled words, appointments hastily written, notes to self, were drawings. A half-finished human head, a dog curled up, a building that Alex recognised as the kayaking club's shed. There was a rough pencilled sketch of an almost naked man asleep, his face resting on his arm, a pillow propped to the side of him and a black thick curved line above his head. The sheets were bundled up low around his waist, hinting at what lay underneath. Near his hip bone was a small dark mark in the shape of a J. The drawing had captured something intimate and private; Alex, feeling a little like a voyeur, turned the page. There was a man fishing and a quick sketch of a large old-fashioned sailing ship, but mostly Maxine drew people's faces. Alex recognised several from the town.

'She was very talented,' said Alex.

Silver's shoulders slumped as she turned her attention back to her food.

It occurred to Alex that the exhibition was another clear link between Bella and Maxine. There were a lot more questions that she would have liked to ask Silver, but she had already intruded enough. At least Vandenburg had talked to the girl but he hadn't been very thorough about it.

Alex stood up. 'I'd better head off. Hope things work out with the gallery for you.'

'Thanks.'

At the doorway, Alex hesitated, looking back.

Silver sat there, downcast, the sun from a nearby window creating a haze of creamy light around her incredible hair. She looked like a portrait painted by a Dutch master.

Unhappy Girl with Quinoa, was the title Alex came up with.

Chapter 8

Just after dawn, Alex walked into a service station restaurant, an hour's drive north-west of Merritt. The term 'restaurant' seemed overly generous, though the crumbs and greasiness of the tables and a discarded grimy serviette gave the impression that someone had once consumed food there. The fact that cars and trucks pulled in regularly for petrol and yet the place was empty of customers suggested that the locals knew better. She had no idea why Tom had picked this awful place and this dreadful time to meet and now he wasn't even here.

Wiping down her table with a different serviette, she sat down and checked her messages. Nothing new. She reread the text from Vandenburg that she got late yesterday, agreeing to finally catch up with her. He had suggested they get a drink tonight. Meeting at the Sail sounded less formal than at the station but maybe he didn't want Kelly to know about it. She had left a message for

Robyn letting her know. There was still no sign of any evidence from the older woman.

Next she opened Instagram on her phone and scrolled through Tom's new girlfriend's pictures again. It hadn't been that hard to find her. She was the backup weather girl for one of the commercial TV channels and sometimes appeared on morning chat shows to provide the all-important blonde millennial's view of the world. Her feed was full of posts talking about her imperfections whereas her photos – of stylised hair, full-wattage smile and coltish legs peeping out of flowing dresses – were designed to show she had none. Her favourite emojis were sparkles, the love heart and praying hands, all of which were on high repeat in any photo with Tom. There was Tom in sunglasses, Tom with his eyes shut and artfully tousled bed hair, Tom laughing, Tom holding a surfboard (Tom didn't actually surf) and – Alex's favourite – Tom hugging a random small child, both of them wearing suspiciously white, crisply ironed but loosely worn linen shirts, #myguy and, best of all, #lawyerlover. Alex snorted over that one and made sure that she didn't accidentally like any of them.

Twenty minutes later, the real-life version of Tom arrived, minus the white linen shirt, and slid into the seat across from her as Alex quickly put away her phone. Tall, tanned, lean, he wore a fitted black shirt and pants, leather jacket, dark glasses and a baseball cap. They were all new. It was like sitting across from someone who couldn't decide if he was a cat burglar or going out to dinner. There was a time when her heart would beat faster at the sight of this man; now she just wanted to get this over and done with.

'You're late,' said Alex.

'And I bet you were early,' he said. 'Ordered coffees yet?' He flashed his perfectly straight teeth.

She shook her head. Alex hadn't been brave enough to disturb the girl sitting up at the register, staring blankly out towards the truck parking area like she was dreaming of her own escape.

'Excuse me,' Tom called out. 'Can we have two flat whites here?'

The girl turned to them, sighed deeply and moved towards the coffee machine.

'What am I doing here?' asked Alex.

'I needed a place where we wouldn't be overheard.'

Why this ridiculous need for all the secrecy? It didn't take a genius to work out that finalising their divorce might have something to do with the arrival of Shantelle.

'How have you been?' asked Tom. He rearranged the bit of his face she could actually see under his cap and glasses, predominantly mouth, to look concerned. 'How's the delightful Denny?'

Denny had hated Tom from the moment they met. She had even written the wrong name on Christmas cards, mixing him up with past boyfriends that Denny had grudgingly liked despite herself. This had upset Alex, infuriated Tom and had resulted in fewer catch ups. At the time, Alex thought Denny had felt betrayed because it was no longer just the two of them. Now, looking back, she wondered if it had been an early warning sign of what was happening in her mother's brain – or perhaps Denny had recognised something that it took Alex some time to realise: that Tom wasn't worth remembering because he was only passing through.

'Sends her love,' Alex said. 'Said next time why don't you come and visit us in Merritt, save me having to get up before five am to drive to the middle of nowhere.'

This was a lie. Denny didn't even know Alex had left the house. She had put a note on the floor outside her mother's bedroom door. If this meeting was quick enough, Denny wouldn't even know she'd been gone.

Tom laughed, though it seemed forced. 'All right,' he started but was interrupted by the waitress putting their coffees on the table. She slopped Tom's onto his saucer, muttered something about cleaning it up, but, looking down at the milky grey coffee, he told her that wasn't necessary.

Alex took a sip. Lukewarm dishwater from a rusty rain tank.

Tom took off his sunglasses and flung his hands wide, as if making a big announcement. 'I'm getting married again.' He paused, an uncertain look on his face.

They had met at the same large law firm. Alex was a workaholic to cover up the fact that she, a latchkey kid from the country, was a fraud who shouldn't be employed alongside the type of people who were related to judges and went to Europe every other year. Tom had been different from the others too, but he was confident – confident enough for both of them.

When Tom decided to become a barrister, he had convinced her not only to do it as well but marry him at the same time. Tom loved grand gestures. She found out during the best man's speech that she wasn't the first person he had asked to marry him, just the first one to say yes. Unfortunately, Tom turned out to be the sort of person who loved the spectacle of weddings but wasn't so interested in the domestic life that came afterwards. It was only in retrospect that she realised he'd needed her help to get through the bar exam and this must have seemed the surest way to guarantee it. Everyone makes mistakes, she told herself, and Tom was the six foot tall version of hers.

'That's quick,' she said.

'When you know, you know,' said Tom. 'No point waiting.'

Theirs had also been a whirlwind courtship. At the time, she had told herself it was romantic; now she realised it was his trademark move. Still, this development seemed hasty even for him.

'Is Shantelle pregnant?'

Tom's mouth opened. 'How did you guess?'

They had talked about having kids but it had all been in the far-off future, when their careers were more established. Now Tom would have his career and kids, just without her. There was a time when Alex would have found this devastating, but in a strange way finding a severed leg on the beach had given her at least some perspective. Worse things can happen.

'I hope you're very happy,' she said untruthfully.

'Phew.' Tom beamed. 'You know, if you met her, you'd really like her.'

Alex thought it would be hard to like a grown woman who used sparkle emojis but she let it pass.

'We're not telling anyone about the pregnancy yet, so if you could keep it to yourself . . .'

'Sure.'

'So,' said Tom, 'are you seeing anyone?'

There was only one way to answer this question and retain a skerrick of human dignity.

'Yes,' Alex lied. 'I am actually.'

'Oh, really?'

Did she detect scepticism or was it merely surprise?

'It's only a recent thing. We're taking it pretty slowly.'

Tom didn't react to the jibe. 'Anyone I know?'

'I don't think so.' She shook her head and tried to look enigmatic so he wouldn't ask her any more questions.

'Is he a lawyer?'

She groped around for something, anything. For some reason, Kiran jogged into her mind.

'A doctor. We met running.'

Tom smirked at this. He definitely had done something to his teeth. 'Running?'

'Well, he was running and I was walking,' Alex corrected. 'We started chatting and–'

'What sort of doctor?' Tom asked.

'What sort of doctor?' Alex repeated.

'I mean, is he a neurosurgeon, a cardiologist?' He was mocking her now.

'A GP,' Alex said. 'Now tell me, does Shantelle know that technically you are still married to me?'

Take that.

A shifty look crossed Tom's face. 'Not exactly. That's why we need to get this done as quickly as possible.' He reached into his messenger bag and brought out a yellow envelope. 'Now, the media might get in touch with you – paparazzi, that sort of thing. Shantelle's manager had a chat to me about it. People love the ex-wife, new love angle. Makes the great unwashed feel better about their own lives. I'll only have nice things to say about you, of course – that I still think of you as a friend and admire you as a lawyer – but you should feel free to be as frank as you like.'

'What?'

'The franker the discussion, the bigger the clicks. It's the way the world works.'

'I hope you aren't asking me to publicly attack your pregnant fiancée so that you get the sympathy and she gets a higher profile?'

'It could be worth a bit of money. Just be vague about when we actually got divorced. No one has the resources to check that sort of thing anymore.'

Alex gazed out the window, taking in concrete and petrol bowsers, trying to find the right way to respond other than throwing a tepid cup of coffee at him.

'Did you talk to Charlie about the case?'

Tom frowned. 'Let's just get this sorted out first.'

'No,' said Alex. 'This is actually important.'

'All right, all right. I talked to Charlie about it and he was pretty keen to know why you were interested. In the strictest of confidence, he's trying to get a reward up for it.'

So typical of Tom to claim to know something that she had told him in the first place.

'Charlie said there was a local cop that kept getting in the way. He could never work out if he was being really helpful or actually obstructing the investigation. Just that he was always there. Even wanted Charlie to stay at his house.'

Alex leant back in her seat, felt the stickiness of the vinyl and, wincing, peeled herself off.

'Was it Kingsley Kelly?'

Tom made his hand into a gun and pointed his finger at her. 'King Kelly. What a name. Charlie sent through some photos. He wanted to know if you had any information about some of the people in them.'

'Do you mean they're suspects?'

'I guess so. I've put his details in here. He's tied up with another investigation at the moment but give him a call in a fortnight.' Tom pulled another envelope out of his bag. 'You've got to keep these pics to yourself.'

'Of course,' said Alex. 'Have you ever met a detective called Vandenburg?'

'Nudge?' Tom asked. 'What's he got to do with it?'

'He's in Merritt at the moment working on a different investigation that might be related to Charlie's. I'm meeting him at the pub tonight for a drink.'

'Good luck with that,' said Tom. 'He's notoriously lazy. Likes to push work off his plate onto other people.'

Pot, meet kettle.

'What's your involvement in all this?' Tom asked. 'This isn't a court case. Have you got a client caught up in it?'

'I'm not at liberty to say,' said Alex.

Tom nodded his head and looked thoughtful. 'You know, I was wondering if you might leave the bar.'

'What made you think that?' Alex tried not to sound outraged. Just because she had thought of it didn't give Tom the right to think it as well.

'Let's face it, there are too many lawyers and not enough work. Solicitors keeping minor matters they used to brief out for, grunt work being sent offshore, robots and computers doing more and more of it, and hardly anyone has the money to run big court cases these days. It's why I've worked hard on developing a public profile. You can't just be a lawyer anymore; you have to be a brand.'

A brand? Alex didn't even want to think what her brand might be. Abject failure with a sideline of dreadful taste in men.

She reached out a hand for the envelope.

'Not so fast,' Tom said, holding it out of her reach. 'Sign the documents first.' He placed them on the table in front of her.

'Really?'

'Really.'

Sighing, Alex flicked through the pages. There were helpful little tags on the side indicating where she should sign.

'I need a witness,' she said.

Tom nodded at the girl who had gone back to sitting at the register. 'Just try to be discreet. Don't show her my name and pay for the coffees while you're there.'

He wasn't even going to pay for the coffees.

Alex got up and walked over to the girl. 'Hi,' she said 'Could I–' but the girl was already putting the amount into the till.

'That's seven dollars,' she said.

Alex got out her phone and paid it. 'I was wondering if you would mind witnessing me signing a document?'

The girl shrugged. Her face gave nothing away, like she'd been asked to do a lot of weird things in her job.

'What's it for?' she asked.

'My divorce papers.'

That got a reaction. The girl looked first at her and then craned her head to look past Alex to Tom. 'You're divorcing him?'

'That's right.'

'He looks like a tosser. You're better off without him.'

Alex glanced over her shoulder and saw Tom had put his dark glasses back on, as though expecting a passing truck driver might recognise him and ask for an autograph.

'I think you're right.'

Back in the safety of her own car, she ripped open the envelope from Charlie Farinacci and pulled out the pictures. The first one was a mugshot of a man in his mid to late thirties, short, cropped hair exposing a scar on his scalp, thick neck and muscular physique. His dark eyes snarled an 'I'm not intimidated by you' back up at her. The name Johnny Ewart was scribbled on the back.

She'd heard that name before somewhere. Grabbing her phone, she pulled up a news report from a few years ago that mentioned drug charges. Alex had met a few Johnny Ewarts, had even defended some of them. What was his connection to Bella?

The next photo was completely different. It was a professional headshot of a man, late forties, early fifties, in an open-necked shirt and blue suit jacket. He could have been styled by Shantelle. The face was too angular to be handsome, the nose a beak, but the eyes were intelligent. There was a half-smile on his face. He was interesting, but what was even more fascinating was the name underneath: Dominic 'Nic' Quirke.

Nic Quirke, the tech billionaire and art enthusiast who seemed to own most of Merritt, including half of Maxine's business, was a suspect in Bella's murder. No wonder people were keeping quiet.

The rest of the pictures were of Bella's body. She was lying face down on fertile soil, a bed of dark brown loam, except her head was angled on its side, eyelids closed, as though she was sleeping. Against the green ferns, dark twigs and detritus on the woodland floor, her skin was a marble white, like she had been carefully placed there, a sculpture waiting to be discovered. Other pictures had a broader viewpoint, taking in the flattened grass beneath her.

The photo Alex spent most time on was a close-up of Bella's head. Golden red hair, long, most of it still tied back at the base of her skull but with strands spilling out, darker at the roots, from blood or shadows.

Despite all her problems, the broken marriage, spluttering career and Denny's dementia, Alex couldn't feel sorry for herself. At least she still had a life. These poor women, Bella and Maxine, weren't as lucky. Robyn might not win a popularity contest in Merritt, but she was right about one thing: Bella's investigation had gone wrong and Maxine's seemed to be headed in the same direction. Alex couldn't stand by and watch that happen.

Chapter 9

'We're going to be late,' said Alex to Denny, as they half walked, half ran towards the Sail. It was like taking a fifty-eight-year-old toddler for an outing, with her mother getting distracted by shop windows, trees and even a cat who stared almond-eyed at them as they rushed past.

Denny had taken forever to get ready, refusing all help. Alex cast some of the blame for their tardiness on her mother's dress. It was dramatic, plum-coloured and had folds so complicated it would befuddle an engineer. Alex thought it might possibly be on back to front but wasn't game to ask.

'Remember I have to catch up with someone while you have dinner with Prue and Tayla at the bistro.'

'Who?' asked Denny.

'You don't know him.'

'Is it a date?'

'No! It's work-related.'

'You've actually got some work?' Her mother sounded surprised.

Alex tried to bottle the exasperated feeling that fizzed up inside her. Denny's memory had been on the blink for most of the day and yet she had a perfect grasp of Alex's failing career.

The Sail came into view. Painted a smart glossy white with black trim, it looked like an enormous box of old-fashioned chocolates. The double-storey building sat on the corner of Merritt's main street.

Alex pushed open the first wooden door and found herself in the front bar rather than the bistro. The average age of the inhabitants was retirement and the only woman in sight was pouring drinks. From the looks that Alex was getting from the clientele, strangers were not welcome. This was the type of place where sticky bar stools were like dogs and loyal to their owner.

One of the men sitting across from the door said something out of the side of his mouth to the bloke next to him, who guffawed in response. It took Alex a moment to realise who it was. Kingsley Kelly. Here he was, surrounded by his gang. You could smell the alpha male along with the beer.

Kelly was the last person she wanted to see, especially when she was planning to talk about him to Vandenburg. Turning quickly, she stopped Denny from coming in. She didn't care if they had known each other for years, like Kelly claimed. Instinctively, she didn't want her mother to have anything to do with him. As the door swung shut behind her, Alex thought she heard someone shout, 'Piss off!' Was it Kelly? Yeah, buddy, she thought, you are a real study in courage.

'Wrong door,' she said to Denny with a smile. 'Let's try the next one.'

And for once in her life, Denny did as she was asked and trotted off.

The bistro smelt of roasting meat and hot chips. Football blared from a television up in the corner. A waving Prue had already arrived and grabbed a table. Tayla looked up from her phone for a nanosecond as they sat down.

'Tayla,' warned her mother, 'put it away.'

'Erin's just texted saying there's a problem with the sound system!'

'It's this protest tomorrow,' explained Prue. 'It's all she talks about.'

'You're coming, aren't you, Alex?' asked Tayla. Her hand lingered over the phone on the table as if she couldn't bear to have it out of her sight. 'It's really important.'

'What's it for again?' Alex asked. 'Climate change?'

'It's our first-ever gig!' Tayla said, outraged. 'Midday, near the rotunda at Fish Hook. Come on, Aunty Den.'

'We'll be there,' said Denny firmly. 'Won't we, Alex?'

'All right,' muttered Alex, who could think of much better things to do, like ringing Kathleen over and over until she gave them a new appointment.

She passed a menu to Denny, scanning the room as she did. She couldn't see anyone who looked like Vandenburg.

Behind the bar was a woman, eyes rimmed in kohl, blonde hair made white by the fluorescent glow of the bar's lights. She worked with cool efficiency, pouring beers, scooping ice, plunking lemon slices in jugs of soft drink and taking money. There was something about her that caught the eye. Alex was about to lean over to ask Prue who she was when Tayla said, 'Here's Theo.'

It was the man Alex had met at the jetty, the Quirke Industries employee. Now he was wearing dark blue chinos and a blue-and-white-striped t-shirt, his curly hair tucked behind his ears. He pecked Tayla on the cheek and then grabbed a chair from the next table and sat down between Denny and Tayla.

'Alex and Denny, meet Theo,' said Prue.

'Actually, we've met before,' a smiling Theo replied. 'Down at the marina,' he explained. 'I had to rescue Alex from Dirk Gardiner.'

'Not Dirty Dirk,' hooted Tayla. 'How did you cope with the smell?'

'That's enough,' said Prue. 'Poor Dirk's harmless, really.'

Tayla rolled her eyes, encouraging Theo to laugh.

Denny was staring at him intently. 'Do I know you?' she asked.

A half-embarrassed grin crept over Theo's face. 'I don't think so.'

'You look familiar.'

It sounded like a cheesy pick-up line. Denny had always been an incorrigible flirt, which had led to moments of extreme teenage mortification for Alex. Someone who, when she was in good humour, was the life and soul of the party, the one who would dance on tables. A string of strangers had made an appearance at breakfast when she was growing up. Rarely did teenage Alex have to scowl at the same man twice. Denny had taken seriously her commitment to just the two of them and rejected all offers of relationships and something more permanent, using her daughter as an excuse. Alex had watched all this and decided her life was going to be different.

'This is Ted's boy, Den,' said Prue gently.

Alex's mother frowned, little grooves appearing at the top of her nose.

'Denny knew your father, Theo,' said Prue. 'In fact, they went to our deb ball together. Made a gorgeous couple. Ted died a few years back, Den. Remember? I told you that.'

Alex flinched at the word 'remember'. There must be nothing more frustrating than having people constantly ask if you remembered something when you didn't.

Theo's face flushed, as though he was uncomfortable with the attention.

Denny reached out a small hand and cupped Theo's chin. There was an immediate contrast of her freckled skin against Theo's deep smooth fisherman tan.

'Aunty Den,' joked Tayla, 'keep your hands to yourself.'

Denny didn't seem to hear. Her expression was one of deep concentration as she stared at Theo. He gave an awkward smile, then looked away.

'Mum,' said Alex quietly. She reached out to lift Denny's arm from Theo's face. Denny dropped her hand but not her gaze.

'We haven't seen you in ages, Theo,' said Prue, trying to move the conversation on. 'Every time I tell Tayla to bring you home for dinner, she says you're too busy up at the lighthouse.' Prue turned to Alex and explained that this was a restoration project that Theo had started. 'His grandfather was the last lighthouse keeper and Theo still lives up at the point, in the old cottage.'

'Actually, I was just talking to Sasha about holding a fundraiser to get the lamp restored,' said Theo.

Tayla gave a theatrical groan.

'It's been a couple of years since the last fundraiser for the lighthouse,' Prue said, after she had glared at her daughter. 'Could run a good raffle for it.'

'Not a raffle,' said Tayla. 'Everyone does raffles.'

'What's your idea then?' Prue retorted.

'Tayla's sick of hearing about it.' Theo smiled at his girlfriend. 'But it will be worth it when we're lying on the balcony at night-time, listening to the lighthouse lullaby.'

'The waves and wind?' asked Alex.

'Torrential rain would be more like it,' said Tayla.

'No,' said Denny, 'he's talking about the light.'

'That's right!' Theo nodded his head vigorously. 'My grandfather used to say it was such a great beam you could hear it rushing past, punching a hole in the darkness. Calling out to all those who were lost, guiding them home.'

Alex pictured little boats dotted in choppy black waters making their way back to the safety of the shore, but then she thought of Maxine in the same water and shivered. No one had rescued her.

'Lighthouses are such a romantic idea,' said Prue.

'Can't you imagine the ocean rolling below and the stars above us?' Theo put an arm around Tayla. She made a face but consented to lean in to his body, holding out her cheek for a kiss, which he gave her.

'They send you mad,' said Denny suddenly.

'Sends me mad,' muttered Tayla.

'What do you mean, Den?' asked Prue.

'That's what my father used to say. Lighthouses were like an addiction that devoured men whole. You could get trapped inside the lens.'

Prue opened her eyes wide at the mention of Jack Walker and shot Alex a questioning look. 'Well, it is a lonely job, I guess.'

'He was probably talking about the old days, when they used liquid mercury to float the lenses,' said Theo. 'Gave the keepers all sorts of hallucinations.'

'We could mention the fundraiser at the protest tomorrow,' interrupted Tayla.

'What's that got to do with climate change?' asked her mother.

Tayla made a face. 'It can be about both. Theo, you are coming?'

'Of course. I want to be able to say that I was there at Hatpin Panic's first-ever gig.'

'I'm the only one who can sing properly, so we're bound to be terrible.'

'Then I really want to be there.'

Tayla lightly punched his arm.

'You should come for dinner, Theo,' said Prue. 'How about next Monday? I'm sure Tayla would love to cook for you.'

'Well, if Tayla's cooking how can I refuse . . .' He stood up. 'Anyone want a drink?'

'I will,' said Denny.

'Is that a good idea with your meds?' Alex asked. She tried to keep her voice quiet so only her mother would hear.

'A whisky, thanks,' said Denny loudly. 'Make it a double.'

'Come on up to the bar with me, Aunty Den,' said Tayla, clearly sensing an opportunity for mischief. 'Let's have cocktails together.'

Alex gave up. Tayla could be in charge of a tipsy Denny. See how she liked that.

'Better order our meals while you're there,' said Prue. 'I'll have the special. What do you want, Alex? My treat.'

'The schnitzel, thanks,' said Alex.

'And a couple of glasses of white wine for us as well.'

'All right,' said Tayla, grabbing her mother's wallet from the handbag swinging off the back of the chair. The three of them wandered away.

'Well, how about that,' said Prue. 'I nearly fell off my chair when Den started talking about your grandfather.'

'That was weird,' Alex answered. Her mother hardly ever mentioned him, even though she lived in their house.

'I think it's a good sign. Let the problems of the past stay in the past.'

Alex ran her fingers through her hair. Could you really leave that behind?

'You know, I've asked your mother to come out to the Sail with us dozens of times, but she never would. It's great to see her engaging with people again. All because you're here, you know,' Prue continued. 'I know it isn't easy, but you've always been one to do the right thing, Alex.'

'Does the right thing include making appointments to visit the assisted living facility? Because we're going to have to do that no matter how many times Mum hides my keys.'

Prue sighed. 'You're here now and that's what counts. Denny was nowhere to be seen when it came to your grandmother. Lucky for her, there were people like Alby prepared to help out. Did you ever meet Alby? He was your grandfather's partner at the surgery.'

Alex shook her head.

'He was always kind to Denny, even when your grandparents treated her terribly. You know, when Denny brought you back for the first visit, Jack told her that she should give you up, that she would make a bad mother.'

'What?' It was as if Alex had turned over a rock and something unpleasant came scuttling out. 'He actually said that?'

Should she be surprised? If someone was going to shame and belittle a small child, then it made sense they would be prepared to say much worse to the mother.

'Dealing with Dr Jack Walker was like talking to someone out of the Dark Ages. I think God was doing everyone a favour when He took your grandfather before same-sex marriage got legislated. Just the thought of it would have driven him apoplectic. I don't know how Alby put up with him for all those years. Worshipped the ground Jack walked on. Are you sure you've never met him?'

'I saw him at Rosie's cafe for the first time a few days ago. I think Kelly said he was just back from overseas.'

Prue nodded. 'The old Merritt fishhook has got Denny back and now Alby. It will get you too.'

Not quite the same as the lighthouse bringing all those lost home. Alex had heard the superstition about the fishhook before; it came from the name of the bay. The more she heard about Merritt, the happier she was not to have grown up here. Still, she smiled at her aunt. 'That just sounds painful.'

'Denny is lucky that Jack died first. If it was up to him, I'm sure he'd have left everything to Alby. He was the surrogate son. It was your grandmother who wanted Denny to have the house. I think it was her way of saying sorry.'

'I wonder if Mum came back because she knew something was starting to go wrong with her memory,' Alex said. It was a thought that had preoccupied her. 'Returning to the place that she remembered best, the house that is clearest in her mind.' There must come a stage when the ghosts of the past would be more real to Denny than the present day.

'Or maybe she wanted to be with the people who knew her so that when she forgets, we can do the remembering for her.'

That was a thought so sad that something seemed to get caught in Alex's throat and she gave an involuntary little gasp. Prue reached over and squeezed her hand and then reached into her handbag, pulled out a hanky and blew her nose loudly.

'Or maybe it's the weather,' said Alex, her voice clotted.

Prue laughed more loudly than the joke deserved.

'Funny how things change.' Prue nodded her head in the direction of Theo and Tayla. Denny was standing beside them slurping down a ludicrously pink cocktail that had a strawberry stuck on the rim of the glass, chatting away to some poor man trying to have his dinner up at the bar. 'Thirty-odd years ago, in this very spot, that would have been your mum and Ted. Poor Ted never got over Denny leaving town. In fact' – she lowered her voice – 'I always wondered if there was a chance that Ted might have been your father, Alex.'

'What?!' Alex stared at her.

Her aunt shrugged. 'That was always my guess, but I'm probably wrong. Usually am, according to Tayla.'

Alex didn't know how to react to this. She turned around in her seat to study Theo. There was a time when she would have loved a sibling; now the thought unsettled her. She remembered her grandfather's only kindly gesture, offering to take her to the lighthouse to meet the ex-keeper's son when she was a little girl. Even as a child she had found it strange that he was paying her attention. Alex could still recall her mother's face and how she'd yanked Alex's arm, pulling her from her chair so abruptly that it toppled over.

Could Theo be her half-brother? There were superficial resemblances between herself and Theo – they were both tall with dark hair – but no stranger was going to assume that they were related. Alex couldn't say that she felt any sort of instinctive connection.

'When we were growing up everything seemed so certain,' said Prue. 'Ted was going to be the next lighthouse keeper like his father and grandfather and marry Denny. But then the lighthouse was shut down, and Denny left town – ran away, really – without a word to anyone, not even me. That was like a fault line in all our lives. Nothing was the same after that.'

Was that why Denny reacted at that long-ago lunch? Was her father reminding her of the path she should have taken? Maybe it had nothing to do with who Alex's father was.

'So what did Ted do instead?'

'Started a mussel business – Fishhook Mussels. Sold them up and down the coast. It failed a while back. Some people said it was climate change, others blamed pollution in the bay. Ted was pretty broken by then; his wife had died of cancer. He drank himself to an early grave, leaving poor Theo by himself at sixteen. Grief, it damages people. I don't think you ever get over it, not really.'

'That's awful. Poor Theo.' Another glance over at him. Leaning against the bar, Theo was smiling at something Tayla had said.

'Well,' said Prue, 'it's all water under the bridge now. He's got Tayla and he's got us for family, God help him.' She noticed a greasy spot on the table and took out a serviette to wipe it away, rubbing it more vigorously than was warranted. 'Anyway, thanks again for meeting with that detective. I really appreciate it. I know Robyn does as well.'

Alex was almost grateful for the change of subject. 'Robyn still hasn't told me exactly what evidence she has about Maxine's death. Instead, I'm supposed to meet up with her tomorrow at the museum.' She tried not to sound too exasperated. It had taken so many phone calls to even get a response from Vandenburg that she wasn't going to delay talking to him and instead decided to return the meeting back to its original purpose, focusing on her concerns surrounding Kelly and his blinkered determination to claim that Maxine's death was an accident.

Looking around the room to check if Vandenburg had arrived yet, her eyes stopped on Theo again.

'Well, the main thing is that we are all out tonight and Denny's with us enjoying herself,' said Prue, glancing towards the trio at the bar. 'Who's she chatting to?'

Alex's gaze moved from Theo to the man eating at the counter. Denny had been prattling away to him for at least ten minutes, a different drink in hand now. Goodness only knew what she was talking about as she threw back cocktails.

'Oh no, that's Kiran.' Alex stood up quickly, nearly tripping over her chair. 'I'd better go rescue him.'

'Hello!' said Kiran as Alex joined her mother by his side.

'Hi,' she said, feeling flustered. 'I hope Mum wasn't interrupting your dinner.'

'Not at all. We've been having a lovely chat. She tells me you've got an important date tonight.'

'It isn't a date!' Alex looked despairingly at Denny, who had pulled the pineapple off the rim of her glass and was now sucking on it. 'And I think you've had enough cocktails for one night.'

'Actually, they're mocktails,' Denny replied. 'Not bad, really.' There was a small smile of triumph on her face; clearly she was delighted to have tricked her daughter. 'See you later, Doc.' And she sauntered off.

Kiran smiled up at Alex, the corners of his eyes crinkling. 'I think it was all an elaborate ploy of Tayla's to keep her away from the hard stuff.'

'And fool me at the same time,' Alex said through gritted teeth.

'How about I buy you a mocktail? Or a cocktail, even? You look like you could use one.'

Kiran had such a lovely shaped mouth, she noticed.

'That would be lovely, but I'd better not. I *am* about to meet someone and it's . . . kind of work-related.'

'Our timing is terrible.'

He had such kind eyes as well.

Aware that she was staring at his face, Alex blinked and looked away, and saw Karl Vandenburg standing at the entrance to the bar, wearing a checked shirt and blue jeans, with a belt buckle that looked as large as his ego threatened to be and a moustache that screamed cop. There were two schooners of beer in his hands. All he lacked was the white Stetson and sheriff's badge.

She raised her hand to get his attention. Vandenburg gave her a nod that was more businesslike than friendly and headed in the direction of the beer garden.

'That's who you're meeting?' Kiran asked.

'Yeah.' Alex sighed. 'I'd better go.'

There was a large fig tree in the centre of the courtyard, fairy lights strung in its crooked branches. No one else was out here, something Alex put down to the fact that all the surfaces were wet from the rain that afternoon. The chairs slumped up against the tables like tired drunks. Vandenburg put his drinks down on the furthest table from the door, grabbed a chair, giving it a good shake, and then put it back on the ground and sat down. Alex did the same.

'Thought you might be thirsty,' Vandenburg said. He pushed a beer towards her.

'How's your investigation progressing?'

'Just about ready to wrap it up.' Vandenburg saluted her with his glass and took a swig of his beer. 'Looks like an accident. She shouldn't have gone out kayaking alone. Boats like that tip all the time. It's something every beginner should know. Coroner might want to issue recommendations but it's not one for us.'

Alex frowned. 'But the autopsy report said she didn't drown. There was no salt water in her lungs.'

Vandenburg, who had stuck his tongue out, pink and fat, to pick up some stray beer foam under his moustache, stared at her. 'How did you get a copy of the autopsy report?'

'But I'm right,' Alex said, not answering him. 'She didn't drown.'

Vandenburg wrapped his large hand around the glass and took a long chug, before putting it back down on the table. 'Ever heard of "dry" drowning? Sometimes when you fall into cold water, an automatic reflex closes the airway. It's a muscle spasm in response to the shock of water hitting the back of the throat. Nothing enters the lungs, not air and not water.'

Alex folded her arms as she considered this. Could Maxine's death have been a random accident? Could Robyn and Lou have got it wrong?

Vandenburg sat there, drinking his beer, looking supremely unconcerned, like talking to her was a waste of time.

'Wasn't there evidence of a blow to the head?' she asked. She had to tread carefully here, to be clear that she wasn't trying to attack his investigation.

'Big wave, boat tips, paddle smacks the head, knocks her into cold water, muscle spasm, can't breathe, all over.' Vandenburg put down his glass on the table, confident he held the winning hand. 'Ocean was rough that day. No one else was stupid enough to go out in it. There'd been a lot of rain, so the water was colder than usual. Mind you, it always seems to be raining in this dump, and Christ knows it's ball-shrinkingly cold down here at the best of times.'

'Did anyone actually see her out in the water? Was there no one on the beach? Any boats out?' She couldn't help but pepper him with questions.

A flicker of impatience passed across his face. 'Phone records have her at the shed.'

'What else do they show?'

Vandenburg threw up his arms in frustration. 'Reception around here is rubbish and the weather is miserable. Lifesavers are only employed to save tourists in summer. This is a pissant town in the middle of nowhere. No one was there to see anything.'

That was exactly what was wrong with the detective's version of events. It was an easy mistake to make if you have never lived in a country town. Alex had lived in several with Denny before heading to the city by herself. There was always someone who saw something.

'Look, I know you found that leg, which must have been upsetting, and it probably feels very important being involved in a crime investigation, but this one's just an accident.' Now he was patronising her.

'Quite a few of Maxine's friends believe she was murdered.'

Vandenburg's smile hardened into something mask-like. Alex could tell he was getting annoyed. 'Are you one of those friends? My understanding is that you never met the woman.'

'Who was the last person to see her alive?' she pressed, ignoring his question. 'What was she doing beforehand?'

'No deal,' he said. 'You tell me why you think it wasn't an accident.'

'Have you heard of the Bella Greggs case?'

'Of course,' he said warily.

'There was salt water in her lungs, even though she was found miles away from the sea.'

Vandenburg tilted his head back, eyes hooded. 'And here we have Maxine McFarlane pulled out of the ocean but with no salt water in her lungs.'

He wasn't stupid, Alex told herself, just lazy. He wants to wrap this up, leave Merritt and get home to his normal life. All things she could empathise with.

'There are rumours that Kingsley Kelly interfered in the Bella Greggs investigation.' She explained to him the story about finding the wings.

Vandenburg listened with his hands clasped behind his head. 'You don't like Kelly much, do you?'

'That's not why I'm here.'

'I have to say he's no fan of yours either. He warned me that you were an interfering lawyer. Told me I shouldn't bother talking to you.'

'That's completely unprofessional. I'm a witness in the case.'

'And that's why I am talking to you now.'

'How have you found him?' she asked.

'He's been pretty good. Sometimes country cops go all territorial, keep things hidden from you. He's been helpful.' Vandenburg nodded. 'Even gave me a lift to the pub tonight.'

That explained what Kelly was doing in the front bar.

'Did you tell him we were meeting up?'

'Was it supposed to be a state secret? Besides, I couldn't exactly keep it from him; I'm staying at his house.'

'What?'

'It's where all visiting police stay.'

Charlie Farinacci hadn't. Maybe Vandenburg *was* stupid.

'It's got a bungalow in the backyard and his missus, Cath, is a decent cook.' Vandenburg rubbed the back of his neck. 'He's a friendly guy. Sits down each night for a beer and chat about the day. He was the one who told me about dry drowning . . .' He stopped there, as if suddenly catching the implication of what he was saying, then continued: 'I mean, are you seriously alleging that Kelly tampered with a crime scene? For Christ's sake, you're a lawyer. You should know there needs to be something more substantial than a rumour before you start throwing that sort of muck around.'

'You're the only person I've told. Go have a talk to Charlie Farinacci about that investigation. See what he thought about Kelly.'

'This is my investigation and I'll decide who I talk to,' Vandenburg said dismissively. 'So far all you've talked about is Bella Greggs. My concern is Maxine McFarlane.'

Alex knew she was doing a poor job of articulating her concerns. She tried again.

'It's possible that the cases are connected. The two women were close. Bella was Maxine's favourite pupil. Maxine was curating an exhibition of Bella's artwork at the local museum, an exhibition that she was worried about because she knew it was going to cause a stir. Kelly even tried to stop it. And there is this,' she said, putting a carefully wrapped square package on the table.

'What is it?' asked Vandenburg.

'It's Maxine's diary.'

Alex had pored over it, trying to decipher its contents, and she had photographed every page.

Before Vandenburg could respond, the door to the garden swung open.

'This is where you got to!' said Kelly. 'Thirsty work all this chatting, so I thought I'd bring you out another beer. G'day, Alex.

I was just having a lovely catch-up with Denny in there. Always enjoyed a party, your mother.'

Alex didn't notice Vandenburg move but somehow the diary had vanished off the table. She stood up and grabbed her damp jacket. 'I should go back and have my meal.'

'Don't let me chase you away,' Kelly said. 'Stay, have another beer. My shout.'

'No thanks.' She turned to Vandenburg. 'Good luck with the investigation.'

Chapter 10

Next day, the weather was dismal, so Denny decided that she didn't want to go to the climate change rally after all.

'But you promised Tayla,' Alex reminded her. 'You said we would go.' She stood looking at the ceiling in the front room to see if rain had got in overnight. It was hard to distinguish the water damage from the cracks in the plaster. This whole house was probably about to fall down around their ears.

'You can go for both of us.' Denny was tucked up in a blanket in front of the television. 'It'll probably be cancelled anyway.'

When Alex looked out the window there was a gloomy haze of grey clouds, but in the distance, a ribbon of blue sky was visible, like the trim on a dress. It held out the promise that there might be sunshine sometime in the next few hours.

'All right, I'll drop in for a few minutes before I meet up with Robyn.'

Denny gave a hollow laugh.

'Well, she's not going to be happy to hear what I have to tell her,' said Alex.

'Good,' said Denny.

Nathan, the young policeman Alex had seen at the beach the day she found Maxine's leg, was in the middle of the intersection in front of the surf club, making heavy weather of directing the traffic as minibuses took up parking bays, disgorging groups of protesters clutching homemade banners. Traffic management was not usually needed in Merritt, and the drivers in the stopped cars were getting impatient.

Alex hadn't expected much of a turnout at the rally, but there was quite a crowd spilling out from the park onto the footpath. Kids from the local high school were there, most in an approximation of their uniform, as if they had just wandered out of class. They stood in tight knots and took selfies with different placards. Surfers in wetsuits carried their boards, and a clutch of grandmothers wearing matching purple t-shirts started up some chanting and waved their posters. Alex's favourite was I'M TOO OLD TO PROTEST THIS SHIT, brandished by a woman in a wheelchair who had to be at least eighty.

Alex could see Tayla standing up the back of the stage next to some musical equipment. She was wearing a fluoro yellow dress with matching leg warmers and had a bass guitar slung about her. Next to her, Erin fiddled with a drum kit.

Another minibus beeped loudly at the policeman directing traffic and then, ignoring his instructions, barrelled through to park next to the others. There was a familiar face at the wheel.

Lou Buckley hopped down from the driver's seat and gave Alex a cheery wave as more people poured out of the side of the bus. He was looking particularly dapper in a crisply ironed shirt and camel-coloured sports coat.

'You've got a lead foot,' Alex said.

'The man didn't know what he was doing,' Lou replied. 'Someone had to take charge. Bit of good news: I got my mower back.'

'Was it Dylan?'

'Course it was bloody Dylan. King Kelly ran the "I can neither confirm nor deny" line, though. Told me there was no need to press charges. I like that!' Lou's tone suggested otherwise. 'It's a two-tiered justice system in this town. Maybe we need to have a protest about that next.'

'Instead of climate change?' Alex asked.

'Bugger climate change. It's all a hoax.'

The crowd was getting larger by the minute. 'Looks like the rest of Merritt disagrees with you.'

'People love a good whinge,' said Lou. 'The bigger the mob, the smaller the brain.'

A blonde woman walked past. She stood by herself, a camera around her neck, acknowledging no one, separate from the large scrum of people crammed in front of the stage. Alex recognised her as the bartender from the Sail. Away from the artificial light of the bar, she looked younger and more fragile.

'Who's that?' Alex asked Lou.

He glanced in the direction she was pointing. 'Sasha Greggs,' he said.

Sasha Greggs. Bella's mother.

A klaxon-like squeak blasted from a nearby speaker. A woman was anxiously tapping the microphone and saying, 'One-two, one-two,' as if she had forgotten that three came next. A murmur of restless expectation swept through the crowd.

There was a purring engine-like noise.

Alex stared up at the sky. A sleek black wasp of a helicopter was approaching.

'Who is it?'

'Only the bloody Messiah coming to save us all,' Lou said, waggling a finger above his head. 'You watch this lot cheer like their bank balance depends on it – mostly because it does.'

The chopper hovered over a nearby oval which, Alex noticed only now, had been roped off. The tail bobbed upwards before it settled into place. With the rotors still moving, lights blinking, a figure emerged. He bent over, moving clear, the wind from the blades pulling at his hair and clothes. The helicopter rose, turned, hung in the space for an instant, then moved higher.

The man was in casual clothes – jeans, t-shirt, a windcheater – but Alex recognised the face. Almost straight away he was greeted by onlookers and was shaking hands and kissing cheeks. It was certainly an entrance, though not an environmentally friendly one.

'Mr Quirke, in the flesh,' said Lou.

'Okay, everyone,' came the amplified voice from the stage. 'Let's start off with a few chants to get us in the mood.'

As the crowd surged forwards, Lou gave Alex a wink. 'Now's the time for me to nip off to the TAB. The dogs are running today.'

'You're not going to stay?' asked Alex.

'I reckon it'll be raining soon.'

It started drizzling just after the Acknowledgement of Country had finished. Three kids from Merritt Primary School were up at the microphone. Alex kept her eye on Nic Quirke, who stood at the side of the stage. Theo Rushall was next to him, looking almost like his bodyguard. Someone brought an umbrella over and offered it to Nic, but he shook his head, remaining focused on the speeches. He clapped loudly when the kids were finished and high-fived them as they got off the stage.

A few more chants were tried.

'WHAT DO WE WANT? CLIMATE JUSTICE!'

'WHEN DO WE WANT IT? NOW!'

And then the anxious woman was back, looking a bit happier. 'Next up is someone who doesn't need any introduction to the people of Merritt. He may not be a local, but we love him all the same . . .'

The rest of the introduction was lost in the noise. Nic Quirke bounded on stage, pushing his wet hair back from his forehead.

'Hello,' he said into the microphone, and got another cheer. There was a beat as he acknowledged the applause and then gestured for the crowd to pipe down.

'How are you all doing?'

He was milking it now.

'It's always good to be back in Merritt. I won't make this long, because the last thing you guys need is an outsider up here telling you what you already know, especially in this weather. I'm here today, and you are too, because we care about the environment.

Merritt is a special place and we want to preserve it for our children and grandchildren. It needs to be cherished and cared for, developed properly for the benefit of the community.'

Nic stood back for a moment, enjoying the performative howls of furious agreement. Alex checked the time on her phone. Robyn would be waiting for her. She was going to have to miss Tayla's band.

'A good friend of mine died recently,' continued Nic. 'Maxine McFarlane was not just a talented artist . . .'

Alex turned back towards the stage, more interested now.

'. . . she was also passionate about the environment. So today I want to do something in her honour. That's why I am announcing plans for a joint project between this community and Quirke Industries for Merritt to be run on one hundred per cent renewable energy. Not in fifty years' time, not ten years, but in five years. It won't be easy, but it *is* possible.'

'Whose money?' came the shout.

Alex searched the crowd for the voice. She thought it was a young man wearing a trucking cap with a hoodie over it, stained dark by the rain. Placards were now covering people's heads, being used as mini-shelters.

On the stage, Nic was still talking as if he hadn't heard. 'Working together . . .'

'How much are you chipping in?' shouted another voice and then another, impossible to ignore now. 'What about the Eden Point Development?'

But the naysayers were drowned out by the rest of the crowd, who reverted to an earlier chant – 'WHAT DO WE WANT?' – and, after a moment's hesitation, amended the response to 'RENEWABLE ENERGY', which was harder to coordinate.

Standing on the sidelines, the anxious woman had progressed to worried. Theo was standing next to her, shoulders hunched against the rain, his face impassive.

Nic put his hands in the air, still smiling. He walked off the stage to general whoops and cheers.

'Sorry, everyone,' the anxious MC began, 'but due to the weather we'll have to postpone the rest of our speakers and the entertainment . . .'

Loud boos followed but people were already starting to peel off.

'Please make sure to sign up to our attendance sheets so we can keep in contact about this important . . .'

Alex, drenched now, ran across the street. The museum and local library sat next to each other, sharing a joint wall, but there was a contrast in the architecture. The library was a sleek modern glass box, whereas the beige-brick museum looked down at heel and neglected, the type of building that would be freezing in winter and too hot in summer. It clearly had never been a candidate for politicians' promises and government funding.

Robyn stood out on the street under the awning, waiting for her. Alex almost expected a telling-off for being late, but instead there was a matter-of-fact nod acknowledging her presence.

'This weather,' said Alex, pushing wet hair out of her eyes.

'At least it cut Nic Quirke's speech in half,' said Robyn. 'If it had been a sunny day, he'd still be going.'

'It was a pretty important announcement,' said Alex. 'And in memory of Maxine.'

'Beware billionaires bearing gifts because chances are you'll end up paying for them.' Robyn looked sideways at her, as she adjusted her scarf like she was about to get down to business.

'I've had my fair share of run-ins with Mr Quirke over the Eden Point Development.'

'What is it?' asked Alex, who hadn't heard anything about it.

'Just his brilliant idea to put an enormous housing development on pristine bushland. He claims that it's all sustainable building and green architecture but then he's a great one for announcements and pretty words like that speech he just gave. I intend to keep on holding him to account. Plenty in this town have put their money in and they've a lot more to lose than Nic Quirke. But that's not why you're here. Come on inside.'

Alex followed Robyn, her wet shoes squelching on the linoleum floor.

'Don't take another step,' said Robyn, crisp lines of disapproval around her mouth, when she noticed the trail of wet footprints. 'I'll get you a towel to dry yourself.'

Alex stood there and looked around as Robyn bustled off. She had heard so much about this museum from Prue but had never bothered to come inside before. Right in front of her was the counter for ticket sales, next to a small gift shop filled with postcards, books, knick-knacks and the sort of floral silk scarves Robyn seemed to be so fond of.

The title of the exhibition had been stencilled on the opposite wall: WHEN WE FALL. An interesting name. It was as if the phrase had been left deliberately unfinished. Fall where? How? Alex tried to complete the phrase – fall in love, fall pregnant, fall apart.

The introduction underneath the heading stated that this was an exhibition about forced adoption in Australia, which made a bit more sense of the title. Perhaps the three examples of falling

Alex had come up with mirrored the trajectory for some of the women who had given up their babies.

There had been a government inquiry into past practices which had led to a formal apology and the exhibition was designed to increase understanding and share experiences.

Alex looked around. There didn't seem to be anyone besides her who wanted to increase their understanding and even she was here for another reason. Prue had mentioned the exhibition was proving unpopular.

Through the clear glass wall separating the museum from the library, she could see seniors reading newspapers and magazines on bright green couches and a procession of young children, parents and prams, as well as wet protesters from the rally streaming through the entrance.

'Here you are,' said Robyn, coming back with an armful of towels. Alex started to rub her hair with one as Robyn mopped the floor with another.

'Pretty quiet day for you,' said Alex.

'Had a local through this morning. Lovely young man named Theo Rushall.'

Alex gave a half-smile of recognition. 'I know Theo.'

'I suspect Prue encouraged him to come along to improve numbers. He was very helpful; came and moved some things around for me out the back.'

Alex walked over to the wall that had a framed version of the National Apology that had been given by the Prime Minister in Parliament. It spoke of hurt and betrayal, shameful practices and grief. 'I guess it's all such a long time ago. People have moved on and they don't want to look back.'

'The type of policies documented here might have officially ended years ago,' said Robyn, 'but unofficially, well that's something quite different. Attitudes don't change overnight. Merritt has always been a hard place for single mothers. Your own mother could tell you that. I expect that's the reason why she left.'

Alex felt a stab of sadness. Because Denny refused to talk about Alex's father, the topic of her pregnancy was off limits too. It was this unspoken subject between the two of them, a locked door that had never been opened. Her mother had always seemed so fearless, Alex didn't want to think of her ever being young and scared or, worse, regretful about having her.

'Sasha Greggs is another one,' continued Robyn. 'I've heard people blaming her for Bella's murder as if that is the inevitable outcome of Sasha being a teenage single mother.'

'What about Bella's father?' Alex asked. 'What happened to him?' But she could already guess the answer. He had disappeared, of course, just like Alex's own father had.

Robyn snorted. 'Don't you know, it's all immaculate conception in these parts. The closest Bella had to a dad was Johnny Ewart. I wish I could say that Johnny was better than nothing, but nothing would actually be preferable to him.'

Johnny Ewart. Alex had seen that name before on the back of a mugshot. He was one of Charlie Farinacci's suspects in Bella's death. Her mother's boyfriend. Something else that felt predictable.

'I met up with Vandenburg last night,' Alex said. 'The police seem to be convinced that Maxine's death is an accident. I expect that's what they're going to tell the coroner.'

Robyn stood there, arms folded, and listened as Alex ran through what Vandenburg had told her in relation to dry drowning. She seemed neither surprised nor disappointed.

'Come with me,' she said, once Alex had finished. 'I want to show you this.'

The two women walked through the first room of the exhibition, into a smaller space.

'There,' said Robyn.

Alex stood in front of an exhibit of some official-looking documents hanging on the wall, rubbing her still-damp hair with the towel.

'There's a reason that this exhibition doesn't just focus on illegal adoptions and includes forced ones. Just because the law is followed, the forms all filled in correctly and people in authority stamp the document, doesn't make it right. See that?' The older woman pointed to the initials *BFA* scrawled on top of a page dated 1961. Alex thought it looked like a hospital medical record. 'That stands for Baby For Adoption. They used to put it on the file of every single young unmarried mother who came in to give birth, without the mother knowing. Didn't matter if she wanted to keep her baby or hadn't made up her mind. Every doctor, every nurse, every social worker would see that and act accordingly. There are hundreds, if not thousands, of pieces of paper with BFA written on them. Officials were deciding what was best for someone they had never met before, knowing nothing about the women or their circumstances. So I'm not interested in whatever that young whippersnapper detective from the city thinks about someone he never met. I *knew* Maxine and I'm sure she was murdered.'

Robyn was a solid rock and had no intention of moving.

'Okay,' said Alex. 'Tell me why.'

They sat together at the front desk of the museum. Robyn pulled a manila folder out of a nearby filing cabinet and placed it between the cash register and ticket sales book. As she began flicking through its contents, Alex could see pages of perfect copperplate handwriting, presumably Robyn's. When she was a solicitor she had learnt to beware clients who brought in reams of notes in their own handwriting. None of this was going to be evidence of anything other than Robyn's own opinion.

'Are you interested in art?' Robyn asked.

Alex thought she'd misheard. 'Art?'

'Do you appreciate art?'

'What has that got to do with this?'

'Everything,' Robyn insisted, getting impatient now, as if this was a classroom and Alex a particularly dense student.

'Then no, not really.'

'That's unfortunate.' Robyn gave her a severe look. 'Because the exhibition that Maxine was organising in relation to Bella's work is at the heart of this.'

'I think you'd better start at the beginning.'

'The exhibition was intended to raise money for Sasha Greggs – that's Bella's mother.'

Alex nodded to indicate she'd got that far at least.

'Maxine was hoping that if we raised enough money, Sasha might leave town and start again. She didn't think much of Johnny.'

'Tell me about him.'

Robyn pursed her mouth. 'Local troublemaker, rumoured to be a drug dealer, if not worse. I know Maxine was worried that he was violent towards Sasha. Even Kelly thinks he's no good. If he could stay permanently stationed in front of Sasha's house, he would.'

Kelly hanging around Sasha's house. It reminded Alex of what Tayla had said about Kelly hanging around Bella.

'I tried to discuss him with Sasha myself, but she reacted badly to what was only a well-intentioned gesture of help.'

Another person to add to the growing list of people whom Robyn had annoyed.

'The exhibition,' prompted Alex.

'We started to collect Bella's paintings. Most of them had been kept in Sasha's shed. Maxine went through them with a fine-tooth comb, turning over every scrap of paper that had so much as a scribble on it. Made sure that Sasha stored the best ones inside the house.'

'Really? Was Bella's work that good?'

'That's one of hers.' Robyn pointed to a picture on the wall next to the gift shop.

It was an abstract, quite small with very delicate brushwork. Edged in dark black-blue, there was a knot of white light, tinged with yellow, at its centre, with lighter shades swirling around it, bleeding elegant watercolour across the paper, suggesting movement.

'Bella was a genuine talent, in my opinion,' said Robyn.

Alex stared up at it. She liked the picture, but at the same time she wasn't quite sure what it was supposed to be about. A storm, perhaps. Night-time. 'What's it called?'

'*Light in the Darkness*,' said Robyn. 'She painted it for young Theo's fundraiser for the lighthouse a few years back and I bought it. Cost me a bit, I don't mind telling you. Still, all for a good cause.'

The lighthouse! That made Alex like it more. It was a good title as well. She always found it annoying when paintings were untitled. Words were important; they helped explain things.

'I look up at that and think it's what we all need to do, be lights in the darkness,' said Robyn. 'That's why I wanted to have this exhibition and why I'm determined to find out what happened to Maxine.'

'Why do you think Maxine was killed?'

Robyn shot her an annoyed look, as if it was self-evident. 'Because she worked out who murdered Bella, of course.'

Alex's heart began to beat a little quicker. 'Who did she say that was?'

Robyn didn't answer.

'She did tell you, right?'

The older woman sat there, lips pursed. 'Unfortunately, no. She didn't say anything.'

So this was all in Robyn's head. Alex shook her own head in frustration, sending droplets of water flying onto the counter. She would just have to tell Prue that Vandenburg wasn't going to pay attention to opinions. Where was the evidence that Robyn had promised?

'Why didn't Maxine take it to the police, then?'

'Artists don't think like the rest of us. She was the sort of person who preferred her art to do the talking.'

'What do you mean?'

'Maxine was painting something for the exhibition.'

Alex nodded. 'Silver mentioned it to me.'

Robyn reached into the file and brought out a typed list numbered from one to twenty. 'These were all the pieces that were going to be exhibited. Look at number twenty, the final piece. It was planned to be at the very heart of the exhibition.'

Alex ran her eyes down the list until she found it.

The work was called *The Accusation*.

'They say a picture is worth a thousand words,' said Robyn.

Was that true? Not in Alex's opinion and certainly not in a courtroom. Alex had spent years working with words. She was comfortable with words, especially when they came in neat, numbered paragraphs, correctly formatted, laying out a position in a logical manner. Pictures weren't quite as convincing. Still, the title made her sit up.

'Have you seen it?'

Robyn shook her head. 'It's not just one painting: there were three artworks – a triptych. Here's the layout that Maxine drew.'

It was a careful bird's-eye view sketch of the museum, numbers neatly placed. Robyn pointed to the three boxes with the number twenty on them.

'A triptych?' echoed Alex. 'Aren't they usually religious?'

'Not necessarily. The term "triptych" just means three works that together create a bigger whole. All I know was one part was an original by Bella, another part was done by Maxine and the last was something they had made together. Maxine didn't want anyone to see it until the opening of the exhibition.'

'Show me.'

'The thing is,' said Robyn, 'they're missing. That's why I put off meeting with you; I was trying to find them. Maxine never brought them to the museum. I went and checked her house and her gallery. There were paintings there, of course, but nothing new that looked like part of a triptych.'

Alex tried to work out the implications of this. There could be another reason why the paintings were missing. What if they had been stolen to sell?

'Would the art be valuable? Financially, I mean?'

Robyn sat back in her chair. 'It depends. Bella is an unknown artist, so it's unlikely her part would be, but depending on what Maxine painted, that could be worth more.'

'So it's possible, hypothetically speaking, someone could have stolen it for the money, not because they had something to hide.'

'Possible . . . but very unlikely,' said Robyn. 'You would have to find the right buyer for starters. Locals didn't have a clue how valuable Maxine's work was. I'm assuming that Silver explained the unorthodox nature of it to you.'

'You mean the fact that Maxine made fancy knock-offs for rich guys.'

'That isn't how I'd describe them.'

'Have you reported the paintings missing to the police?' asked Alex.

'Not yet,' said Robyn. 'There is one place I haven't checked yet.'

'Where?'

'Sasha's house. I know that Maxine visited her a couple of days before she died.'

'Then perhaps you should ask her if she knows anything.'

Robyn gave her a tight smile. It was the type of smile that the partner at her old law firm used to give her late on a Friday afternoon when he asked for something to be done by first thing Monday and knew it would take the entire weekend. 'Unfortunately, Sasha has made it abundantly clear that I'm not welcome at her house. I was rather hoping *you* might ask her. If she understood it could help to find Bella's murderer, I'm sure she'd cooperate – especially if she knew a lawyer was involved.'

Just then the phone rang and Robyn reached over to answer it in her best telephone voice. Alex stood up and walked away, almost relieved at the interruption. Already this was bracket creep for favours. She'd talked to Vandenburg at Robyn's behest. Now the woman wanted her to visit the mother of a murdered girl.

Distracted, she began to walk around the rest of the exhibition and read some of the stories documented. Each was a small sad tale of devastation. One woman described the loss of her child as a wound that never healed.

Standing there, she thought about her grandfather wanting to have her adopted out, telling Denny that she'd be a bad mother. It was such an awful thing to say, Alex had found it hard to believe. But now she understood. In a world where it was so easy to separate mothers and babies, no wonder he thought that was acceptable. That his own social standing was more important than his grandchild. She should ask her mother about that time before those experiences slipped out of Denny's mind permanently. She could add that to the to-do list that already included hassling the assisted living facility, organising to sell her grandparents' place, sending more pleading emails to Glenys for work and taking solicitor friends out to lunch on her second credit card, the one only to be used in case of emergencies, in the hope of drumming up some work.

'Another booking to see the exhibition,' Robyn called out to her as she put the phone down. Her voice echoed through the almost empty room. 'Poor woman was crying, saying she had to give up her baby over fifty years ago. The people who tore these families apart should be held to account.'

'Yes,' agreed Alex, though she knew they wouldn't be. It was all too long ago and impossible to prove.

'Just like something needs to be done to find the person who murdered Bella and Maxine.' There was a note of triumph in Robyn's voice, as if she had laid the bait and hooked her catch. 'So you will visit Sasha and ask about the paintings?'

Alex knew she had been beaten.

Chapter 11

Alex was scrolling through healthy recipes on her phone, trying to decide what to cook for dinner. Denny sat with her in the kitchen drinking tea but not expressing any interest in the different meal options that Alex suggested. Definitely loss of appetite, Alex thought. She'd have to tell Kiran at their next appointment.

'Robyn took me around her exhibition today,' Alex said, putting the phone down. 'The one about forced adoption,' she added, in case Denny had forgotten.

Her mother became very intent on her cup of tea. Alex could feel the tension but she soldiered on.

'She said Merritt was a hard place for single mothers.'

Denny sat up in the chair, back ramrod-straight. Her eyes darted from the tea, past Alex to the fridge and then back again.

Alex could sense she was getting ready to escape. Why was this topic so hard for her to discuss?

'What would Robyn know? She doesn't even have children,' came the clipped reply. The telltale signs of anger were there, the hollowed cheeks and set jaw. 'Always presuming to talk about things she doesn't understand.'

Alex wanted to reach out to her mother, to wrap her in a hug, ask her what it was like then and tell her how brave she was to raise a kid on her own. For a moment this seemed a shimmering possibility, but then reality hit and her courage failed. Denny would only push her away and tell her to stop being ridiculous. There was a gulf between them that was too wide to bridge. She deflected momentarily. 'Robyn mentioned Sasha Greggs. Do you know her?'

Denny blinked, looking at Alex suspiciously, as if this were some sort of test. 'Works down at the pub. The blonde one.' She hooked her fingers into the cup's handle but didn't pick it up. 'Her daughter was the one that was killed.'

'Bella.'

Her mother nodded and then raised the cup to her mouth. Her hand shook slightly. Denny was getting frail.

'Did you know Bella?'

Slowly, the cup made its way back to the table. 'Never met her. Bit of a wild one, people said. Used to protest the logging. No wonder she ended up dead. Merritt doesn't like mouthy women.'

'Is that why you left?'

Denny flashed a look at her daughter but Alex wasn't quite sure how to read it. Anger? Fear? Words, thought Alex. What I want is words. I want to understand. She waited in silence for her mother's reply.

'I had my reasons,' Denny said at last. A hesitation and then, 'What about Sasha?'

Subject dismissed, not to be discussed. Alex gave up. Perhaps she would never know what her mother had been through, maybe Denny had forgotten those memories already.

'Robyn wants me to talk to her,' Alex said. 'Apparently, some paintings of Maxine's are missing. Sasha might know where they are.'

'Got you running her errands now? Typical. Give her an inch.'

'It's more complicated than that,' said Alex, even though she thought Denny could have a point.

Alex's phone began vibrating on the table.

'Probably Robyn ringing with more jobs for you to do.' Denny gave a knowing half-grin. 'Now that she's got her hooks into you, she won't let go easily.'

But it wasn't Robyn. It was Julie at the police station, asking for Alex to drop by as soon as possible. She couched it in terms of a demand rather than a request. Perhaps Vandenburg was having second thoughts and had decided to give her a better hearing?

'I'll be there in twenty minutes,' Alex told Julie.

'I'm going out,' she said to Denny. 'I'll pick up some fish and chips on my way home.'

That got the biggest smile Alex had seen all day, though whether it was for the food or the fact Alex was leaving it was hard to tell.

Julie's eyes lit up as Alex entered the police station.

'Oh, hello. I'll let them know you're here.'

It was ominously polite and Alex had logged the 'they'. This had the hallmarks of an ambush, which was confirmed when she was shown into Kelly's office. Kelly was sitting behind his desk, fingers digging into his forehead, which looked even more lined than usual. Grey skin under his eyes suggested that he hadn't been sleeping well. Vandenburg was leaning against the wall, an arm carelessly propped up on the filing cabinet, an unreadable expression on his face.

An empty seat on the other side of the desk looked like it was meant for her. It felt like the start of an interrogation.

'Did you give this to Detective Vandenburg?' Kelly asked without preamble. He pushed a clear evidence bag containing a book across the desk towards her. It was Maxine's diary.

Her stomach clenched but she kept her face impassive. 'Yes,' she said. Say as little as possible until you know what this is all about, she warned herself.

'And Karl here tells me you are questioning the quality of the investigation into Bella Greggs's death.'

She could sense Vandenburg shifting uneasily behind her. What exactly had he told Kelly?

'No.' She would not let this man railroad her into something she didn't say. 'I'm sure Charlie Farinacci conducted the investigation as thoroughly as he could under the circumstances.'

She waited to see if Kelly understood the implied criticism of him in her words.

They were like petrol on a fire.

'What is that supposed to mean?' Kelly replied in a tone of righteous indignation. 'Who do you think you are,' he thundered, his words becoming blurred with anger, 'interfering in matters you do not understand?'

But Alex had been yelled at by bigger dickheads than Kelly. There were solicitors, legal partners she had worked for, opposing barristers and even judges. The type of men who relished the lacerating rebuke. From them, Alex had learnt the art of detachment, how to let the insults wash over her. And so she watched unmoved as Kelly progressed into full-blown rage.

Alex wasn't blind to the failings of the justice system. She knew that sometimes the courts got it badly wrong. Policing was a hard job. Particularly for country cops, who worked far more hours than they were paid for, in a role that was part social worker, part enforcer, part diplomat. But still, she was gobsmacked by Kelly's behaviour now. It was clear that something very strange was going on. He seemed unhinged. Alex could feel her own temper rising in response. More than anything else, this man was a gatekeeper. If he interfered in a murder case, then the courts, the part of the justice system that she was most interested in, as problematic as they could be, were irrelevant. The matter would never even get there.

'What have you got to say for yourself?' asked Kelly.

'Only this,' Alex said, standing up. 'Your behaviour is completely unprofessional and I will consider lodging a complaint against you. Why are you fighting so hard to dismiss the connections between Maxine McFarlane and Bella Greggs?'

There, she had said it out aloud.

Her unrepentant tone pulled Kelly up short.

'There *is* no connection. Maxine drowned. It was an accident.'

'Is that the official finding of the investigation or just your preferred outcome?' She turned to look at Vandenburg for confirmation.

If he was uneasy about how this meeting was going, Vandenburg didn't show it. He returned her gaze with no hint of shame.

'You are just a smart-arse city lawyer who doesn't know the first thing about what is going on here!' Kelly jabbed the air with his finger. 'Under no circumstances are you to involve yourself in police business any further. Do you understand me?'

This wasn't a court, where she would be given the opportunity to speak, to present a different case. There was no judge here who was obliged to listen to both sides of the argument. Kelly had shaped the facts that were known into a story and he controlled the narrative. The only way she was going to persuade anyone that he was wrong would be if she found out what happened to Maxine herself – and right now, staring at an apoplectic Kelly, there was nothing in the world that she wanted to do more, other than possibly punch him.

'If only I had a pair of wings to fly away from here,' she said.

As she turned to leave, she saw Kelly's mouth drop. She had hit the target.

Alex left the room, closing the door gently behind her – though it was tempting to slam it so hard that every window in the place shattered. But she would not give Vandenburg the satisfaction. She had been told he was lazy, but this was something different. They had talked about concerns around Kelly and he had gone straight to the man and told him everything.

Moving down the corridor, she saw Julie hurrying back to her seat. The woman had probably been standing outside the office door, trying to eavesdrop. Her head remained suspiciously bowed as Alex walked out.

Right now, Alex hated just about every person in the building.

'Alex!'

She had reached her car when she heard someone calling her name. It was Vandenburg. The temptation to run him down, reverse over him and then run him down again was overwhelming.

'It wasn't me,' he said. He held his hands palms facing her as if to indicate surrender.

Ignoring him, she opened the car door.

'Hang on, hear me out.' He reached for her arm but withdrew when he caught sight of her expression. Instead, he held on to the door, apparently certain she would not slam it on his fingers. Brave move.

'I'm not interested in anything you have to say,' Alex snapped.

'It was Nathan, the young constable here,' he said. 'I asked him if he knew about Bella Greggs's case. I thought he might have heard those rumours about the wings. When I got in this afternoon, he was already in Kelly's office. There wasn't any time to warn you. I was ambushed as well.' He took his hands off the door, more confident now that Alex was going to keep listening.

'Kelly just said that you were the one who told him,' Alex reminded him.

'I couldn't lie about it when he asked me straight out. I need to retain his trust if we're going to get anywhere. If you're right about those wings, this is some serious shit – a murder investigation compromised right from the start by the officer in charge.

Besides,' he continued, eyes sliding away in admission, 'he's been on my case to wrap this up quickly, wanting me to endorse the "dry drowning" theory.'

So, it was only a theory now? That, at least, was progress.

'Didn't notice you coming to my defence in there,' she said. 'This is your investigation, not Kelly's. You could have told him that he was out of line.'

Vandenburg's jaw hardened. He turned away and took several loud breaths as if to calm himself.

'Was there anything in that diary you gave me?' he asked. 'I've flicked through it. As far as I can see it's just a bunch of drawings.'

That was what Alex had thought until she got to the final page.

'Flicked through it?'

'I've been busy.'

Her turn to exhale.

'The last appointment Maxine wrote in it was at the Eyrie,' she said.

'What the fuck is an eyrie?'

'It's the name of Nic Quirke's property up in the bush. He was also one of Charlie Farinacci's suspects in Bella's murder.'

'Quirke? That tech guy who part owns the art gallery?'

At least he had got that far.

'He seems to have money all over Merritt. It's like it's some sort of weird personal vanity project. He just gave a big speech at the climate change protest saying how sad he was about Maxine's death. You need to interview him.'

Vandenburg frowned. 'Anything else?'

For some reason, she was not quite prepared to tell him about *The Accusation*. She didn't need to, she reasoned; not yet.

Vandenburg had delayed wrapping things up. Hopefully, that would give her enough time to find the paintings and see if they supported Robyn's hypothesis. Instead, she mentioned something else that had occurred to her.

'A teenager by the name of Dylan Ferris was the one who supposedly saw Kelly take the wings off Bella's body. Kelly has been giving him preferential treatment. Just in the last week, he refused to bring charges against him, despite Dylan being caught red-handed with stolen property. You need to see if he'll make a statement about what he saw during the search for Bella.'

Vandenburg let go of the car door and shoved his hands in his pockets.

'Bella Greggs isn't my case.'

'They're connected.'

'How can you be so certain?'

'Maxine was an artist. She drew all over that diary: sketches of people, places she'd been. It's like a visual record of each day. Guess what she drew on the day she was killed?'

'Surprise me.'

'A pair of beautiful black wings.'

Chapter 12

Alex read each passing street sign. It was early Monday afternoon and she was driving out of town up into the hills. There was a property advertising pony rides and several signs that promised hot chips in large block letters. Slow drops of water dimpled the windscreen. The entire place felt damp.

There was a knot in her stomach. She had spent the weekend worrying about what to say to Sasha, let alone what would happen if Kelly found out what she was doing.

Caught up with her own thoughts, Alex didn't see the bicycle. As she turned into Sasha's street, it seemed to come out of nowhere and nearly ran into the side of her car. A narrowly avoided disaster.

Slamming on her brakes, she swore so loudly that the boy looked at her, helmet swinging from his handlebars. He stared at her: blond hair, chin-length, knotted, under a dark beanie. Heart thumping, Alex recognised him as the boy who had sat across from her at the police station. Lou Buckley had said his name was Curtis. Curtis leered and then gave her the middle finger before slowly cycling around the car and up the hill, standing up on the pedals to grind his way forward.

Breathing hard, Alex pulled into the street.

The cul-de-sac was on the outskirts of the town, surrounded by bush, a world away from the gentrification of Merritt's main street. Some brick, most of them fibro, these were houses that had Rottweilers and German shepherds rather than automated security systems. She double-checked the address Robyn had given her. Yes, she was in the right place.

Behind the chain-link fence, long grass surrounded the house, the garden overgrown. There was a rusting Bedford truck next to an old brick garage. As she parked out the front, Alex tried to imagine what it must be like to have police on your doorstep telling you that your daughter was dead. Who would have done the death notification? It was most likely to have been Kelly. He was the senior officer in charge of the search and the person who had found Bella.

Kelly.

What else did he know about that death? Could it be guilt that was driving his erratic behaviour? Was it fear?

The house, painted yellow with green trim, was old, with small windows and a wraparound verandah. It felt isolated, somehow separate from the rest of the street. Alex was still sitting in her car staring when a knock on the window made her jump.

It was Erin, the waitress from Rosie's coffee shop.

Alex got out of the car.

'Hi,' Erin said. 'Thought it was you.'

'Hello,' said Alex. 'What are you doing out here?'

'I live here.' Erin pointed to a small fibro house behind her. 'What's your excuse?'

'Just dropping in.' Alex nodded in the direction of Sasha's house.

Erin made a surprised face. 'You picking up from Johnny?'

'Picking up?' Then, realising what Erin meant, Alex shook her head. 'No, nothing like that. I'm here to see Sasha.'

'Oh, right. She'll be there.'

Robyn had told Alex that Monday was Sasha's day off from working at the pub. 'Is Johnny home as well?' she asked.

Erin shook her head. 'He does the day shift up at the sawmill.'

'Does he get a few visitors dropping by?'

'Enough,' said Erin. 'Used to be pretty bad, but he's been quieter lately.'

'Turning over a new leaf?' Alex tried to make a joke of it.

Erin gave a half-smile. 'Wouldn't go that far.'

Alex was about to say goodbye but then thought of something. 'So you must have known Bella?'

If Erin found the question an odd one, she didn't say. 'She was one of my best friends.'

'What was she like? It's just that I saw one of her artworks at the museum and I can't stop thinking about it.'

'Bella was like anchovies,' said Erin. 'You either loved her or you hated her. Occasionally both at once. She was really passionate about everything. When she wanted something she would go for it at a million miles an hour and wouldn't listen to anyone who tried to stop her. It was impossible to be bored around Bella, and that's saying a lot in Merritt. I sometimes wonder what she'd think if she could see me now, still living at home, working as a waitress.'

'I'm sure she would have liked Hatpin Panic.'

Erin smiled. 'Yeah, she would have loved that. Probably would have fought like hell with Tayla, though. They never got on.'

'Why?'

'I think they were jealous of each other.'

Alex could understand Tayla being jealous of Bella and her artistic genius and loud opinions, but why would Bella be jealous of Tayla?

'They probably would have got over that in time,' Alex said.

Erin gave a sad smile. 'We'll never know.'

As Alex walked through the gate towards the house, the green front door opened and Sasha came out onto the verandah. She was wearing denim overalls with a blue t-shirt underneath, a thick Aran-style cardigan and a wary expression. Her blonde hair made an untidy wispy halo around her head.

Even at a distance Alex could sense the grief radiating off Sasha. Prue had said something about it damaging people. Sasha was a perfect example of that.

'I know who you are,' Sasha said. 'Denny Walker's girl.' A low voice, deeper than her narrow frame would suggest.

At least she didn't ask if Alex was a lawyer, like most of Merritt's residents.

Alex had searched online to get some sense of what Bella was like, and there was no doubting that this was Bella's mother, with the same wide dark eyes in a narrow face. Luckily, the girl had a knack for getting attention at logging protests and rallies. Trawling through clip after clip of poorly shot, wobbling footage, Alex had seen Bella marching along the main street of Merritt; Bella up in a tree, refusing to come down; and, of most interest to Alex, Bella standing next to a cop car out in the bush. She was wearing her black wings, talking animatedly to the camera about how the police had just raided their camp. In the background, in a high-vis police uniform, his arms folded, sunglasses resting on the top of his cap, was Kingsley Kelly. His eyes flickered over to Bella from time to time, a look of bemusement on his face. Alex had watched that piece of footage over and over again.

If Maxine was a person who didn't deal in words, Bella was a person who had an abundance of them.

'What do you want?' Sasha asked.

'I want to talk to you about Maxine McFarlane,' said Alex. 'Can I come in?'

Sasha stood there for several seconds, staring at her, then she turned and walked into the house, leaving the front door open behind her. That was enough of an invitation.

Inside, rooms painted in different colours – brick red, bright blue, a sunny yellow – branched out on either side of the hall. Underfoot, the floorboards gleamed and creaked loudly. Sasha led the way to a large open-plan kitchen and living room full of clutter. A shabby green velvet couch sat beneath the window, littered with mismatched cushions. A black pot-belly stove was in the corner, a small woodpile beside it. Pots and pans dangled from a large hanging wooden rack that had clothes drying on top of it. And, finally, there were pictures, postcards, paintings and photographs on all the walls and surfaces.

This was a house that had once been happy in a way that Alex's grandparents' house had never been, but now it felt that the happiness had calcified, like flowing lava turning into rock and ash.

'Do you want a cup of tea?' asked Sasha.

She was slowly thawing.

As Sasha boiled the kettle, Alex wandered around the room, looking at the photographs. They made up a disjointed history of an interrupted life, jumping back and forth in time. On the mantelpiece, a breathtakingly young Sasha was holding baby Bella. The baby stared bemused into the camera with her enormous eyes and a moon-round face. In a photograph on a side table, Bella was a schoolgirl with a constellation of acne on her chin. There was a class photo nearby and Alex recognised not just Bella but Tayla, Erin and Silver, the latter with a fountain of wild red hair sprouting from her head.

The kettle whistled. Sasha opened cupboard doors and clattered crockery as Alex searched for something more recent. It was the feathers that caught her eye. Bella's skin was painted a ghostly geisha white. Her lips were a slash of dark crimson and curved demurely, her hair piled up in a fraying bun. It would be an arresting image even without the huge dark wings that sprouted from her shoulders. Made up of a patchwork of black feathers, they were so large they were only partially in the shot. There was nothing sleek about them, as Alex had imagined. Rather, they were ragged and looked more like flapping shreds of paper than feathers, but the effect was dramatic and unsettling. She was a fallen angel. A witch.

These had to be the wings that Kingsley Kelly had supposedly removed from Bella's body.

'I took that one,' said Sasha, noticing her interest. 'We were down at the logging protests.'

'Those wings are amazing.'

'There was a woman at the Tasmanian protests almost twenty years ago who did something similar, except her wings were white. Bella wanted a more gothic kind of look. It took her ages to collect that many feathers. She dyed them all black herself. Maxine helped.' Sasha poured milk into a small enamel jug and brought it to a round table in the corner of the room, along with two steaming cups. Alex sat down opposite Sasha.

'What happened to the wings?'

Sasha's expression closed, a curtain being pulled down.

Too early, thought Alex. I've got to take this slowly.

'Why are you here?' Sasha asked bluntly. 'What's Maxine's death got to do with you?'

Alex had rehearsed various ways of explaining her interest, none of them mentioning Robyn. All of them seemed to fall apart now she was sitting across the table from Bella's mother.

'I found Maxine . . . part of her,' she answered. That was the moment when Alex had become involved, whether she liked it or not. 'There are questions surrounding her death.'

Sasha's eyes narrowed. 'Kingsley says that it was an accident.'

'Do you believe that?' asked Alex.

The other woman stared into the middle distance, lost in thought. Alex waited for an answer, or more questions, but they didn't come.

'Maxine dropped by the day before she died,' the other woman said eventually. 'She was stressed about the exhibition but didn't go into details. She had decided to head off for a few days to have a break.'

'Why did she come over if she didn't want to talk about what was bothering her?'

'She wanted to go through Bella's paintings. She hadn't quite finalised the list for the exhibition.'

That seemed odd, given that Robyn had a numbered list of the paintings and a layout showing how they were to be displayed.

'Did she tell you that she was painting something special for it herself?' Alex asked.

Sasha nodded.

Not wanting to sound too eager, Alex took a sip of tea before asking, 'Did she show it to you?'

Sasha shook her head. 'She wanted me to see it properly exhibited. I think she was worried I might not like it, but she said it was the truth as she saw it. She did give me this.' Sasha got up and pulled a postcard off the fridge. She passed it to Alex.

It was a print of a painting. The setting was a cliff looking out over the sea. There were people in the foreground – a farmer, a shepherd and a fisherman – and animals, and in the harbour below there were ships with great billowing sails crewed by tiny dots of sailors.

Alex turned the card over. The opposite side was blank.

'It's a painting by Bruegel,' Sasha explained. 'I looked it up. He was a Dutch painter in the 1500s.' She tucked one leg under her as Alex looked at the postcard again, studying it more carefully this time. Perhaps Robyn would know what it meant.

The farmer was ploughing the field with a barrel-shaped horse. His head was bowed, concentrating on the ground. Down the hill, closer to the sea, the shepherd was paying no heed to his flock, which strayed dangerously close to the water's edge. Instead, he leant on his staff, gazing at the sky. The fisherman had his back to the viewer, his face invisible. The sun was almost setting on the horizon, a half-circle of lemon in a faded sky. Alex could barely draw a stick figure. How was she supposed to decipher this? But then she recognised something. It was the fisherman. She had seen that figure before. Maxine had drawn it, or something very much like it, in her diary. Alex was sure of that.

'It's called *Landscape with the Fall of Icarus*,' Sasha said.

Another painting's meaning changed by the title.

Sasha stretched across the table and pointed at a spot in the lower corner. Between the fisherman and the closest ship were two bare legs, the rest of the body having already disappeared into the water. One was really only a foot, almost gone, the other leg desperate not to do the same, thrashing about enough to create foam, but the viewer could sense the dragging inevitability of the body being sucked down. In the next instant the leg would be swallowed, and the sea would once again become a blank green canvas and, like the people in the painting going about their tasks, looking the wrong way, no one would notice what had happened.

Icarus. Wings. Feather.

The words scrolled through Alex's head like she was once again reading the online tattoo encyclopedia's post for the first time. She stared at those small painted legs. It must be a reference to Bella, but in her mind's eye she couldn't help but replace the image with what she saw on the beach that day with Denny.

'Why did Maxine give you this postcard? What does it represent?'

'I think it was about how Bella died and everyone in the town pretended nothing had happened.'

Here it was, the opening. 'Some people are saying Maxine found out what happened to Bella and that's why she's dead,' Alex said carefully, her heart beating faster.

The words twisted and turned in the space between them.

'Really?' said Sasha. Her face became a mixture of hollows and grooves, old before her time.

'I'm worried that it is a possibility.'

'What does that Detective Van-der-something say?'

'He's still investigating.'

'They're still investigating Bella's death. Haven't got too far. You heard about the reward?'

Alex nodded.

'Maybe the million dollars might help. That sort of money would go a long way in Merritt. Not that Kelly agrees.' Sasha frowned and crossed her arms before continuing. 'He wants me to ring up the detective and tell him I oppose it.'

'The reward could bring new information. That's why Farinacci is applying for it.'

'Kelly doesn't like Farinacci.' Sasha picked up her cup of tea but didn't drink. 'He doesn't like you much either. Said you were trouble. I was supposed to ring him up if you got in contact.'

'Perhaps he's the problem,' said Alex quietly.

Sasha sat there and didn't say anything. She had a way of tilting her head back and sticking out her chin so that her eyes were gazing down but still looking straight at you. There was a wariness to her, a vulnerability. 'He likes telling people what to do.'

'Do they listen to him?'

'In this town, most of the time.'

'Not me,' Alex replied.

'Not me either. Not anymore. But why are you interested?' Sasha asked. 'You never even met Bella or Maxine.'

Alex couldn't quite articulate an answer that she thought Sasha would understand, though she could think of several. Her aunt had asked for help on behalf of her interfering boss. Alex's life was a mess and this gave it purpose. Doing this distracted her from thinking about her mother's memory loss. Take your pick.

Instead she said, 'The pictures that Maxine was creating for Bella's exhibition have gone missing. Do you know where they are?'

Sasha rubbed her eyes. 'Have you asked Robyn Edgeley at the local museum? She was involved in the planning and seems to know everything going on in this town.'

'She can't find them either. They're not in Maxine's house or her gallery.'

'Maxine might have put them in Bella's room with the other pictures when she was here,' said Sasha. 'I don't go in there much.'

'Can I check?' Alex stood up, waiting to be shown the way, but Sasha remained seated.

'I didn't say that you could see them.' The words were barbed. Here was a person who trusted no one.

'If we can find those paintings, then maybe we'll discover the truth about what happened.'

Sasha gave a derisive laugh. 'Now you sound exactly like Maxine.'

'But don't you want to know what really happened to Bella?'

'Every day I deal with the truth that my daughter is dead, and there is nothing you or anyone else can do that will bring her back. And now Maxine is dead. How many more dead women is the truth worth?'

Alex sat back down. The question unsettled her. She'd accepted that the truth might cost a million dollars in the form of a reward, but she had never thought the price would be measured in the terms Sasha described. No more dead women, she thought: that was the point. Whoever had done this needed to be stopped before anyone else died. But she couldn't think of the right way to express it to Sasha.

Sasha sighed and stood up. She took her cup over to the sink and poured it out.

'Sasha, I'd still like to see Bella's artwork,' Alex tried. 'Please.'

She waited for the woman to respond. Would Sasha agree? Or would she throw her out and ring Kelly?

'Why?' A sudden burst of fury charged through the room. This was the real Sasha: a volcano of grief and rage. Alex had pushed Sasha to the brink and now she could almost feel the anger take shape in the air.

Alex picked up the postcard and held it up. She pointed to each of the figures in turn: the farmer, the fisherman, the shepherd. 'Because I can't be like them.' The more she had looked at the picture, the more it seemed to her that these men were complicit. It was no accident that they missed Icarus's fall. They had chosen to avert their eyes.

There was no such thing as an innocent bystander.

Sasha stood there, quivering with emotion, but then she sagged. Her defences had been penetrated. 'All right. Her bedroom is this way.'

Chapter 13

Sasha hesitated by the closed bedroom door. For a moment Alex feared she had changed her mind and would prevent her from going in.

Instead she said, 'We fought the day she left.'

'What about?' asked Alex.

'I told her if she wasn't careful, she'd end up like me: failing school, pregnant. I just wanted her to have a better life, an easier life, but she reacted like I meant having her was the worst thing that ever happened to me.' Suddenly upset, Sasha turned away.

'Bella would have known you didn't mean it like that.'

'How do you know? You never even met her.'

How did she know? She was Sasha's age, maybe older, and she'd never even had a baby let alone had to wrestle with a teenager.

'Because I was seventeen once with a single mum,' Alex said. 'We fought almost every day.'

Seventeen. That had been the start of them pushing each other away. Alex choosing a path that led to university, law, Tom and now divorce. None of which she had thought possible when she was seventeen. Seventeen. The time when everything was wonderful, and everything was terrible; a time of first loves and broken hearts, of ideals and absolutes, worrying that life was passing you by when it had barely started yet. There was no such thing as even ground when you were seventeen, and Bella was going to be seventeen forever.

Alex reached out a hand to open the door and Sasha did not stop her.

The room was sparsely furnished, with only a single bed and a cupboard. The pictures were stacked against a wall, except for one hanging over the fireplace.

It was a drawing, black ink on canvas, of a young woman lying on a bed, nude, elbow bent, hand propping up her head. Her hair, the only part of the image that was coloured, flowed down her body in fiery gold torrents, covering her chest, but her arse was bare as were her legs, though she wore thick woollen socks on her feet. Her face had a wistful expression. A big flamboyant B was scrawled in the corner. The girl in the picture was a far cry from the gothic harpy with the black wings.

Bella had been dead for two years, but she was still here in this room.

'That's my daughter,' said Sasha.

A self-portrait, and it was stunning. Here was the person Tayla claimed could drive you crazy, whom Silver said was a drama queen and Erin had described as an anchovy. Up until now, Alex had thought of Bella as a schoolgirl, but this was a young woman, sexy, alive and knowing.

'Maxine found it,' Sasha said. 'I'd never seen it before. She must have drawn it not long before she died. Maybe she had wanted it to be a surprise for me. Max wanted to exhibit it, but I said no. This is where it belongs.' Sasha pressed her lips together so tightly that they seemed to disappear. The tension from the start of Alex's visit was returning to her body.

'I saw her painting of the lighthouse at the museum,' said Alex. 'She was very talented.'

'She found out that we had an ancestor who was a keeper and got all excited. Bella had been obsessed with that lighthouse ever since she was a child. She was delighted to hear about the family connection. Mind you, most of the town is related to one keeper or another.'

Was a love of lighthouses genetic? Did Alex's own interest in the lighthouse come from a relative who was a keeper? Ted Rushall came into her mind but she forced herself to focus. Right now she had a job to do.

'You can stay here with me if you like, but you don't have to,' Alex said, crossing her fingers that Sasha would leave her in here alone.

Sasha hesitated but then disappeared without a word. Alex listened to her footsteps disappear up the hall.

It took a moment for her to realise that the bed in the drawing was the same bed in this room, a curved black wrought-iron bedhead. Another reason why Sasha had kept the picture in here, Alex supposed.

She walked over to the window and looked outside. An old brick garage was in danger of being swallowed by a climbing rose. A large oak tree nearby had a rope swing tied to a branch. There was a dilapidated wooden fence that was caught in the act of falling down, the grey palings darkening in the wet. Several currawongs, black wings folded like businessmen's umbrellas, hopped busily across the grass. Their calls echoed in the bushland.

The Wyld was only a few kilometres up the road from here. Sasha probably drove past the place where her daughter's body was found most days. No wonder Maxine thought she should move.

Alex grabbed the paintings resting against the wall, moved back across the room and sat down on the single bed. The mattress sagged and the bedhead squeaked in protest.

Every girl had a secret internal life that her mother knew nothing about, a rebellion of sorts. What was Bella's and had it got her killed? She looked back up at the painting on the wall. It had been a secret and seemed an odd present to give to your mother. This was a very different Bella from the one people had described to her. Here she was contemplative, even a touch sad. If Alex had to guess, she'd say painted Bella was waiting for her black inked lover to turn up and he was late – but maybe Alex was projecting her own fears and desires onto the canvas. Really, it was like trying to work out Mona Lisa's smile. *Light in the Darkness* suddenly popped into her mind. The words sounded vaguely biblical, but that was what Alex wanted: something to shine a light and make sense of these deaths.

Slowly she began to work through each of the pictures propped against the wall. A handful were framed. Alex assumed these were the ones chosen for the exhibition. Robyn should be able to confirm that. She took photos of each of them with her phone.

There was everything from detailed oil paintings to rough pencil sketches. Lots of drawings from school. Silver with her masses of hair. Erin chatting to Tayla. One of Theo in footy gear. Lots of Sasha – Sasha reading, Sasha doing the dishes, Sasha sitting in a chair. A particularly poignant one was a painting of a much younger-looking Sasha laughing at a toddler, Bella, who was dressed in a pink sundress with thin little straps tied in bows.

Her phone buzzed. A missed call from Prue. Reception was patchy up in the hills. It had probably gone straight through to voicemail. Alex would call her back once she finished here.

Eventually she put all the pictures back against the wall. There was nothing by Maxine and nothing by Bella that suggested triptych, but then Alex wasn't the best person to judge that.

As Alex was returning the paintings to their position against the wall, a photo that must have been stuck to the back of one of them was dislodged and fluttered to the floor. Alex picked it up.

It was a close-up of three people standing in front of a wide brown river. There were city skyscrapers in the background. A boat painted in jaunty colours, the type to take visitors out on the water for an hour or so, was just visible in the background. This was a snap taken by a passer-by or a tourist of a family on holidays in the city. Bella in pigtails, no older than two, was smiling at the camera, wearing the same pink sundress as in the painting Alex had admired. Sasha was standing to one side of her, laughing, just as her daughter had drawn her. But in the photo there was a third person, someone who was missing from Bella's version. Sasha wasn't laughing at her daughter. Instead, she was turning to look at the man standing there, a dapper straw hat on his head. He was lifting Bella up, his hands around her waist, holding the child close like she belonged to him.

For the moment of that photo, the man and woman had forgotten that the picture was being taken. The photographer had clicked on an off-beat, too early or too late. It was only the child who stared straight into the camera. Perhaps the photographer had called out to her. The adults, though, only had eyes for each other. The man had his mouth open, caught mid-sentence, telling a joke perhaps, and Sasha was laughing in response.

It was a tender, revealing moment, an informal family portrait. A father, mother and child having a holiday in the city, away from the prying eyes of their home town. The father wrapping a protective arm around his daughter while talking to the mother, who smiled right back at him. When we fall in love, thought Alex.

The only problem with this story was that the man in the photo was Kingsley Kelly.

There was the sound of a car engine outside. She heard hurried footsteps. Sasha suddenly appeared in the doorway. The weather in the room changed as if a storm was about to hit. 'Did you find anything?' she asked.

It took Alex a moment to realise she meant Maxine's paintings and shook her head.

'Don't mention Maxine or the exhibition,' said Sasha. 'Just say you came for coffee.' The words were hurried, almost coming out jumbled.

'As long as you don't tell Kelly I was here,' Alex replied equally quickly. Sasha's relationship with him had become a lot more complicated in the last five minutes.

Sasha gave her a hard stare but then nodded her agreement.

The front door opened, and Alex heard someone kicking off their shoes.

'Bloody birds are trying to get into your veggies again!'

Sasha turned towards the male voice. Alex quickly slipped the photo into her pocket. This would need to be the subject of a much longer conversation, but there wasn't time for that now. Instead, the two women moved swiftly back to the living room.

'Sash?' The voice was impatient now. 'You here?'

By the time Johnny Ewart reached the doorway, belligerent, barrel-chested and bearded, wearing a muddy rain jacket, a hi-vis shirt underneath, the two women were sitting at the kitchen table. It was a different Johnny from the mug shot that Tom had given her. More defenceless somehow, like he wasn't quite the hard man he liked to pretend to be. The same white scar still bisected his hair.

'Didn't know we were expecting company.' He didn't sound too happy about it.

'Actually, I was just leaving,' Alex said. She tried to keep her tone friendly and bright.

Sasha stood up so hastily that the chair scraped the floorboards.

'Don't let me scare you off,' said Johnny, but the face he made suggested that was exactly what he wanted to do.

'Alex just dropped by for a cuppa,' said Sasha.

Coming closer, Johnny rubbed a hand on his trousers and then put it out. 'John Ewart.' His hand was rough, with splinters of skin coming off it. He gripped hers hard. 'And what do you do, Alex?' he asked.

'I'm a lawyer.' The question had been so unexpected that the words were out of her mouth before she could stop them. 'But that's not why I'm here in Merritt. I'm just in town because my mother has been unwell.'

'We met at the pub the other night,' Sasha cut in. 'Thanks for dropping by. I'll see you out.'

Alex followed her down the hall.

Sasha pushed open the screen door. 'Wait,' she said and retraced her steps.

When she came back, she thrust something at Alex. 'Keep it,' she whispered.

Glancing down, Alex realised it was the postcard of *Landscape with the Fall of Icarus*.

'Maxine had a studio up at the Eyrie,' she said in a low voice. 'Not many people know that.'

'Nic Quirke's place?'

Sasha nodded.

'We should talk again,' Alex replied quietly. She dropped her hand, patting her pocket to make sure that the photograph was still hidden.

Johnny came out on the verandah and stood next to Sasha, putting his arm around her shoulders. Sasha stood there, shivering like a greyhound in the cold. She looked shrunken somehow compared with the woman Alex had met earlier that day. The afternoon had taken a layer of skin off.

A grimy silver SUV with thick tyres was now parked beside the Bedford. On the back of it was a bumper sticker of a tree stump and a chainsaw with the caption: DON'T WORRY. I HUGGED IT FIRST.

As she climbed into her car, Alex saw Johnny say something to Sasha, who shook her head in reply. He pulled out his phone as he walked over to his car but Sasha stayed where she was, raising her hand, so that when Alex drove away, she could see her in the rear-view mirror.

Chapter 14

A wooden sign with chiselled block letters, blackened with moisture and age, welcomed Alex to the Wyld, home of Jackson Falls. The place was almost empty, with just one other car in the dirt car park. The tourist buses that came for the waterfall only a five-minute walk away had gone for the day.

Alex sat in her car and stared at the photo.

Kingsley Kelly was Bella's father. She was certain of that, if little else. Sasha had kept it a secret all these years. Why? Prue had mentioned Kelly was married and that his wife couldn't have children. Was that the reason? It explained Kelly's interest in Bella at least.

Putting aside the town scandal potential, what did it change in relation to the investigation? Everything? Nothing? She needed a walk to think through this new information.

It was probably only a couple of hours or so until sunset. The shadows were already lengthening. She could walk to the spot where Bella's body was found and get back before it grew too dark.

Opening the boot, she grabbed her hoodie and pulled it on, then began flicking through the documents from Charlie Farinacci, which she'd been keeping in there to prevent them being caught up in Denny's Bermuda Triangle of lost items. She soon found what she was looking for: a photocopy of a map that marked the spot where Bella had been found. Shoving all the documents into her backpack, she slung it over her shoulder and walked up to the tourist board at the start of the path that showed the different routes. The quickest way to the spot she was looking for was to head down to the riverbank and then walk alongside it.

Stepping into the bush felt like entering a portal into another world. Here the bushland gave way to lush green rainforest, fed on a combination of waterfall mist and the ever-present rain. Alex stopped to look at a fallen giant of a tree that lay next to the path, furred green. Long dead, it teemed with smaller forms of life. She had the impression that if she stood there long enough, the moss might start creeping over her. There had been talk last election about logging jobs in the area and according to Prue the Wyld had been in the political crosshairs. It was one of the campaigns Bella had been involved in. At least Nic Quirke's investment in the town seemed to have quietened the chainsaws for the time being.

Walking down the two hundred and forty stone steps, holding on to the metal railing, Alex felt a drop in temperature, and before long she heard the dull roar of the water. Even the quality of light changed to something soft and mysterious. At the bottom, the temperature now cave-cool, she watched the gushing bridal veil of water racing down the cliff, flowing white amid the static green.

In the ferns not far from the rocky trail along the river, Alex caught sight of a man with a bucket beside him. He was bent over and seemed to be searching through the plants.

'Hello,' she called, her voice raised to compete with the background thunder of the falling water. 'Have you lost something?'

The man straightened up, wiping his muddy hands on his trousers. He was elderly, with glasses, wearing a pair of old overalls and muddy work boots, a camera slung over his shoulder. Alex had last seen him talking to Kelly at Rosie's cafe. It was Dr Alby Sadler.

'Lost something? Oh no. Found something would be more accurate.' He lifted the bucket and showed it to her. 'The definition of a weed is a plant growing in the wrong place and these definitely don't belong here.'

'You've got a big job ahead of you if you're planning to weed the Wyld.'

'That would take several lifetimes,' Alby said. He pulled out a handkerchief and mopped his face with it. There was a wispy silver stubble on his wrinkled cheeks. 'A volunteer group used to meet regularly but that seems to have fallen apart while I was overseas. I was only intending to bushwalk, but when I saw these, I just couldn't stop myself. Always keep a bucket and trowel in the car.'

'I'm Alex Tillerson,' she said. 'I think you knew my grandfather, Jack Walker.'

Alby scrutinised her. 'You're Denny's daughter?'

'That's right.'

'I'm very pleased to meet you,' he said, and gave a little bow. 'Have you moved to Merritt?'

'I'm visiting.'

'I've just returned from a stint volunteering overseas. What's the saying? Doctors never retire, they just lose their patients.'

Alex laughed politely. 'Are you enjoying being back?'

'Yes,' said Alby. 'I missed the place.'

'The old fishhook.'

He nodded. 'Something like that.'

'Well, I'll leave you to it,' said Alex.

'You don't wish to join me?' Alby asked. 'Plenty of weeds for the both of us.'

'Sorry, I'm on a bit of a quest.'

Alby glanced at the sky. 'You'd want to be back before dusk. It gets dark quickly this deep in the valley.'

'I will,' said Alex.

She turned away, past the sign that exclaimed about the possibility of flash flooding, slippery rocks, falling trees and snakes, accompanied by cheerful cartoon illustrations of each potential calamity, and began to walk across the rocks towards the dirt trail beside the river. The going was slower than she expected, as she was forced to clamber over branches and tree roots, and the way was slippery with mud. At times the path splintered off into smaller, more incoherent versions of itself, disappearing into the bush. Alex decided it was safest to stay close to the river.

Her mind wandered as she walked. Putting aside the implications of the photo for a minute, the next step had to

be checking out the Eyrie for Maxine's pictures. This was
another place where Robyn wouldn't be welcome, given her
vendetta against Nic Quirke, so Alex guessed that she would
have to be the one to go, since she couldn't imagine convincing
Vandenburg to get a search warrant for it. Her best bet was
to approach Nic Quirke directly; he'd been a good friend of
Maxine's, after all.

Having worked out the way forward, she tried to appreciate
the solitude, but after forty minutes of walking with no real sign
that she was getting closer to her goal, she sat down on a tree
stump, hot and sweaty. Stupidly, she hadn't brought a drink bottle,
which she now regretted. Somehow, being next to flowing water
only made her thirstier.

Cliffs ran along the other side of the river. From where she sat,
it was impossible to see the top of them, as they were screened
by ferns and trees. Whoever had put Bella by the river must have
been a local who knew the area well. It all looked the same to
Alex. She glanced again at the maps. There was a handwritten
note about a tree in the water. Pulling up her backpack, she
kept going.

Just as she was beginning to think about turning around,
she saw it. On the opposite bank was a fallen tree with tangled
branches submerged in the river. There was a dirt ledge – another
feature that had been noted on the map – just above the water.
Large dense foliage with ferns as tall as trees lay behind it, and
rocks covered in bright green slime sat alongside. If the river had
been running higher, Alex might never have found it.

Such a lonely place. Someone had carved a cross into a nearby
tree surrounded by a thick blanket of greenery. Even though it

confirmed she was in the right spot, the symbol unsettled her. It didn't belong here. A cross meant churches, gravestones and rituals. This place was ancient, wild and far less human than that. It had its own private language, one she did not understand, other than sense that here was a place where death and life went hand in hand.

What must it have been like to swim across the water towards your dead daughter? For the first time, she felt a pang of sympathy for Kingsley Kelly.

Alex pulled out the photo that was still in her pocket. The magical combination of chemicals, paper and light that captured memories, turned back time and revealed secrets. She stared at the younger Kelly's face and tried to see a family resemblance, but could find nothing – except for the hair, perhaps – then tucked the photo away.

Crouching down, Alex put her hand in the water. The river was cold. She could see it ran fast in the middle. You would have to be a strong swimmer to make it across. Denny had told her stories of swimming in this river, but only in the summer and much closer to town, where it widened and was more tranquil.

Alex pulled out her phone. No reception, just like Dylan had told Silver. The missed call notification flashed again, followed by the message that she had received in Bella's bedroom. She would have to remember to call Prue back when she got to the car.

There was a rustle behind her. Listening, Alex was sure she heard footsteps and turned to look back the way she had come, expecting to see a hiker moving through the bush, following the same trail she had. But no one appeared.

More rustling and Alex's skin prickled, a sensation that worked its way all up her spine, a feeling that convinced her she was being watched.

'Hello,' she called.

Only birds replied, high up in the trees overhead. When she looked up, she couldn't see them, so it felt as if they were ghostly voices, shrill and alarming. Alex felt even more aware of how isolated this spot was. Glancing back at the river, the water seemed more treacherous now. Could she get to the other side if she had to? Better to stay on land and leave that as a last resort. She looked around, then grabbed the sharpest rock she could find. Gripping it tight, she felt the hardness of it press against her skin. Carefully, step by cautious step, she moved closer to the bush, and then she spotted it: a pair of eyes looking at her.

'What do you want?' she shouted, raising an arm, prepared to throw.

Shadows in the green, movement as the person in the bushes turned and began to run. Alex caught sight of light hair underneath a beanie. It was the guy on the bike, Curtis, who'd almost collided with her car. Had he been spying on her?

'Wait!' she yelled, but he kept moving.

Instinctively, fuelled by adrenaline and a sudden burst of fury, Alex set off in pursuit, pushing her way through the ferns, hurdling low-lying logs, the ground soft and slippery, the path disappearing into overgrown grass and bush. He was faster than she was but the adrenaline gave her wings and there was a momentary exhilaration to being the hunter. But all too quickly her anger dissipated and the rational part of brain caught up, telling her to stop. This path led away from the river and the direction from which she had come. She had no idea where it was taking her and what might be waiting up ahead. Alex stood there breathing hard, almost dizzy with confusion about what had just happened. Was it a teenage prank or something more sinister?

She began to retrace her steps back to the river, feet clumsy now, hands clutching at nearby branches for extra support as she began the laborious trek back to the car park.

It was dusk by the time she climbed the steep stairs. The mist had made its way through the fabric of her clothes to settle clammily on her skin and the straps of her backpack chafed her under her arms. All the excitement and curiosity inspired by the day's discoveries had disappeared.

A figure was standing beside her car, peering inside.

'Hey!' she yelled. 'What are you doing?'

He turned, and she saw it was Alby.

'I'm relieved to see you,' he said. 'I was starting to think something terrible might have happened.' He gestured at the car. 'I was about to ring the police.'

The passenger-side window had been smashed. Splinters of broken glass glittered inside the car. The glove box dangled slack-jawed, and the contents were strewn across the seat and footwell. The boot was dented but still locked. Scrawled across the windscreen were the words: *FUCK OFF BITCH.*

Alex froze in shock.

'And whoever it was slashed your tyres as well.' Alby pointed to them. 'All four, I'm afraid.' He conveyed the information precisely, as if handing her a diagnosis.

'Did they damage your car?' Panic began to rise up like boiling water turning to steam.

'Not a scratch. Perhaps I disturbed them.'

Alex forced herself to think logically about this. It felt more sinister than just mindless vandalism.

'Did you see someone hanging around – late teens, on a bike?'

He shook his head. 'No one. You should call the police, or I could drive you to the station.'

The police station was where she had seen Curtis for the first time. Lou had said he was waiting for Kelly to give him unofficial community service. Was this an example of it? Had Curtis followed her to Sasha's house and then here under Kelly's orders? Any sympathy Alex felt for Kelly vanished in an instant. There was very little point in reporting the damage to her car, she decided, because there was every chance that Kelly knew exactly what Curtis was up to.

'Thanks for the offer. If you could give me a lift back to town that would be great.'

Alby headed to his car while Alex popped open her boot and grabbed the remaining bags and remnants out, putting them into her backpack. She had taken Charlie's file with her. Was that what Curtis had been looking for?

She decided to leave the inside of the car untouched. Vandenburg could arrange for fingerprints to be taken. Sighing, she took a couple of pictures of the damage. Would insurance cover this? Luckily she had decided to renew it after all but there would still be an excess. Where would she find the money?

'Did you fulfil your quest at least?' Alby asked, as they left the car park. His car groaned and spluttered as he changed gears.

Alex was too frazzled to lie. 'I wanted to see where Bella Greggs's body was found.'

'Bella?' Alby frowned.

'Did you know her?'

'You could say that,' he answered. 'I delivered her.'

'Oh,' said Alex.

'She came out screaming and in a rush, if I remember correctly. Not dissimilar to her mother, it must be said. Sasha was nearly born in a loading bay and almost didn't need my help at all.' Alby kept his eyes fixed on the road ahead. 'I was working in Timor at the time of Bella's death so only heard about it afterwards. Very sad.'

The engine strained and revved.

'Apologies,' he said. 'The car is old, a bit like me.'

How old was Alby? Mid-seventies? He must be at least fifteen years older than Denny but somehow they seemed the same vintage. It made Alex realise that her mother had aged badly in the last couple of years whereas Alby seemed strong and relatively youthful.

Alex waited for him to quiz her about her interest in Bella, but he didn't.

'You must come into the house and say hello to Mum,' she said eventually. Surely Denny would still remember him. The way Prue talked about him, Alby seemed to have been an unofficial family member.

Before he had a chance to answer, her phone started pinging with messages; they were finally in range of a signal. Glancing at the screen, she saw there were a number of missed calls, all from Prue. With a sinking heart, she dialled Prue's number.

'Where have you been?' Prue asked.

'What's wrong?'

'There's been an accident. Denny's been run over!'

Chapter 15

'What happened?' Alex demanded.

She stood in Prue's kitchen while Alby examined Denny in the guest bedroom.

Prue took a deep breath and began again. Denny had been on the main street and stepped out into traffic. She'd been looking the wrong way.

'The poor driver was hysterical.'

'And Denny was at fault?'

'That's what Kingsley said. He wanted to call an ambulance, but your mother wouldn't let him, so he contacted me to come and take her home instead. I tried the doctor's surgery but they were all booked up. They were going to ring back if there were any cancellations.'

'What was Kelly doing there?' This was the part that worried Alex the most.

'Apparently the two of them had been having lunch together at Rosie's. Denny said he had rung her up to suggest it.'

What was Kelly playing at? Was this some sort of payback for her visiting Sasha?

'It could have been so much worse,' said Prue, shaking her head.

'Now do you see why we need to get her to move into assisted living?' replied Alex.

'Have you got an appointment there yet?'

'Kathleen left a message for me this afternoon. She's been away sick but we should be able to go up there next week.'

'Your mother can stay here tonight and we'll talk about this tomorrow, after everyone has had some rest,' Prue said.

Alex poured a glass of water and then headed back to the guest bedroom.

Denny was sitting up on the bed, her face as pale as a sheet, eyes closed as Alby carefully manipulated her foot. To Alex's relief, Denny had not only recognised Alby but had agreed to let him examine her. At the sound of Alex's footsteps, her mother opened one eye and gazed around the room, owl-like.

'Took your time,' Denny said, her voice faint.

Alex handed her the glass of water and crouched down to look at the injury. Bruises, purple and black, were already appearing.

'Watch the foot,' said Denny irritably. 'It's very painful.'

'I'm not touching it. How did it happen?' She wanted to hear it in her mother's own words.

'I was simply trying to cross the road and some idiot drove into me, of course. Luckily, I stepped back and they only got my foot.'

'Very lucky,' said Prue, appearing behind Alex.

185

'Yes,' said Alby, who got up slowly, looking at Denny over the top of his glasses.

'How is she?' asked Alex.

'Don't talk about me like I'm not in the room,' retorted Denny.

'She seems her usual self.' Alby gave Alex a ghost of a wink.

'How's the pain?' he asked Denny.

'Bloody awful.'

'Well, I don't think anything is broken, but best to have an X-ray. I'll write you out a referral for the morning.'

'Come and have a cup of tea, Alby,' said Prue. 'It's the least we can do for your trouble.'

'That would be most welcome,' said Alby and followed her out.

'What were you doing at the shops?' Alex asked. 'You said nothing to me about going to the shops.'

'I don't have to tell you,' said Denny, her voice truculent. 'You don't need to know everything.'

'*Everything?*' This was the final straw; Alex was at breaking point. 'You never tell me *anything*! How many secrets can one person have? How about you tell me . . .' She almost said it. It had come into her head out of nowhere: the forbidden subject that hadn't been raised between them in years. Who was her father? Was it Ted Rushall, as Prue had suggested? She could feel the words on her tongue, the needle-sharpness of them, but she bit them back. This was not the time.

'What are you talking about?' her mother demanded, suddenly furious. 'Of course I don't need to inform you of my every move. I'm not a prisoner. I'm allowed to go outside. Looked after myself fine before you arrived, and I'll do it again once you go.'

It was the first time Denny had mentioned anything about her leaving.

'I can't go while you're like this.'

Denny tried to sit up straighter but the effort of moving made her wince in pain. 'This will be right in a day or so,' she said. 'Then you can go back to the city where you belong. I never asked you to come to Merritt. I don't need you.'

Alex should have expected Denny to push her away, yet it stung all the same. She swallowed to steady herself then, as if her mother hadn't spoken, she told her, 'Prue says it's fine if you stay the night. Alby is going to drop me home to pick up your medication and pyjamas now.'

Alby's car pulled up out the front of the house. In the darkness it looked almost abandoned.

'I can remember the first time I ever visited.' He nodded towards the front door. 'It was an informal job interview. I was invited for Sunday lunch straight after church and I wore my smartest clothes. Your grandfather had strong views about dressing appropriately.'

'It sounds as though he had strong views about a lot of things.'

Alby smiled. 'He did, he did, and he wasn't afraid to share them. Something Denny has inherited. I'm glad she has come back to live here again and that this house remains in the family.'

'Yes,' said Alex, reluctant to enlighten him about her plans to sell.

'I used to eat here every Sunday after church. Your grandmother was a very good cook. Your mother would be on washing-up duty, and if I had the time I would dry the dishes for her. It's a shame you didn't get to know your grandparents better. I know your mother had her difficulties with them, but they were very kind to me.'

'Would you like to come inside?' asked Alex. 'See the place again?'

Alby shook his head. 'I haven't been inside that house since your grandmother died. So thank you, but no. Perhaps another time.'

Whether it was because of what Alby had said or the fact that she hadn't been alone in the house without Denny, the ghosts of her grandparents felt even more present than usual. 'Not now,' she mumbled to herself, pushing away memories of her grandfather, red-faced with fury, railing about some misdemeanour, and her grandmother, silent and disapproving. Alex was hurrying around trying to find things to pack in Denny's overnight bag when the doorbell rang, making her jump.

'Who is it?' she called anxiously as she switched on the porch light.

There was a hesitation and then, 'It's Dr Seth . . . Kiran.'

Opening the door, she found a puzzled version of the doctor on the doorstep.

'Sorry,' he said. 'I wasn't sure anyone was home. There wasn't any car in the drive.'

Fuck, she had totally forgotten about the car up at the Wyld. She hadn't phoned Vandenburg or even tried to find a towing company. Alex groaned.

'Bad day?' asked Kiran.

'Shocking.'

As she led him into the living room, she explained about the damage to the car, remaining vague about why she was up at the Wyld in the first place. 'It wasn't till Alby Sadler was driving me back to town that I received Prue's messages about Mum.'

'That's why I'm here,' he said. He had heard about Denny's accident and thought he'd better drop over to see if everything was all right.

'That's kind of you,' Alex said.

'Only for favourite patients.'

Kiran was dressed in what Alex thought of as his doctor's clothes, slightly crumpled after a busy day but still businesslike. They suited him. Alex became aware of just how sweaty, muddy and dishevelled she was.

'God, I'm a mess,' she said.

'I have some phone calls to make. I can take care of them here while you go have a shower and get changed, and then I'll drop you back at Prue's.'

Alex stumbled to the bathroom and looked at herself in the mirror. Worse than she had thought possible. She looked like a crazy woman. Quickly she showered, changed into jeans and a sweatshirt, combed her hair and finished packing the bag for her mother.

'Thanks again,' she said, returning to the living room. Kiran wasn't on the phone; instead he was standing looking at the photos peering out from tarnished silver frames on the mantelpiece. Alex had often studied them to see what she had inherited from earlier generations. These people were all gone now, handing on their characteristics like they were playing pass-the-parcel, first to Denny and now to her. Maybe, when you considered that dementia was at least partially genetic, that parcel might be more like a ticking time bomb. Her favourite photo showed her mother in her late teens, standing beside her father and a man she now recognised as a younger version of Alby in front of the doctor's surgery. A scowling Denny with a handbag over her shoulder, her long dark hair pulled back off her face, arms crossed as if trying to put a barrier between her and the world. It seemed to sum up her mother perfectly.

'So that's the famous Jack Walker,' Kiran said, pointing at another photo. It was one taken on her grandparents' wedding day. Her grandfather stood in the centre, his bride next to him almost as an afterthought. He wore a three-piece suit and a half-smirk, looking quite proud of himself. Her grandmother had a tight anxious smile. Perhaps she was already regretting the day or concerned about what came next.

'I've heard a lot about him,' Kiran said.

'I'm sure he would have appreciated you making a house call to check on his daughter,' replied Alex.

'I'm not sure he would have approved of having me in his house.'

'Don't worry,' she said glibly, 'he never approved of me either.' But then she paused. 'What do you mean?'

'Apparently he had interesting views on race relations and white superiority.'

Was that true? She had no idea. It felt like Kiran was rebuking her in some way, but if it was a rebuke, it was gently done.

'I never really knew him.' It was a weak response and she instantly hated herself for it. *Don't blame me, I've nothing to do with him other than living in his house.* 'Is racism a big problem in Merritt?' she asked. Erin had implied as much at the coffee shop, she remembered.

Kiran shrugged. 'You do get those people who ask you very nicely if they could please see a "proper" doctor. Some don't even ask nicely. It happened more when I first started here. I had thought it was getting better, but only this week Alby asked if he could come back to work in the clinic and patients are already ringing up trying to book him.' He gave the same sort of smile that her grandmother had done all those years before.

Alex didn't know what to say. Should she apologise for her grandfather, a man she was pretty sure she would not like or agree with on almost anything? She decided to concentrate on the issue of Alby. 'Maybe you could remind him that it's your practice now, not his.'

Kiran made the sort of face that suggested this wasn't Alex's problem to solve. 'It can't be easy for Alby,' he said. 'I think the overseas organisation he was working for has told him he's getting too old for field work. It must be hard to hear when until now your skills have always been in demand.'

'He has to retire sometime.' Alex was getting more strident now, she wasn't even sure why.

'And do what? He hasn't got any family. His work is everything to him. Take that away and there's not much left. You must see it in the law: people who can't accept when it's time to let go.'

That shut Alex up. He could be describing her. Perhaps it was time to let go of being a barrister and do something else, like Tom had suggested. She had always expected that there would be much more to her life than just her mother and her career, but it hadn't worked out that way, and right now she seemed to be in the process of losing both.

'I'd better get you back,' said Kiran. 'It sounds like Alby took care of Denny for now but she really should have an X-ray tomorrow.'

'Okay,' said Alex. 'I'll have to borrow Prue's car to take her.'

'Give me your keys and I'll see if I can get your car towed to the local mechanic tonight. New tyres and replacing the window shouldn't take too long.'

'Really? At this time of night?'

'Being a doctor does mean you know everyone in town.'

Alex quickly hunted around in her handbag for the keys. 'I can't thank you enough,' she said, and in giving him the keys, somehow ended up holding his hand.

They both stood there not moving, Alex suddenly very conscious of her fingers in his. In the moment, all the events of the day disappeared and she felt a surprising flicker of desire running through her body. She leant forward, thinking to kiss his cheek in a gesture of thanks and gratitude for his help, but Kiran moved his head and her lips ended up at the corner of his soft open mouth. The unexpected intimacy both disturbed and intrigued her. Pulling back, the pressure of his lips still tingling, her gaze locked with his. His eyes were nut brown, shining, with long dark lashes. They smiled at her. Meanwhile, their hands remained entwined as if they had been fused together. The tough calluses on his skin surprised her.

'Should we be doing this?' he asked.

'Probably not,' she answered, her mouth curving into a small smile, but then, as if compelled by a magnetic force beyond their control, a surge of shared electricity, a loop completed, they kissed again and again, mouths, tongues, shocking and tender all at once.

'You took a bit longer than I thought,' said Prue. 'And you're all flushed. Don't tell me you ran here.'

She was sitting on the chair next to Denny's bed. Denny said nothing, as if her mouth had been Velcroed shut.

'I got a lift,' said Alex. Her body still thrummed and it was enough of a distraction to distance herself from Denny's earlier remarks.

'Theo's coming for dinner. I almost forgot I invited him. Maybe I should have asked Alby to stay as well.'

'He seemed happy to head home.'

'Well, he was always a bit of a loner.' She nudged Denny gently. 'Remember we used to call him Saint Alby behind his back when we were young?'

Denny gave a slight nod. Her eyes were red-rimmed with tiredness.

'There was always a touch of the missionary about him; still is with all his volunteering overseas. Mind you, he was a hopeless businessman. Your father used to give him a terrible time about running the practice into the ground.'

'Dad was a bully,' said Denny. Her voice sounded stronger than she looked, which reassured Alex.

'He bullied everyone,' Prue agreed.

'Not me,' said Denny. 'I left. Alby helped me, though. He found a job for me up north, encouraged me to study nursing and kept it all a secret from my father. Must be the only time he went against him.'

It was like a little chink of light from a darkened room. The door was ajar for the first time. Was Denny attempting to extend an olive branch?

'Saint Alby, like I said.' Prue stood up. 'You've had enough excitement for one day. Time you got some sleep.' She fussed over the bedcovers until Denny told her sharply to stop, her eyes already shutting.

'She's a tough old thing.' Prue closed the bedroom door. 'Today must have been a shock for her but she'll come good. Come on, it's time to eat.'

Theo sat at the long table. In his collared shirt and with slicked-back hair, he seemed bigger in these surroundings, as though he didn't belong indoors.

'This is delicious,' said Theo, as Prue brought over his plate.

'You haven't even tried it yet,' teased Tayla.

'Enough from you, miss,' said Prue. 'I thought you were on cooking duties tonight but apparently music is more important. Theo, you know you're welcome here any time.'

Alex sipped her glass of wine and felt some of the tension of the day leave her – or was it excitement? The last hour or so had confused her.

'What did you get up to today?' asked Prue.

The question was directed at Theo but Tayla was the one to answer. 'I had band practice.'

'Yes, we know,' said Prue. 'Most of the street knows.'

The garage had been co-opted as the new band rehearsal space.

'We're definitely getting better,' said Tayla.

'Hmm,' said her mother. It was no doubt designed to be noncommittal but seemed to settle on being critical. Tayla opened her mouth in protest, so Prue very quickly added, 'And you, Theo?'

Theo swallowed as he nodded. 'I was welding up at the lighthouse.'

'Must be hard to make time for that with all your other work,' said Alex.

'I mostly do it at night. Luckily there's no one around to complain about the noise. Even got this one helping me pressure-wash the inside walls the other day.' He stretched out and put an arm around Tayla.

'I'd do it more often if it wasn't for the dog,' she replied.

'What's wrong with my Luna?'

'More like lunatic,' said Tayla. 'She is terrifying,' she told Alex. 'I'm always worried that she's going to take a bite out of me.'

Theo laughed. 'She just wants all the attention.'

'Like some others I could mention,' said Prue.

'Now that the Eyrie is just about finished, I've got more time to focus on raising the money for the light,' Theo continued.

The Eyrie. Alex had forgotten about Theo's connection to it. Perhaps she could ask him about the paintings. 'Someone mentioned the Eyrie to me today,' she said.

'Theo didn't just help build it,' said Tayla. 'He designed it as well.'

'That's an exaggeration,' Theo said. 'It wasn't all me, not by a long stretch. Lots of people were involved.'

'I'd love to see it.'

'Oh, Theo can organise that,' said Tayla airily, like it was no bother at all.

A frown passed over Theo's face, which suggested he wasn't nearly as confident.

'I understand Maxine McFarlane used to paint up there,' Alex said. She tried to keep her tone casual but it was hard.

'I didn't know that,' said Prue. Her face took on a pinched look at the mention of Maxine.

'Apparently there are still some of her pictures up there,' Alex said. 'I promised Robyn that I'd pick them up for her. It's important to keep them all together for Maxine's estate.' That was a lie, but a convincing one, Alex hoped. From the look on Theo's face, though, she wasn't sure it was succeeding.

'Paintings?' Theo's fork was forgotten in mid-air, hovering between mouth and plate.

'Robyn didn't mention that at work,' said Prue.

'Would you know where they are?'

'I don't actually go up to the Eyrie that often now. Only when Nic needs me to.'

'You're up there tomorrow remember, supervising the fire drill,' said Tayla, nudging him. 'Alex could drive up then.'

'If you'd prefer, I can ring Nic Quirke and discuss it with him,' said Alex. Quirke was probably very particular about who entered the Eyrie.

'Tayla has been very community-minded and decided to volunteer for the rural fire brigade,' Prue explained to Alex, with a sceptical undertone.

'It's important to give back to the town,' agreed Tayla. She held out her arms in a saintly pose.

'Nothing at all to do with getting paid time off work.'

'That didn't enter my thinking at all.' But then Tayla gave a wicked laugh as she rubbed her hands together like a pantomime villain. Out of all of them, she seemed in the best mood. 'I won't be the most useless one there, though. Apparently King Kelly has made Dylan Ferris and Curtis Stevens join as well. It's informal community service.'

'God help us if all that stands between Merritt and a bushfire is the three of you,' said Prue.

Tayla made a face at her mother. 'Anyway, we'll be gone by midday. Alex could come up to the Eyrie then.'

'That will work perfectly,' decided Prue. 'We can get Denny's X-ray done in the morning and then I'll come round and keep an eye on her when you head off. It's a bit of a hike out to the Eyrie.' She looked at Theo expectantly.

He had a worried expression but then slowly nodded. It seemed everyone, outside of Tayla, found it impossible to say no to Prue.

Theo and Tayla left shortly after dinner.

'It's so isolated up there on the point,' Prue explained to Alex as they cleared the plates and began on the washing-up. 'It's good for Theo to have company.'

'He seems pretty serious about Tayla.'

Prue shrugged as she began scraping the plates into the bin. 'I suspect he'd marry her tomorrow if he could. It's Tayla I worry about. She can barely decide what she wants to do next Friday night.'

'She's young,' Alex said, as she wiped down the table. 'There's all the time in the world.'

'Oh, sorry,' said Prue. 'It's probably tactless of me to talk about marriages when you're finalising your . . . oh, well you know.'

'Don't worry,' answered Alex. 'The divorce documents have been signed. I'm putting all that behind me.'

'It's just that Theo's had to grow up so quickly. You saw how he was at dinner tonight. Always on his best behaviour and so grateful for the slightest thing. It's like he thinks that if he doesn't say thank you five times, he'll get booted out. I'll admit I wasn't a fan of their relationship at the start, Theo being a couple of years older and that was just for starters. Ted, God rest his soul, was a right mess towards the end and Theo was practically bringing up himself. I was strict with them – probably too strict, really, looking back. There was no staying over at his house, bedroom door always kept open, no driving around at night in his car, curfews, you name it. Tayla really hated me for a while there. She was sure that Theo would find someone else. But he didn't. I was surprised he stuck around, I admit it, but then I realised that we're the closest thing to a family he's got. There's no one else.'

The cutlery clattered together as Alex put the basket into the dishwasher and then pulled out the higher rack to start stacking the glasses. What if Theo did have one family member left and it was her? That could be a lot of responsibility . . . But, then, she only had Denny and maybe one day Alex would lose her. Perhaps she needed another family member as well.

'And I don't like him working for Nic Quirke,' continued Prue. 'The way Theo talks about him, it's like he's a substitute father. I remember when he first got the job with Nic. He was that excited, gave him something to be proud of. Now, there's all sorts of muttering around the town about Quirke's big announcement at the rally. All very exciting, but what about his earlier promises, like the development at Eden Point which has been at a standstill for so long?'

If Prue was representative of town sentiment, it seemed that the gloss was coming off Nic Quirke's gold. It only made Alex more curious to check out the Eyrie in the morning.

Prue closed the dishwasher and then turned it on. There was the buzz of it starting and then a whoosh from the water. 'Anyway, what are you up to with Robyn? I don't know if I did the right thing getting you mixed up in her plans. You were only supposed to go talk to that detective on her behalf and now she's got you tracking down missing paintings. Maybe you need to draw a line.'

Alex decided not to tell Prue about the trip to Sasha's and the vandalised car. 'Robyn means well,' she said.

'Her heart is in the right place,' Prue conceded. 'Before you arrived, she rang up to check how Denny was going.'

'That's nice of her.'

'They even talked for a little while.'

'Mum didn't hang up on her?'

'I just handed Denny the phone and ran for the door to miss the yelling. She's mellowing, your mother. Putting the problems of the past to rest. I mean, she had lunch with Kelly, talked on the phone to Robyn and then had a quiet chat to Alby tonight.'

'Maybe she did hit her head after all.'

'Don't joke about that. Mind you, it wasn't just Denny acting strangely – something was up with Robyn at work today.'

'What do you mean?'

'She just seemed very pleased with herself, saying that she had made some real progress. Wouldn't say with what, mind you.'

'Could it be in relation to Maxine's death?'

Prue shrugged.

As she stood to leave, Alex thought about ringing Robyn when she got home but decided she was too tired. She'd drop in to see her after the trip to the Eyrie – hopefully she'd be able to show her some paintings.

Chapter 16

The road narrowed, becoming bumpier with potholes. Tar gave way to dirt. Cultivated fields and pastures were replaced by thick dense bushland and Alex had to slow to take the tight corners. The sat nav had given up once she was in the hills proper, and as she glanced down at her phone she saw the reception had too.

Following the instructions Prue had given her, she'd headed out of town in her aunt's car, having made up a story about her own having a flat battery. Hopefully, Kiran's mechanic would have it fixed soon. Another thing to add to the credit card. She'd phoned Vandenburg first thing that morning and told him about the damage. He promised he would look into it but she didn't have much confidence that it would be a priority. She considered telling him she was heading out to Nic Quirke's property to look for Maxine's paintings, but in the end decided to wait until she knew whether or not there was anything there.

After about half an hour, she turned off onto a private track surrounded by a forest. There were no markers, no letterbox, no sign to indicate that this was the Eyrie. She was not convinced that it was the way to the Eyrie, but she took it anyway.

Massive gums towered above her. A thick undergrowth of ferns threatened to creep out over the track and swallow it up completely. It was actually sunny today, for the moment at least, but there were still thick mud patches. Driving out here in heavy rain would be treacherous, if not impossible.

The place was isolated and more than a little unsettling. The only comfort was the thick tyre tracks in front of her, gouging a deep impression in the mud. The rural brigade's fire truck, Alex thought, which suggested she was in the right place.

After two kilometres or so, the track ended. There was no sign of a house, but she saw a car parked nearby, a muddy four-wheel drive with a blue QI logo on the side. As she pulled in next to it, she heard a loud crack. It sounded like a gunshot. She switched off the engine.

Silence.

Getting out of the car, she looked around but couldn't see anyone.

'Hello?' she called.

The word echoed around her.

'Theo?' Her voice was more uncertain now.

She listened hard but there was no answering call.

The wind was caught up in the leaves high above her head. It sounded like the white noise of the ocean. Looking around, she was surprised to see a mixture of trees: pines and firs as well as the ubiquitous eucalypts. All of them were huge and Alex felt suddenly inconsequential. She could see quick dark velvet blurs moving among the leaves, busy wings swooping between the branches. There was a scuffling in the undergrowth, the sound of small feet moving fast. Yesterday, those sounds had heralded Curtis spying on her in the Wyld. Just the reminder of it made her adrenaline spike.

Walking around the car, she called again, and then even the scuffling stopped, like everything was holding its breath.

It's an animal, more scared of me than I am of it, she told herself.

Perhaps she could use her car horn to get Theo's attention? But there was something discomforting about this blanket of quiet that made her reluctant to disturb it. Alex checked the other car. The driver's door was unlocked. Opening it, she noticed a single cartridge on the footwell of the passenger seat. Had someone loaded a gun in a rush? It must have been a shot she had heard.

A noise behind her, the sound of a foot on a stick.

Whirling around, she saw Theo.

He was standing further away than the noise suggested, in a clearing in the trees. A pair of binoculars hung around his neck and in his hands there was a rifle.

'Sorry,' he called, coming closer. 'You been waiting long? I was taking pot shots at a few cheeky rabbits.'

Alex tried to get her heart out of her throat and had to swallow hard before talking. 'Only a few minutes. Really, I just got here.'

Guns were perfectly normal in the country, she thought. Get a hold of yourself.

'Come on then,' he said with a grin.

She followed him along a track leading through the bush.

'Do you often go rabbiting?' she asked.

'First thing in the morning is better, but the fire brigade was here then.'

Walking towards Theo, Alex caught glimpses of small wedge-shaped buildings in the surrounding bush, sitting on steel legs above luscious plants and ferns.

'We call them the Bird Boxes,' said Theo. 'That's Nic's office.' He pointed at the one nearest. 'The others are self-sufficient homes. Each of them runs off solar power and has a roof garden where you can grow herbs and veggies. They can even be fitted with an aquaponics system to breed mussels and yabbies.'

'Who's going to live in them?'

'These are just prototypes. The plan is to use the design for the development at Eden Point. Revolutionary, really; it'll be the future of housing.'

'Is that the development that's been delayed?'

'Don't listen to town gossip,' said Theo. 'Nic's a visionary. The best thing that has happened to Merritt in a long time.'

'He seems to have got quite a few people offside. Are you sure it will go ahead?'

'If you believe in something, you've got to be prepared to back it all the way, no matter what the obstacles. Don't under-estimate Nic and don't underestimate me.' The words came out surprisingly bitter.

'Sorry,' said Alex. 'I don't mean to imply anything.'

'You can do all these things right and yet this town will still think that you're the worthless child of a drunk. But forget about them – come and take a look at this.'

They walked down the slope until the trees thinned and then disappeared, the ground changing to slate-grey rock – and then suddenly the world dropped away as a panoramic view opened up and they stood at the edge of a cliff. Before them was an enormous valley.

'So this is how the Eyrie got its name,' Alex said.

Theo pulled the binoculars from around his neck and passed them to her. 'I think of this as Paradise Rock, because from here you can see Eden and the lighthouse.' His lips curved in a half-smile at the cheesy joke, he pointed to the stretch of blue sea on the horizon. Far off beyond the trees, she could see the dark slope of the headland.

Bringing the binoculars up to her eyes, she felt the cool weight of metal on her face. Dishwasher-dirty clouds were gathered out at sea but eventually she found a fingernail blade of white.

Light in the Darkness.

'I saw a painting of the lighthouse at the museum,' she said, as she adjusted her focus. 'Do you know it?'

'Yeah,' he answered after a hesitation. 'The one Bella painted.'

'Did you know Bella?'

'Not well. Only because of Tayla really.'

'Weren't you at school with them?' Once again, she found the lighthouse and then moved her gaze across the ocean to the next section of visible coastline. Around the corner was Beacon Beach. The thought of it jolted her and she quickly turned her head back the other way.

'I didn't spend much time at school, gave up altogether once Dad died. Started working instead and got lucky. Greatest office in the world when you get to have a view like this.'

'It is an amazing landscape,' Alex said.

'The area around Merritt is actually one of the best places in Australia to adapt to climate change. That's why Nic's here. It's unlikely to go into drought, there are strong wind currents for power generation, stable water temperatures, a lack of air pollution and dependable food sources with the salmon farm.'

'Still the threat of bushfires,' Alex said, 'but I guess nowhere is perfect.'

'Even New Zealand has earthquakes and look how many tech billionaires have invested there. That's why Nic encourages the fire drills out here, and he's talking about buying more equipment, like drone spotters and a second lightweight fire truck, making it easier to move around the hills and on the fire tracks. He's got a plan to keep this place safe.'

Alex swung the binoculars back to Eden Point and the lighthouse wobbled into view. 'I always wanted to climb it,' she told Theo. 'The lighthouse, I mean.'

'Any time you're free, come on over.'

'And it was your grandfather who was the last keeper.'

He nodded. 'We scattered his ashes off the top of it. My father's too. I want it to still be there for mine one day.' Theo rubbed the side of his face, his mouth twisted like barbed wire. 'Perhaps I shouldn't say this, but Tayla mentioned something about how maybe my dad . . .'

'Yeah?'

'Could be . . . um . . . your dad.'

Alex's first instinct was to shut this conversation down, to deny everything, say she didn't have a father, but she forced herself to stay quiet. She kept her eyes fixed on the horizon.

'Maybe you don't want . . .' Theo tried again, but then stopped. 'This is harder than I thought it would be.'

She glanced at him out of the corner of her eye. He was nervous. Hands balled into fists, body tense. One wrong word from her and he would walk away.

'Maybe you're happy with your life the way it is with your mum. I mean, it's not like Dad and I are prize additions to any family, and you're some fancy city barrister.'

She turned and looked at him properly then. For the first time she caught a glimpse of the abandoned boy Prue had told her about. 'Just so you know,' she said, 'my divorce is about to be finalised, my husband's already engaged to be married to someone else, I have no money in the bank, the fancy barrister career is on ice, Denny's got dementia and I'm avoiding dealing with all of that by getting caught up in a wild-goose chase for missing paintings. In short, I'm a failure.'

There, she had admitted the truth out loud and the world had not fallen in on her. The sun was still shining. The trees below them stood there unchanged. Alex breathed out, and for the first time in a long while she felt a moment of pure relief. On a whim, she cupped her hands around her mouth and shouted the word 'failure' and listened to it echo down into the valley, breaking up into indistinct sounds before fading away altogether.

Theo stood there looking at her, mouth open in shock, but then he laughed. 'Feeling better?' he asked.

Alex nodded.

Something that was hard to put into words passed between them. A sort of understanding or connection that hadn't been there a few minutes earlier.

'That's quite a list,' Theo said. 'Any of it retrievable?'

Alex thought for a moment. The marriage was a lost cause and there was nothing she could do about Denny.

'All I need is one big case.'

'What are you doing here then?' asked Theo. 'You should be back in the city hustling to find it.'

'I'm here to get Mum organised, even if she doesn't think she needs it. And I guess I promised Robyn,' Alex said. It sounded ridiculous now she said it aloud. Prue had been right. She needed to draw the line.

Theo shook his head. 'Well, then I guess we better see if we can find some of Maxine's missing paintings for Robyn. You can at least tick that one off the list and then get on with fixing the other important stuff.'

'Any theories where they might be?'

'I've got an idea.'

She followed Theo along a path running parallel to the cliff top. Was it possible that she could lose a husband but find a half-brother? It seemed too weird.

They passed by a swimming pool cut into the cliff. Roughly oval in shape, edged with the matching rock from the landscape, it looked almost like a lagoon. The sun danced lightly across the water. It was the sort of pool that you would want to sit in, glass of wine in hand, and gaze down the valley, all the way across to the ocean.

'Nic wanted the water to be accessible for helicopters in case of a bushfire,' said Theo. He was also retreating to safer topics of conversation, but there was a bond there, newly forged, Alex could feel it. Whether this was familial or something else, she had no idea, but it was there.

'Part of his fire plan?' she asked.

'The original idea was to build it jutting out off the cliff and have a glass bottom so you could swim out over the view. Thank goodness he rethought that. Still, it's a nightmare in practice. Solar heating's on the blink, filters keep buggering up and that water's like ice. Fixing it is on my to-do list.'

'That must be disappointing for Nic.'

'You know,' Theo said, with a laugh, 'I don't think he's noticed. He's never used it.'

They went deeper into the forest, walking steadily up an incline until Theo stopped and waved his arm like a magician introducing his next trick.

'Nic wanted to build something that fitted in with the Eyrie, so here is the Nest.'

It was something out of a fairy tale, like stumbling across a gingerbread house or Sleeping Beauty's castle, except that it also appeared to be airborne. There among the trees, an enormous burr of sticks – shaped like a gigantic Russian fur hat – floated in the air above them, four metres off the ground.

As she walked closer, the secrets of the design were revealed. It had four trees as supports, each reinforced with steel rods. Alex moved directly under it, craning her neck to look up into the tangle of branches crisscrossing over one another. She walked all the way around and couldn't find any opening at all. It was a dense thicket, a knot, a puzzle waiting to be solved.

'It's based on a hotel in Sweden,' Theo told her. 'Nic flew in the original architects and builders. Couldn't tell you how much it cost. It's an extremely rich man's folly.'

'And Maxine painted in *there*?'

'I don't think Nic actually knew what to do with it once he built it, so in the end he let Maxine use it. They were pretty close.'

'It's extraordinary.'

'I find it a bit claustrophobic, like being trapped in a submarine. More fun to look at it from the outside.'

'How do you get in?' Alex ran her hand down the bark of one of the trees.

Theo walked over to the tree opposite. There was a discreet black box like a security system sitting flush in the trunk. He pulled out a swipe card and waved it over a sensor. Alex could hear the whirr of a mechanism and then a trapdoor opened in the Nest. A retractable stepladder began to descend.

Theo gave her a mock bow. 'It's all yours. Just come back along the path to the lawn and give me a shout when you're done.'

Alex put her foot on the first rung. It was made from thin wire like a coathanger but felt sturdier than she expected. Impatient now, she began to climb. Stopping halfway up, she looked about her. Theo had walked back down the path and out of sight. The trees felt closer from this height, like they had huddled around to hide her. She took a deep breath and then continued her ascent.

Chapter 17

Alex emerged into a curved space made entirely of wood. A creeping smell of turpentine and oil paints tickled her nose and gave her the premonition of a lingering headache if she stayed too long. Someone had been painting in here – a good sign.

The walls arched upwards above her head to form a dome, like the inside of a nut, though the roof was lost in darkness. What light there was came from outside, through the narrow windows, but it was broken, weak, crisscrossed by the outside branches, resulting in faint illuminated pools on the wooden floor while the rest of the space remained deep in shadow. Alex had once seen photographs taken of the inside of a violin. The small wooden interiors had been cleverly captured to look like an empty concert hall, but they had seemed warm and inviting, an appreciation of the talent of its maker, whereas this just felt creepy. It was like she was intruding into an abandoned attic, cleared of clutter, so that even though it was a tall space, Alex wanted to hunch over, so as not to disturb whatever might be lurking here. How on earth did Maxine work here in such a dim light? She needed to check the walls for a switch.

Close to where she was standing there was a bench with brushes and paints. Next to it, a large white drop sheet was draped over an easel.

A hummingbird flutter of her heart. Was this one of the paintings? It might even be all three of them lined up next to each other.

She reached for the cloth then hesitated, suddenly uneasy about what she might find. Robyn had told her that the piece was entitled *The Accusation*. Who exactly was Maxine accusing?

Taking a deep breath, she pulled back the sheet.

Landscape with the Fall of Icarus.

It was a giant version of the postcard. Whatever Alex was thinking she would find, it wasn't this. A woman who supposedly despised copying had just done exactly that. Maxine must have spent hours and hours reproducing a painting from the sixteenth century.

Robyn had convinced her that these paintings would be the missing pieces of the puzzle, but instead it was a giant dead end. And yet Alex couldn't take her eyes off it. The painting demanded attention. In this claustrophobic enclosed space, Maxine had created a wide-open world of sky and sea. The postcard had been inadequate in conveying the depth and movement of the picture. Here, in the gloom, the artwork almost glowed with the light of a setting sun, the luminous green of the sea and the tiny perfect brushstrokes of the trees. The nearest ship was crosshatched with the detail of the rigging, the stitching of the sails. An enormous flag curled like a ribbon through the air as sailors clambered up to the crow's nest. One sailor clung to the foremast, getting ready to lower another sail.

It was a perfect copy of a masterpiece and it was of no use at all.

Alex looked for the dark kernel of the picture, those flailing legs emerging from the sea, fighting death and failing. As in the original, Maxine had included tiny little perfect feathers floating above the ocean, the remnants of Icarus's wings – but these feathers were black, Alex noticed, instead of the foamy white of Bruegel's original.

This picture didn't represent the death of Icarus anymore.

Frowning, she took a step back, trying to take it all in as a whole. Something was odd. What else had been changed?

As she studied it, she saw the bay in the background, the one the ships were heading to, was shaped like a fishhook. The village bore more than a passing resemblance to Merritt. There was Eden Point and the lighthouse.

Alex took her phone from her pocket and brought up the photo she had taken of Sasha's postcard. Maxine had changed something even more fundamental than the setting, she realised, as she compared the Bruegel with Maxine's version.

The men were different.

The farmer was still walking down the slope behind his horse, ploughing the field with a crescent of his face visible, the rest covered in hair and a cap, but his clothes had changed and so had the shape of his body. Now he wore a grubby old jacket instead of the long tunic and leggings. There was a hint of something bright underneath the jacket. Alex peered at it. This farmer had been dragged into the twenty-first century wearing high-vis.

The fisherman had his back to the viewer, private and unknowable. Once again, though, the clothes had been changed so that he wore a more contemporary red beanie and a drab overcoat.

She needed to take this painting and show it to Robyn; the museum director might know who these men were.

Finally, she turned to the shepherd, the only one whose face was fully visible to the viewer. Alex recognised him at once. It was Nic Quirke.

She took a few photos of the three men with her phone before switching on the torch app. She held the light up to the picture, staring at Quirke's face. What did the name mean? Was Maxine saying that the tech billionaire was responsible for Bella's death?

Whether it was a trick of her imagination or the flickering torchlight, it looked as if Nic Quirke, the modern-day shepherd, was staring in amazement at something behind Alex.

Turning, Alex followed his gaze. There was a giant shadow on the wall. Slowly, slowly, she moved towards it, holding up her phone.

Hanging from the ceiling, misshapen and broken, drooping and bedraggled, yet radiating a crude, primitive kind of power, was a pair of black wings.

The wings Bella was wearing when she died.

Chapter 18

The trapdoor banged open and the lights came on. Whirling around, Alex instinctively put her arm up to shield her eyes from the brightness.

Nic Quirke stood there.

'What exactly do you think you are doing?' he demanded.

Alex's heart, already beating fast, began to run wild. She blinked hard until Nic came properly into focus. He wore a linen suit, expensive, lightweight, perfectly cut; the sort of suit no one in Merritt owned.

'Don't come a step closer,' she warned. 'The police know I'm here.'

'Good,' retorted Nic. 'That saves me a phone call.'

'What?'

'I want you charged with trespass, fraud and attempted burglary. You are on my private property, having fed Theo some bogus story about being a lawyer involved in the winding up of Maxine's estate, and I catch you red-handed trying to steal her artwork!'

'I'm not trying to steal anything.' Alex decided to bluff it out. 'And for your information, I *am* a lawyer – though the part about the estate might actually in some sense be, um . . .'

Nic almost smiled. No, it was more like a smirk. 'I am the executor of Maxine's will.'

'Oh,' said Alex.

'If you're not here to steal things, would you mind explaining to me what exactly you are doing here?'

'All right,' said Alex, 'but only if you can explain the presence of these wings, which were taken from a crime scene.'

Nic stopped short and stared up at the wings, momentarily lost for words. He shook his head. 'I have no idea what they are doing here.'

'You've seen them before?'

'Yes,' he said, frowning now. 'Bella Greggs was wearing them the day I first met her. She was perched on top of a wooden tripod, styled as a strange sort of Angel of Death.'

Stuck in this space, Alex found it easy to feel the Angel of Death vibe. 'That's quite a first meeting.'

'She was an extraordinary person. A very strong personality with lots of ideas. Fearless.'

He moved past Alex to stare up at the wings. She looked up as well.

Bella and Maxine had worked on them together and with that thought something clicked. These weren't just wings, they were another part of the triptych. Alex had presumed it would be three paintings but that was wrong. Here was the second piece. Delighted at the revelation, she pushed on with her questions.

'And did you talk to Bella that day?'

'Yes, but not until the police shut the protest down. An older officer, Kelly, was in charge. He seemed to know Bella well.'

Quite the understatement, thought Alex.

'I ended up driving Bella home. I went inside and met Sasha, told them I liked what Bella was doing and asked what I could do to help. Bella needed money so I agreed to donate regularly to her cause.'

Nic Quirke had made regular payments to a schoolgirl who ended up murdered. No wonder Farinacci had listed him as a suspect.

'As for the wings,' Nic continued, 'truly, I have no idea what they're doing here. I presume Maxine put them up. She asked for a space that was out of the way, where no one would interrupt her. She was insistent that it be completely private.'

'What about the painting?' Alex gestured at it. 'How do you explain that?'

Nic stood in front of the picture. 'Bruegel,' he said.

'*Landscape with—*'

Nic held up a hand to silence her. 'I know it,' he said. 'It's a strange choice. Art historians think that the one in Belgium is only a copy of a now destroyed original, so it's probably not by Bruegel at all. So this is like an artistic joke, a nod from one master copyist to another. But, then, the whole image is really just a visual joke.' He stood there, arms folded, completely absorbed by the picture.

'A joke?'

'The artist is playing with the viewer – the way your eye is drawn to the farmer and his horse's arse first.' He waved a hand at them. 'And it broadens out into this enormous landscape, with everything seeming bucolic, with the sheep, fishing and beautiful ships sailing past, but then we begin to get hints that all is not well.' Nic pointed out a sword next to the farmer and a disembodied head in the bushes nearby. 'And then, finally, at the last moment, you see the punchline that changes every-thing.' A dramatic gesture taking in the drowning boy. 'People always think of Icarus and how those wings failed, but they forget Dedalus, Icarus's father and inventor of the wings. See how the shepherd is looking at the sky? There was another version of this picture that suggested he was looking up at Dedalus, still in flight. Legend has it he kept flying to Sicily after the accident. Not everyone has to fall.'

It was easy to hear in his voice that Nic thought he and Dedalus might have a lot in common.

He stopped talking, his gaze resting on the shepherd who was staring up at Bella's wings. From the stunned expression on his face, Alex was convinced he had never seen this painting before either. He looked at it for a long time. The silence stretched out like a piece of elastic until Alex broke it.

'This painting was to be part of the final piece of the Bella Greggs's exhibition,' Alex said. 'Maxine called it *The Accusation.*'

Nic's tongue darted out and licked his top lip. Not so confident now, thought Alex.

'I must say, Max was quite flattering in her portrait of me.' Despite the sign of nerves, his voice was calm. 'I'm not nearly as gormless as Bruegel's shepherd.'

Admittedly, that was true. The Nic in the painting looked quite knowing, with a wry half-smile on his face, similar to the expression he wore now.

'Can I ask who the other two are, the farmer and the fisherman? Don't tell me I'm the only one who's recognisable.'

'What if you are?' pushed Alex, even though she was sure he wasn't. 'Why do you think Maxine put you there?'

'You ask a lot of questions,' said Nic. 'Questions that I am not obliged to answer.'

'It seems to me that she is accusing you of something,'

'Whatever that is,' said Nic, 'it isn't murder. She had a lot of moxie, Bella; I was sad to hear that she'd died. But Maxine's death is the real tragedy. Whatever conspiracy theory you've concocted in your head, you can forget about me. There's no one who wants to know what happened to Maxine more than I do. So, if you've quite finished making your own accusations, I'd like to go call the police.'

'You're still going to report me to the police?' Alex was outraged. If Nic made a formal complaint, she could be charged and perhaps lose her practising certificate.

Nic swore underneath his breath and then shook his head like Alex was a crazy woman. 'I meant I'm going to ring that Detective Vandenburg who's been leaving me messages for the last few days. If you're right about the wings being from a crime scene, I imagine he will want to see them. Now, after you . . .' And he ushered her towards the stairs.

Alex climbed down the metal ladder then, finally back on the ground, breathed deeply. That place had given her the creeps. It was a relief to be outside again, to take in fresh air. She looked around at the trees and then at the sky. There was a heaviness to it which suggested rain.

A shout and Theo came walking towards her, a tight expression on his pale face. Alex felt a pang of regret. She had probably got him into a lot of unnecessary trouble with Nic.

'I'm sorry,' she began, but he interrupted her straight away. 'Prue just called me on the satellite phone. The police are looking for you.'

Nic was clambering down the ladder now.

'Everything is fine,' Alex assured him. 'I've spoken about it with Nic. We were just about to call them.'

But Theo looked as far from fine as possible. He seemed too stunned to take in her words.

'There's been another murder,' he said. 'A body has been found at Maxine's gallery.'

Chapter 19

It started to rain hard on the way back into town. From the passenger seat of the four-wheel drive, Alex could see Theo's expression, strained and bewildered, and felt something catch in her throat. Here was someone who had suffered so much and he was about to suffer more. Theo was a local boy and likely to know whoever was dead.

Who *was* dead? Alex's mind had already rushed towards Silver. She imagined Theo must be thinking that as well. What must Tayla and Erin be feeling? And how was all this going to look for Nic? Already under suspicion for Bella's death and now two people murdered who had business connections to him – to say nothing of the painting and the wings at his property. Had he been telling the truth when he agreed to cooperate with the police? He had insisted on staying behind at the Eyrie and she was in no position to compel him to come with them.

'What did the police say?' she asked Theo again.

He shook his head. 'All Prue told me was that someone had been killed at Maxine's gallery and the police wanted to speak to you straight away.'

A deep-veined dread crept over Alex. Until now she had been able to separate what she was doing from the violence that had been done, even though she had seen part of a dead body. Maxine's death had already happened before Alex got involved. Sasha had said the truth could cost more lives and it seemed she was right. This was far more dangerous than Alex had realised.

Theo reached the end of the track. Swinging the car onto the road, he accelerated through the gears to race along the potholed road. Alex wanted to tell him to slow down but her throat seemed to have closed over with fear. Who had been murdered?

Thunder rumbled overhead.

'It won't worry us,' Theo reassured her. 'It's already heading out to sea.' But his voice shook all the same.

He drove expertly, taking the corners well, though Alex's stomach lurched with every turn.

As they passed the sign welcoming them to Merritt, Alex leant back in her seat and forced herself to think about something other than what was waiting for them. Her mind settled on the painting. The painting wasn't suggesting that Nic killed Bella, she realised; if anything, from the way he was represented as the shepherd, it seemed to accuse him of looking the other way. So, if Maxine wasn't accusing Nic, who *was* she accusing? It was then Alex remembered something crucial that she had forgotten: *The Accusation* was supposed to be a triptych, composed of three parts. One part was painted by Maxine, which presumably was the picture Alex had just found; a second part was made by Bella and Maxine together – that must be the wings; and the last part was created by Bella herself. The first two items were in the Nest, but the third was still missing.

Driving up the main street of Merritt, nearing the turn into Hope Street, Theo said, 'Over there,' and pointed up ahead.

Police cars were clustered around the library. A tight knot of people was standing behind the crime scene tape.

'That's not Maxine's gallery,' said Alex. 'Prue must have heard wrong.'

She stared out the window as they pulled in beside an SUV with tinted windows. Nathan, the young policeman Alex had met on Beacon Beach, stood at the barrier, drenched from the rain. Alex got out of the car and ran towards him.

'Vandenburg arrived about half an hour ago,' Nathan said. 'Head into the library. I'll let him know you're here.' He lifted up the crime scene tape.

She was about to ask who had been killed when there was an eruption behind her. A man with a baseball cap hung out of the SUV Theo had parked beside.

'How come you're letting her go in?' he roared.

It was Johnny Ewart. Alex took a step back.

'Because the detective says so,' called Nathan. 'Head home, mate, there's nothing to see here.'

Johnny got out of his car, slamming the door hard. 'You,' he yelled at her, and Alex knew he must have recognised her. 'She's an undercover cop, isn't she?' he demanded, addressing Nathan. 'That's why she was at my house.'

Johnny began charging towards her.

All of a sudden Kelly was there, standing in front of Alex, his finger pointing straight at Johnny. 'Fancy a night in the cells, mate? It's been a while since you came for a visit.'

Johnny stood in front of him, right up close so they were nose to nose. 'You've been fucking spying on me again, haven't you, Kelly? Always trying to get me because I've got something you want.'

'Get back in your car and drive away or I'll book you for being a public nuisance. Might even search your car as well. Never know what we might find.'

Johnny's eyes bulged in fury and Alex took another step back, worried he was about to take a swing at the police officer, but Johnny managed to restrain himself and headed back to his car. She didn't wait to see what he did next but started moving towards the library. Kelly jogged to catch up with her.

'You took your time,' he said. 'Where have you been?'

'That's none of your business,' Alex retorted, all her fears morphing into a stabbing anger. Kelly was the reason her mother was injured. Kelly was responsible for her car getting trashed. Kelly, for whatever reason, had tampered with Bella's body and stuffed up that homicide investigation, and was doing the same to Maxine's.

'On the contrary – Merritt is my patch, so it's my job to know what goes on here.'

'Your patch has another dead body on it,' said Alex. 'Did you find this one as well?'

'What exactly are you implying?'

'Just so you know, I've found Bella's wings – the ones you took from the crime scene. If there are any fingerprints on them . . .'

Kelly's face went from rage to grey, which was all the confirmation Alex needed that Dylan's version of events must be true.

She hurried away, not stopping until she was inside the library.

Looking across into the museum, she could see people in full protective gear walking around. Forensics had already arrived. Vandenburg was among them. Alex raised a hand to get his attention. He jogged through the doors, grabbed her arm in an iron grip, and half marched, half dragged her towards the librarian's office, shutting the door behind them.

'What?' asked Alex, wrenching her arm free.

'The records on her mobile have her phoning your house several times yesterday. Tell me you spoke to her.'

Alex stared bewildered. 'Who are you talking about?'

Vandenburg breathed hard, looking straight at her. 'Did Robyn Edgeley speak to you around midday yesterday?'

She stared back at him, her mind a total blank.

'What did you talk to her about?'

She shook her head. 'I wasn't home then and Mum was out. But . . . you can't mean that it's Robyn who's been murdered.'

Vandenburg seemed close to tears. 'Yes,' he said, and gave a jagged sigh.

Alex gaped at him. 'What happened?'

'The librarian noticed that the sandwich board wasn't out on the pavement after opening time so went to check. She found the museum locked but used her key to get in and found Robyn's body. A doctor tried to revive her, but it was too late. They called Kelly, who rang me.'

'Do you have any idea who did it?'

'Her husband said Robyn left for work early this morning because she was going to meet with' – Vandenburg flicked open his notebook – 'Kiran Seth.'

Alex's mind was reeling. 'Kiran? Why would he be meeting Robyn?'

'Her husband didn't know. Who is this Seth guy? Do you know him?'

Alex felt sick. The first time she'd met Kiran was on the beach, she remembered, right before she found Maxine's leg. 'He's my mother's doctor. Are you saying he's a suspect?'

'Someone is trying to track him down at the moment.'

That wasn't a no.

Alex shook her head. It was impossible that Kiran was involved in this. Robyn's death must be connected to the murders of Bella and Maxine. Did Kiran even live in Merritt when Bella died? Then she was struck with the memory of Robyn telling her about the run-ins between Quirke and herself.

'I just saw Nic Quirke,' she told Vandenburg. 'You need to organise a search of the Eyrie straight away before he tries to get rid of the painting.' She told Vandenburg what she had found.

'Quirke is like the fucking sun,' said Vandenburg, his voice bitter. 'Everything revolves around him.'

'What do you want me to do?'

'Go to the police station and wait for me there. I'll try to get Quirke's place searched as soon as possible.'

As Alex walked up the street, she tried to make sense of what had happened. Robyn must have uncovered something about Bella's and Maxine's deaths; it was the only thing that made any sense. Kiran had nothing to do with either woman. But a small voice in the back of her mind reminded her that she barely knew him.

There was the sound of an engine behind her, and Theo pulled up alongside. She leant in through the passenger window.

'You heard?' she said.

'Why would anyone want to kill Robyn?' He sounded shocked. 'I don't understand. She's just a poor defenceless old lady.'

Alex shook her head. Her eyes stung with tears. 'What are you doing now?' she asked.

'Picking up Tayla and taking her back to the Eyrie to drive Prue's car home,' he said. 'Have you got the keys?'

Alex fumbled in her pocket and passed them through the window. 'Thanks.' She was making a habit of leaving cars behind and forgetting all about them. Then she remembered that Kiran still had her own car keys. There was a house key on that ring as well. How could she be so stupid? Should she tell Vandenburg?

No. Kiran couldn't be involved. It didn't make any sense. Not when Robyn had spoken about the hostility between herself and Nic.

'When did you know Nic was coming to Merritt today?' she asked Theo.

'When he turned up, but that's not unusual. Look, Nic's a good guy. He was just angry you were on his property without him knowing. That was my fault, not his.'

If Theo kept blindly following Nic, he could find himself in a lot of trouble. Alex had to protect him from what was going to happen. 'The police want to interview him and they're going to search the Eyrie, so if you know something about him, anything at all, now's the time to tell them.'

Theo rested his head back on the seat, closed his eyes. He looked so young and helpless. For a moment Alex thought he might cry.

'Are you saying that I'm working for a murderer?'

'I think it's possible,' she said.

When she reached the police station, Alex found Dr Sadler sitting alone in the waiting room. She noticed that there was blood splattered on his shirt. His demeanour seemed unruffled when he said hello, but as he took a sip of water from the glass in his hand, she noticed his hand was trembling.

'Ridiculous,' he said. 'I've seen so many dead bodies, and yet look at me – I'm all shaken.'

'I think that means you're human,' said Alex, sitting down beside him. 'Are you all right?'

'Just taking a moment before I head home. I've already provided my statement.'

'Was it you who tried to resuscitate Robyn?'

'She was already dead when I got there. I'd been in the library reading the papers.'

'I'm sure it will be a comfort to Robyn's family that you still tried. Had she been dead long?'

He shook his head. 'An hour perhaps, not much more than that.'

That would have made the time of death around 9 am. Nic hadn't got to the Eyrie until midday. What had he been doing that morning?

'How was she killed?'

'Struck over the head with a walking stick. I believe it might belong to one of the volunteers. It was lying beside her body.'

The hand holding the water glass was trembling harder now, so Alex took the glass from him and placed it on the counter, then came back and put her own hand on his. There was blood smudged across the cuff of his shirt, she noticed. The attack on Robyn must have been brutal.

'I've known Robyn for over forty years,' he said, almost to himself. 'That it had to come to this . . . It's not fair.'

'I'm so sorry,' said Alex.

His face twitched at her words, as if he had almost forgotten she was there.

A subdued Julie appeared and gestured for Alex to go through the door that led into the offices.

'Are you sure you're all right?' Alex asked Alby as she stood to go.

The old doctor nodded slowly. 'Don't worry about me,' he said. 'I'm fine now.'

Alex wasn't sure she would ever be fine again.

Chapter 20

Julie sat her in a space that looked like a disused junk room but which Vandenburg seemed to be using as an office. It was small and smelt of cigarette smoke.

Time passed and Vandenburg didn't show up. Alex went over to the window, dirty with rippled glass that looked like it hadn't been opened this century. She pushed on the frame. It took several heaves to get it to budge and she kept it propped open with some old phone books. Who even had phone books anymore?

She tried not to think about Kiran. Instead, she looked at the picture of Johnny Ewart stuck up on one side of a whiteboard, along with Nic Quirke. On the other side were photographs of Maxine McFarlane and Bella Greggs. Robyn Edgeley would be joining them. Poor Robyn who drove people crazy but was only trying to do what she thought was right. Alex sat in a chair facing the whiteboard and stared at them, overwhelmed by a feeling of helplessness, until her phone beeped, dragging her back to the present. She pulled the phone from her bag to discover it was running on empty. There was a charger helpfully set up on the wall beside her. As she bent down to plug it in, she heard a knock on the window. Kiran was standing outside peering in at her.

Instinctively, she lurched backwards.

'Sorry,' he said. 'I didn't mean to scare you.'

'That's okay.' Her voice shook.

'What are you doing here? I saw you from the car park.'

'Helping the police.'

'About Robyn?'

She nodded. 'You were supposed to meet her this morning.' It came out as an accusation, which she didn't regret. Kiran owed everyone some answers.

'That was the plan,' he said. 'She rang yesterday afternoon and told me we needed to talk.'

'What about?' Alex demanded, almost shouting.

Kiran looked puzzled. 'Are you all right?'

'Robyn's dead,' she said. 'Of course I'm not all right. None of this is all right. What did she want to talk to you about?'

He shrugged. 'I don't know. She said it was a confidential matter. I told her to come see me at the surgery but she didn't want anyone to see her. She suggested I come to the museum first thing this morning.'

'What time was your meeting?' asked Alex.

'Eight. But when I arrived she wasn't there. The place was locked up, so I left a message on her phone and headed in to work instead. I feel terrible. She must have already been dead.'

Could that be true? Alby had estimated the time of death as
9 am, but Kiran was there an hour earlier. Was he lying to her?
She walked over to the window and peered through it to get a
better look at him. He said he felt terrible, but he didn't seem
that upset. Shouldn't he be? Robyn was a patient of his – perhaps
even a friend.

'What did you do after that?' Alex asked.

'I told you: I went to work.'

'Did anyone see you there?'

'What are you talking about?' asked Kiran.

'The police will want to know,' Alex said. 'They'll be asking
everyone.'

'Do you know what happened? Someone told me that it was
a burglary gone wrong.'

A burglary? Who on earth could think this was a burglary?
She looked at Kiran, incredulous. Was he just fishing for information? She had already stuffed up by telling Kelly about the
wings. Right now she needed to keep her mouth shut.

'Anyway, I just wanted to let you know that your car is ready
to be picked up from the mechanics.'

'Thanks.'

'They told me what was scrawled on the windscreen. Have
you told Kelly about that?'

Alex wanted to shake him and scream that she hadn't needed
to talk to Kelly: he was the one who had ordered it done. Kiran
didn't have a clue what was happening in this town. Unless he
did. Unless he was part of it. She swallowed hard.

'Look,' Kiran continued, 'I've got to give my statement and
then get back to work, but when this has calmed down, we should

have a drink or dinner and talk about what happened . . . you know, last night.'

Last night. It seemed light years ago. She could feel her face redden at the thought of it. It hadn't felt like a mistake at the time, in fact the opposite, but looking at it now, from the sobering environment of a police station, it certainly seemed to be one.

'I'm not sure that's possible,' she replied. 'I've got to get Mum organised and there's so much else going on. It's just not great timing.' As if to demonstrate her point, her phone started pinging behind her as messages flooded in.

'Oh,' he said and straightened up. The initial look of disappointment changed to something harder with eyes narrowed and jaw set. 'Well, if you're too busy . . .'

'Wait.' Alex was making a mess of this and was now uncertain whether she wanted him to go or stay.

'Take better care of yourself, Alex.' Then he dismissed her with a shake of his head and turned away.

'Kiran,' she called after him, but he didn't stop, and she watched as, shoulders hunched, hands in pockets, he walked away.

Suddenly, Alex felt worse than she had thought possible. Slumping down on the floor, back to the wall, she sat there. Her chest felt tight as if something hard was stuck in it. Kiran was right about one thing: she did need to take better care of herself.

Her phone gave another beep. She had to pull herself together and take charge of the situation, starting with her messages. Prue had left most of them, so she texted back telling her aunt where she was and that she'd be home soon. The last message was from her clerk. It was the first time Alex had heard from Glenys in two weeks. Desperate for a distraction, she hit reply and heard the phone ring.

'Can you get back to the city tomorrow?' Glenys asked, dispensing with any of the usual pleasantries. 'You're only three hours away, right?'

'Why?'

'Maxwells need an urgent injunction in the Federal Court by Friday. Do a good job and they might keep you on for the trial. All their usual go-tos are busy. I can send you through all the information. They'll want a conference tomorrow morning. You could do it by video link, but it would be best to go into their offices and introduce yourself.'

This was the one case she needed. The part of her to-do list that was redeemable. Maxwells was one of the biggest law firms in the city. Alex had been dreaming of being briefed by them ever since she started at the bar. Even Tom hadn't managed to nab a Maxwells brief. She would finally beat him in something. It would also be the perfect reason to leave this mess behind her, including Kiran. After all, Vandenburg was the one getting paid to investigate the murders in Merritt. She'd found Maxine's painting; there was nothing else she could do now. As for her mother, Prue had said she wouldn't mind taking care of Denny, and Alex could come back to Merritt next week, or the week after.

But as she opened her mouth to agree, her gaze was caught by the photos that stared out blankly from the whiteboard. Maxine seemed to be looking straight at her, a gentle reproof, as if she knew that Alex was about to walk away.

'I can't,' Alex muttered.

'What?' came the incredulous reply. 'This is Maxwells! Once you get on the books there, you're set.'

'It's just bad timing.' The second time she had said words to that effect in five minutes.

'Alex, you've been pestering me for any work at all and you're turning this down? You're not doing your career any favours. I talked you up to them.'

'It's just . . .' But she couldn't think of the words to explain.

'Perhaps I should try Tom. He'd never knock back an opportunity like this.'

Not Tom! The thought that he might end up with her perfect Maxwells injunction was too awful to contemplate.

'No, don't call Tom – I'll do it! I'll do it!' It meant she wouldn't sleep for two days, what with driving back to the city and then prepping for the meeting, but she'd make it happen.

'Good. I'll get them to email through the file for you to read.'

Alex put her head in her hands. She didn't really know what to do first. Ring Prue and explain that she had to go? Pick up her car? She would give Vandenburg another twenty minutes, she decided.

The time ticked by. Alex spent it trying to work out where that final part of *The Accusation* might be, so she could tell Vandenburg where to look next. Prue texted her about Denny, who had become distraught when she heard about Robyn's death and had gone back to bed.

I've booked her into see Dr K tomorrow.

Another reason to leave, thought Alex. Prue could take Denny to the appointment. It wasn't like Denny would care. Alex would wait until she got home to explain about the urgent work. Her aunt would understand. She always did.

When half an hour had passed, she texted Vandenburg to ask him where the hell he was.

The reply came immediately. *At Eyrie now. Secured painting. Found this in Quirke's study.*

A pixelated picture was attached. Alex clicked on it and then her mouth dropped open.

It was Bella. Vandenburg had taken a digital image of a physical photo of her. Alex could imagine him standing over it, hand shaking slightly as he took it.

The photo was similar to the painting she had seen at Sasha's house – perhaps the last picture Bella had ever created. But if that painting was a modest nude, this photograph was an adults-only full frontal. Bella stood facing the camera, hair piled up on top of her head, leaving nothing to the imagination. It had been taken in Bella's bedroom; Alex recognised the bedhead and the partial view of the cupboard door.

This must be the real reason Nic had been paying Bella. Finally, they had the answer. She felt a mixture of rage and relief. You were more than double her age, she thought. They were closing in on him now and she could leave Merritt in good conscience.

Grabbing her bag, Alex walked to the door, which seemed to open of its own accord to reveal Kingsley Kelly.

'I was just leaving,' Alex said.

'Not so fast.' Standing in the doorway, he seemed bigger all of a sudden, an immovable object blocking her way. They stood face to face for a moment, and then he stepped into the room, closed the door behind him and locked it.

Alex thought about punching him. She thought about screaming. But either of these options might get her arrested. Instead she moved backwards towards the window, putting the desk between them, all the while keeping her eyes fixed on him. There wasn't the usual aura of authority and bluster about him; instead, he looked desperate. She had never seen him like this before.

'That crack at the library,' he said, 'asking me if I had found another body. You don't honestly think I had something to do with Bella's death?'

'No,' she answered. 'But you haven't been telling the truth in relation to Bella.'

Kelly stared down at her, a kind of dullness behind his eyes. 'And what do you think the truth is?'

She didn't have the energy to play his games. 'I found this in Bella's bedroom among her paintings.' Alex reached into her bag, pulled out the photo of toddler Bella in Kelly's arms and put it on the desk. 'You're her father, aren't you?'

It was like seeing someone get slapped in the face in slow-motion. Kelly's head jerked back and then he pushed himself away from the table like he wanted to put distance between himself and the picture.

'Why did you move those wings?' Alex asked.

Kelly didn't answer for a long time, and when he did, his voice was hoarse.

'When I saw her lying there, at first I thought it must have been an accident or suicide. I knew all anyone would talk about was those wings. I didn't want my daughter to be turned into some kind of sick joke. So, I hid them. I wasn't thinking, not really. It was just an instinct.'

Was this true? Or had he been trying to hide his connection to her? A proper murder investigation would have discovered he was Bella's father. His secret would have finally been exposed.

'You can't be sure how people would have reacted.'

He shook his head. 'Know where I grew up before we came to Merritt? A lovely little place in the South Australian wheat belt – Snowtown.' His jaw tightened. 'People want to change the name now, all because some murdering degenerates from out of town thought it was a good idea to hide bodies in barrels. I wasn't going to have weirdos, tragedy tourists, coming to Merritt just because of those fucking wings. Some dickhead journalist wannabe making a name for themselves with a ten-part podcast series that would trash Bella's reputation and rip apart this town and the people in it for other people's entertainment.'

'You gave the wings to Sasha,' Alex said, wondering why she hadn't worked it out before.

'And Maxine found them in the shed and talked Sash into giving them to her for that bloody exhibition. I told her not to, and I asked Maxine to leave Bella's paintings alone, to let her rest in peace, but she didn't listen. She never liked me. For a bohemian artist type, she was pretty judgemental when it came to extra-marital affairs.'

'She knew you were Bella's father?'

'You can't keep any secret in this town, no matter how hard you try. Always some busybody around trying to interfere, people who don't take no for an answer. People like Maxine.' He paused for a moment. 'And you.'

Alex ignored the jibe. 'You told everyone that Maxine's death was an accident.'

'I was wrong about that,' he said. 'It wasn't until you said to my face that the two were linked that I stopped trying to deny it.'

Alex could barely believe what she was hearing. Finally, he was admitting that he'd got it wrong. It should have been a moment of triumph, but too many people had been hurt. Robyn was dead and she still wasn't certain that she could trust him.

'Why did you ask Curtis to spy on me and trash my car?'

Kelly looked blank and then shook his head slowly. 'I don't get teenagers to do my dirty work.'

'You had lunch with my mother. What was that about?'

'I was trying to protect you,' he said, voice rising in exasperation. 'I told Denny that you needed to give up this amateur sleuthing and go back to the city for your own safety. The last person who tried to work out what happened to Bella ended up dead. I didn't want to have to do a death knock on your mother's door.'

Could that be the reason why Denny had told her to go?

'I *am* leaving,' she said. 'I'm heading off tonight – but not because of anything you did.'

Kelly moved away from the door, as if giving her a clear path to head off straight away. 'Can't say I'm sorry.'

Kelly might not be a murderer but he was an arsehole.

He waited until she was almost at the door. 'I've got an idea who might have set Curtis on you.'

'Who?' she asked, not even bothering to turn around.

'Johnny Ewart.'

And Alex remembered what Lou Buckley had said that first day she had met him in the police station waiting room. Curtis was in trouble because he'd been hanging around with Johnny

Ewart. Did Curtis see Alex parked in front of Sasha's house and ring Johnny? Was that the reason that Johnny had come home early? Did Johnny tell him to follow Alex's car and then scare her in the Wyld? That wasn't just possible, it was plausible, especially given Johnny's behaviour in front of the library.

'I was already planning on paying Johnny a visit after today's little outburst,' said Kelly. 'This gives me another reason. I might head up to Sasha's now.'

There was a pile of paintings in Bella's room. Alex had been looking for a painting by Maxine when she went through them, but now that had been found. The last part of the triptych had been created by Bella. There was no better place to hide a needle than among other needles, and Maxine had visited Sasha before she died to go through the pictures again. What if, rather than looking to take paintings away, she'd in fact been putting one back? Alex had been distracted by the photograph first time around. She might have missed something important. Now she knew what the other two parts of the triptych were, perhaps she would recognise the third when she saw it.

She glanced at her watch. There was just enough time to do this before she left Merritt.

'I want to say goodbye to Sasha,' said Alex. 'I'll go with you.'

Chapter 21

As they drove down Sasha's street, Alex saw Erin out the front of her house, mowing the lawn. Kelly parked the car.

'Johnny's SUV isn't here,' he said. 'Probably reckoned I'd come up to see him after the scene at the library and shot through.'

'What are you going to do now?'

'Sasha won't tell me where he is,' said Kelly. 'I'll check with Erin, see when she saw Johnny last.'

'I'll head inside and chat to Sasha,' Alex said, glad of the chance to talk to the woman on her own. She still didn't trust Kelly enough to tell him why she was really here.

She walked down the path to the house. 'Sasha,' she called through the screen door, peering through the mesh. 'It's Alex Tillerson.'

Her words echoed into emptiness.

She tried the screen door. It was unlocked. Country living was supposed to be about leaving your front door open but this seemed wrong. Perhaps Sasha wasn't at home either. Would she have taken off with Johnny? Alex hoped not, but then Sasha clearly had terrible judgement when it came to men.

Walking down the hall, she called out again as she peered into empty rooms. Sasha wasn't in the bedrooms or the living room or even the kitchen. Alex headed to Bella's bedroom.

Pushing open the door, she stopped short with a gasp. Someone had been here. The nude above the fireplace, the one that resembled the photo Vandenburg had found hidden at the Eyrie, had been slashed. Someone had taken a knife to it, slicing Bella in two, leaving the canvas hanging down like a lower lip.

'Sasha,' Alex shouted, more urgently now.

There was a sound, muffled, agitated. A door banged, and then silence.

She should go find Kelly.

But as she left the room she heard another sound. Voices.

Alex walked back through the kitchen and living room and pushed open the back door. She jogged down the steps and turned the corner.

There in the long grass, between a tumbledown dairy shed, Johnny's truck and the chook pen, was Sasha. She was kneeling on the ground and above her stood Johnny, white singlet, jeans, thick chain around his neck, his eyes crazy wild, veins popping. He was pressing the muzzle of a black gun against the back of Sasha's head.

Time seemed to stop and the rest of the world receded. Alex could hear nothing but the thump of her heart in her ears.

'Put the gun down, Johnny.' Her voice was calmer than she felt but the words broke apart like mist and he didn't take any notice at all.

'Where's your uniform, copper?' he asked. 'Or don't you need it when you're just dropping by for a cup of tea? Coming around here, telling Sasha to spy on me.'

His tone was bitter, hate-filled. Alex shouldn't be the one trying to negotiate with him. Should she retreat?

He stretched his mouth, half-grin, half-grimace. 'That interfering bitch Maxine used to come around for cups of tea. Look how she ended up. That's what happens to people who poke their nose into things around here.'

Sasha was injured, Alex saw, blood running down her face. Her head drooped. Alex couldn't walk away.

'I'm not the police,' Alex said, her voice louder now, firmer.

'What are you then?'

'I'm an out-of-work barrister.'

'What? Someone who makes coffee?'

For a wild second Alex thought everything would be all right. Yes, she would say, I am a barista, and then Johnny would put down the gun and Sasha would stand up and they could all go inside, but instead Johnny just looked angrier because he thought she was trying to make a fool of him.

'A lawyer,' she said. 'I told you that when we first met. We can talk this through.' Her voice was sounding more confident now. 'No one needs to get hurt.'

Where was Kelly? Surely it shouldn't take that long to ask Erin a simple question.

'Curtis saw you at the police station,' shouted Johnny. 'And you've been going round asking questions about Bella and Maxine. Why are you doing that if you aren't a cop?'

Because I'm an idiot, thought Alex, not taking her eyes off the gun in his hand.

'That's right,' she said. 'I have been asking questions. That's how I know that the police are about to make an arrest – and it isn't you.'

'Then why's my picture on a whiteboard at the station?'

Alex flinched.

Johnny's laughter bordered on hysteria. 'That Julie's got a big mouth. Told Sash down at the pub. Told everyone. People are looking at me like I killed Bella and Maxine and now that old bitch at the museum. Kelly's setting me up.'

'I know you didn't kill them,' she assured him. 'That's why I'm here. Like I said, the police are about to arrest someone – I came to tell Sasha that.' This was wishful thinking, but she had to get Sasha's attention.

'Liar,' snarled Johnny.

'There's been a breakthrough,' Alex continued. 'The police are searching Nic Quirke's property right now. I wanted Sasha to know before it became public. This must have placed a terrible strain on you both. So just put down the gun then we'll go inside and I'll explain what happened.'

Sasha lifted her head. There was a cut on her forehead and her left eye was already swelling shut. 'Really?' she asked, such longing in her voice.

Johnny kicked out at Sasha and grabbed a handful of her hair, snapping her head back so that all Alex could see was a tight jaw and long neck. 'She's lying, stupid. Don't you understand that?' But he didn't sound as sure now. Alex had a flashback to Maxine's painting. Johnny had the same build as the farmer, with an air of repressed violence hinted at by the sword nearby.

'I'm not lying,' Alex said and took a step closer. 'Put down the gun and we can talk out here if you like.'

Johnny turned the gun on her. Alex's blood turned to ice.

'Come any closer and I'll kill you,' he said.

Out of the corner of her eye, she saw Kelly appear around the side of the house and felt a wave of relief wash over her – until she noticed there was no service revolver in his hand.

Where's your fucking gun? thought Alex. Why don't you have it out? Why haven't you shot him already?

'Put it down, son,' Kelly said, with a low growl of warning.

Johnny swung his head around to face him. The bluster was beginning to falter. Looking uncertain now, he swung the gun from Alex to Kelly.

'I told you if you hurt Sasha you'd be answerable to me,' Kelly said, unperturbed. 'Let her go.'

All Johnny's attention was on Kelly now. Alex took another few steps forward. If she could get to Sasha, she might be able to pull her to safety.

Johnny let go of Sasha's hair. She slumped sideways and almost fell over.

'Sasha, go to Alex,' said Kelly.

There was such authority in his voice that both women responded to it. Sasha scrambled across the grass, half crawling, half walking. She was a bloody mess, whimpering in pain and fear. Alex moved towards her, hand outstretched, one eye still on Johnny.

'Why do you care so much, Kelly?' Johnny was still acting tough, but Alex could tell he was scared now. 'I might not have done everything right, but I didn't knock up some seventeen-year-old and tell her to keep it secret. Took me a while to work out why *you* were so interested in Sash and Bella.'

'Get behind me,' Alex hissed at Sasha, readying herself to push the woman out of harm's way if need be.

'How long did it take, Johnny?' asked Kelly. 'Who do you think paid for this house you've been living in? Certainly not you, you weak fuck.'

'Who killed my daughter?' Sasha grabbed at Alex, frantic.

There was a loud *smack-smack*. A shot fired and then another in reply, so close together they were almost in unison. An explosion of birds, fast-flapping away at the noise.

Alex found herself reacting instinctively, flinging herself forward to push Sasha to the ground. Alex looked upwards, stared at Johnny. He hadn't moved. Where was Kelly? Johnny's eyes met hers. Slowly, he put a hand to his chest as if he was going to introduce himself and then he turned the palm towards her. It was red with blood.

Sasha pushed her violently away and Alex's world lurched sideways. She heard Sasha start to scream as Johnny began to crumple in slow motion.

Craning her neck around, Alex could see there was a gun in Kelly's hand now.

Sounds came in and out. She could hear Sasha keening,

crouched beside her on all fours. Time passed. It could have been seconds. It could have been years.

Slowly, she got to her feet. Her limbs felt heavy as lead. All she could do was stare at Kelly. Eventually, he turned, the gun still in his hand and now pointed at her.

What had he done? What was he doing now?

She could feel her heart racing in her chest, blood throbbing in her body. She opened her mouth to plead, to cry, but no words came out.

Kelly exhaled and shook his head, a strange expression of grim determination on his face as if steeling himself, and then, still looking straight at Alex, he slowly, very slowly, placed the gun on the ground at his feet.

Chapter 22

The paramedic sat Alex and Sasha on the verandah and wrapped them in space blankets. He cleaned up Sasha's head wound. A big man – a Kiwi from the sound of him – he was methodical and calm. He didn't say much and Alex was grateful. If she had to talk now, she would start crying and might not stop.

He told them that they would need to be taken to Durrell Hospital for observation. 'Once we get sorted out here,' he added, giving her a sad little smile.

She tried to nod her head in thanks but it was almost impossible.

Kelly waved the paramedic away when he tried to assess him. He had been standing quietly, leaning on the Bedford, smoking a cigarette that he'd bummed off Nathan. Vandenburg, as acting officer in charge, had been asking Kelly questions in a low voice and writing down the answers. When he arrived, Alex wanted to know if they'd found anything else up at the Eyrie, but she just couldn't bring herself to ask. It was like her mind was a sieve and everything had drained out. All she could think about was the surprised look on Johnny's face when he saw his own blood on his hand and the fact that, for a nanosecond, she'd thought Kelly was going to kill her as well.

Nathan took the ambulance officers around the back of the house to where Johnny must still be lying on the grass. They carried a gurney between them. Suddenly, Alex felt sick. Her stomach muscles clenched. Standing quickly, she threw up into the rosebush, until there was nothing left inside her. Breathing hard, she wiped her mouth with the back of her hand. All she could taste was acid.

The paramedic came back with a water bottle and passed it to her.

Alex started to shiver.

Sasha shook her head when he offered one to her. 'No thanks.' The puffed-up skin around her eye was coloured like a sunrise, her voice so flat it made Alex wince to hear it.

Vandenburg returned from the back garden, said something inaudible to Kelly, and the two men walked over to the squad car. Vandenburg opened the rear passenger door. He glanced at Alex, making a what-the-fuck-just-happened kind of face. Nathan went to the driver's seat. Kelly turned and Alex thought he was about to say something to her, but he only looked at Sasha, grief on his face. Sasha's face was stony in return.

A visibly uncomfortable Vandenburg gestured to Kelly, who nodded. Then, after a moment's hesitation, the senior sergeant ducked his head and climbed into the car. The engine started.

The two women stood there watching as they drove away. Neighbours had come out by now to see what the fuss was about. Alex saw Erin standing by her gate. In the distance, she noticed a lanky teenager on his bike. Curtis stuck his finger up at the police car as it passed by.

Vandenburg headed back around the side of the house. Surreptitiously, Alex moved next to Sasha. Witnesses should be kept separate, she knew, so this was her only chance to get answers before more police arrived.

'No one is about to get arrested for Bella's murder,' Sasha said. 'You lied.' The words came out of the side of her mouth in a harsh whisper, as if it was too painful to talk normally.

'I was trying to convince Johnny.'

'So many people are dead,' croaked Sasha. 'I told you that would happen and you still don't know who killed Bella. You're never going to find out.'

'That's not true. The police really have made a breakthrough; I wasn't lying about that. They're up at Nic Quirke's property now. We're getting closer.'

She was using the word 'we' as if she was part of their investigation.

'You really think Nic killed my daughter?' Sasha turned to her in disbelief.

'Was it possible that he was sleeping with Bella?' Alex asked. It was a question she wouldn't have asked so bluntly earlier, but having watched a man die in front of her, the time for sensitivity seemed over.

'Is this about the money he gave her? Farinacci made a big deal about that. It was for her *activism*. He never tried to hide it.

He even asked my permission first.' A hesitation and then, 'But she was sleeping with someone. I found condoms in her bag and confronted her. She told me it was a boy from school. I wasn't happy about it. That's what we fought over the morning before she died.'

'Did she say who?'

Sasha shook her head, grimacing in pain. 'Told me it was none of my business.' A single tear trickled down her face, making a trail through the dirt and blood.

'It couldn't have been Nic Quirke?'

'No,' said Sasha. 'I don't think she'd lie to me about that. She knows the history between me and her father. Bella used to tell me that there was a power imbalance, that nothing was equal about it. She saw how one person paid the price and the other got off scot-free. My daughter was clever . . . way smarter than me. She'd never have repeated my mistakes.'

Alex didn't have the heart to point out that this could be exactly the reason why Bella wouldn't tell her mother she was sleeping with Nic Quirke.

'That's how you feel about Kelly?'

'Falling in love with him was the stupidest thing I ever did. Having Bella was the best thing. At least he supported me in that. Said if I kept my mouth shut he'd give me money. He lived up to that at least. His money bought us this house. It was going to put Bella through art school. It would have worked out for us. She would have made something of herself, not ended up as a barmaid like her mother.' Her words became choked with emotion.

'What about Johnny?'

'Johnny wasn't so bad. Sure, Bella fought with him, but no worse than any other stepfamily. He never laid a finger on her. It was Kelly who caused trouble. He couldn't stand the fact that Bella might have a dad who wasn't him. Made sure Johnny couldn't get a job around here, except for a few shifts at the timber mill. Wanted to force him to go back to dealing so he could bust him. And now my Johnny is dead too.'

'He was a violent man!' Alex couldn't believe she had to say it. 'Look at what he just did to you.'

Sasha rested her elbow on her knee and stared to chew on her thumbnail. It was like she was ageing in front of Alex's eyes. 'Johnny couldn't cope with the rumours that he was responsible for Bella's death. Went back on the gear. Became paranoid. That bitch Julie from the station told everyone he was a suspect. That's why all this happened.' She was starting to shake. 'Just one shit thing after another. People don't tell you that. They think bad things happen and somehow there's karma and good things will balance it out, like you'll win the lottery or something, but that's not how it works. Badness only brings badness. Death leads to more death. Everything just snowballs into one giant fucking disaster.' Her eyes lifted to meet Alex's. 'But Kelly better not try and fit Johnny up for what happened to Bella and Maxine and Robyn. None of that is on him.'

No amount of spin was going to turn Johnny Ewart into a caring stepfather and a loving partner in Alex's view; the guy had pointed a gun at both of them less than an hour ago. But what Sasha said did bother her. She hadn't seen who had fired the first shot, though she had assumed it was Johnny, in response to Kelly's goading. Alex opened her mouth to ask Sasha if she knew, but then shut it again. Sasha had her own axe to grind here.

'We fought that afternoon, Bella and me,' Sasha said, her voice almost a whisper now. 'It was terrible. I was so angry at her. It was Johnny who got worried when she didn't come home. We got in touch with all her friends but no one knew anything. Johnny thought she might have turned up at Kelly's place to confront him. But he hadn't seen her either. Both of them went out searching that night and then they found her the next day.'

Tears ran down Sasha's face, enormous tears now. Her eyes darted around in distress, refusing to settle on one spot.

Unable to cope with the woman's naked grief, Alex turned away to watch Vandenburg talking on his phone. No doubt following the checklist. A police shooting needs to be played by the book because everyone is watching. Ethical Standards, Coroner, Office of Police Integrity. Stuff it up and it would hang around your neck like a noose for your entire career. Vandenburg would only be babysitting this one, though. He just needed to get through the next few hours and then he could hand it over to someone who was more senior in rank than Kelly.

Forensics arrived and headed through to the backyard. Alex waited to do the walk-through of the incident, but then Vandenburg came past and told her that it wouldn't be done until the next day. The official investigator wanted to do it in person. There was no chance she would be leaving town, she realised.

The two women sat together, stunned, watching the activity.

'Do you still want to find out who killed Bella?' Alex asked quietly. Nathan was standing not too far away, at the front door.

'Of course,' Sasha said, keeping her gaze fixed straight ahead as if Alex hadn't spoken at all.

'I need to get into your house. I have to check Bella's room again. There's something I might have missed.'

A moment's pause. 'What do you want me to do?'

'If I try to go in now, Nathan might stop me. All of this is a crime scene. I need you to create a diversion.'

Sasha glanced up at him and then stood up, took a step forward and collapsed.

'Oh my God,' yelled Alex. 'Sasha's fainted.'

There was movement straight away. Vandenburg came running from the back garden and Nathan raced down the stairs. Alex moved backwards, ostensibly to give the ambo more room to come in and assist. Then, while everyone was occupied, she opened the front door and slipped inside.

She gave herself five minutes tops.

Running down the hall and into Bella's room, she headed straight for the paintings stacked against the wall. She knew what two parts of *The Accusation* were. Surely she would recognise the third if she saw it.

She began to go through the paintings one by one, trying to avoid looking at the slashed picture of naked Bella up on the wall. Johnny must have done that in his paranoid, drug-fuelled rage. Sasha could talk all she liked about Johnny being a good stepfather; only a psychopath would be so destructive.

Landscapes, the pictures of Sasha, the girls from school, Theo holding a football and grinning, Bella when she was three. She got to the end and began again. There was nothing here that fitted. Nothing that made sense.

'Alex.'

Vandenburg was standing in the doorway.

'I can't find it,' she said. 'The last piece of the triptych.'

'We've got him,' said Vandenburg. 'It was Nic Quirke. The search is still ongoing, but there was child porn on his computer as well as the photo of Bella. He didn't even really try to hide it. It was like he wanted us to find it; maybe he thought he was above the law. The guy made billions in tech and yet didn't even encrypt it. He liked them young – and when Bella was no longer young enough, or maybe threatened to expose him, he killed her. Maxine worked it out. She was so certain she made a painting about it and he killed her. If only we'd got there early enough, we could have saved Robyn.'

Alex sank down on the bed, trying to absorb this. Child porn? That was repugnant. But she wasn't sure she bought it. Was Quirke really so arrogant that he wouldn't even try to hide it? He must have known that the police would be coming to the Eyrie once they learnt of Maxine's paintings. He'd had all afternoon to cover up any illegal activities. She tried to square it with the man she had met earlier. Nic Quirke might be a killer, but he didn't seem stupid – and Vandenburg was wrong about Maxine's painting, Alex thought. It was accusing Nic of something quite different.

Vandenburg sat down next to her on the bed.

'We can stop now,' he said. 'It's all over.'

But she knew in her heart he was wrong about that as well.

Alex left a message for Glenys saying that she wouldn't be leaving Merritt. She didn't even bother to explain. It was hard to care about a commercial injunction now.

Denny worried her as well. The accident had done damage. Her mother's foot would slowly heal but her mind might not. Alex decided to keep the circumstances around Johnny's death from her for the time being, because Robyn's murder seemed to have shaken something fundamental in her brain, causing tremors of confusion. There was one terrible moment over breakfast the next morning when she mistook her daughter for a stranger and told her about how she had a little girl, a good girl who was no trouble at all, as if Alex could magically exist as an adult and child at the same time. It was all Alex could do to nod her head and say that was nice.

Prue was so worried she called to ask Alby to come over, but when he arrived Denny locked herself in her bedroom, hysterical, refusing to come out until he had gone. When she did emerge it seemed that all the fight had gone from her and she spent the rest of the day sitting on the couch, staring blankly at the television. Alex rang Kathleen again and finally got an appointment for a tour of the facility in a couple of days' time. Prue, who felt responsible for involving Alex in the investigation into Maxine's death and its aftermath, took charge. She dropped by the real estate agent and they seemed confident that a quick sale of the house would be possible. Prue told her the gossip around town assumed that Johnny was responsible for the murders of the three women and that was why Kelly had shot him.

An enormous bunch of flowers arrived late in the afternoon with a message asking her to get in touch. Alex was a little bewildered to find that they were from Tom, but after staring at them hard for five minutes, she went on his Instagram and found that his fiancée now had a YouTube channel. Shantelle was branching out into a web series and wanted to interview people for one titled 'Messy Exes'. Alex assumed that it was likely she would be the focus of episode one. Glenys texted that she'd arranged for another barrister – not Tom – to take the meeting at Maxwells. Alex didn't reply.

Kiran visited to check on Denny. Now that Nic Quirke was the chief suspect, Alex felt so ashamed that she could ever have considered Kiran a murderer she could barely look him in the eye. After he had finished with her mother, she overheard him talking to Prue about the warning signs for PTSD. He was never going to talk to her about getting coffee or going out to dinner again, and Alex felt both relief and disappointment in equal measure.

At midnight, she was lying in bed, still wide awake, when the phone rang.

'I couldn't sleep,' said Vandenburg.

She didn't bother to tell him she couldn't either.

He told her what had happened since he had found the photos. Nothing good, it seemed. Forensics had reported that there were no fingerprints on the photo of Bella – not Quirke's, nor anyone else's, for that matter. An army of expensive lawyers had arrived and were making their own accusations.

'They're saying that we planted the child porn to get Quirke charged and that the search might not even be legal,' Vandenburg said. Alex could hear the panic in his voice.

'What about the DPP?'

'The prosecutors say we don't have enough evidence yet to charge him. There needs to be more.'

Vandenburg was fraying at the edges and the case was falling apart. All this suffering would be for nothing. Robyn had been murdered and they were still no closer to the truth. Sasha's dire warning had come to pass.

Chapter 23

When Alex arrived at Merritt Police Station the next day for her formal interview, the place was buzzing with too many people in a variety of uniforms.

The interview room was already stuffy when she walked in. Julie gave her a glass of water. Alex didn't bother to say thank you. Julie was lucky that Kelly had shot Johnny; otherwise, she might have been the person under the microscope for talking about the investigation. She should be sacked.

Introductions were made and Alex could feel all eyes turn to her. Everyone in the room looked tired. One officer shoved a biscuit in his mouth as he fiddled with the video, and then swore, calling it fucking rubbish, crumbs flying out.

Alex sat alone on her side of the table, the only woman in the room once Julie closed the door. She could have sought legal representation, but she'd decided not to, reasoning that surely she was an adequate enough lawyer to supervise her own witness statement. Now, though, she had the feeling that perhaps she wasn't even up to this. Her blue suit and red silk shirt, her work armour, felt like they belonged to someone else.

Brett Patterson was running the investigation. She had met him earlier when they recorded a walk-through at Sasha's house. Vandenburg had told her that Patterson was Homicide's go-to man for heading into minefields. Politically astute, well liked, he had enough credit in the bank to charge a fellow cop with murder in the extremely unlikely event that he might have to. Big head, square glasses, not much neck, Patterson possessed the physique of a rugby player and the brains of the coach.

'Let me know if you need a break at any time,' he said.

Underneath the table, her leg jiggled.

'How long have you known Senior Sergeant Kelly?' he asked.

'A couple of weeks,' she answered.

'But he's been a long-standing friend of your family.'

Was he a friend? She had spent most of the time thinking of him as the exact opposite of that and she wasn't sure that her opinion had shifted. 'I think everyone knows everyone if you live in this town. All I can tell you is that I had never met him until the day on the beach when we found Maxine's remains.'

Before that day, she'd thought the worst things in the world were being divorced with an ill mother and a flatlining career. Now she knew things could get so much worse than that.

Patterson nodded to the other officer, who switched on the video.

He methodically took Alex through the statement that she had already given, pausing where there were gaps, but Alex didn't try to fill them in. Every barrister knows that trick. Don't anticipate, always wait for the question, and never ever volunteer information you aren't asked for.

It was a strange feeling being on this side of the table, having to provide answers rather than ask the questions. She felt light-headed at the unreality of it and kept sipping the water. Even an interrogation done with kid gloves was still an interrogation. Alex could feel beads of sweat collecting under her arms.

'Did you see who fired first?' Patterson asked.

'No, I didn't see that.'

'What did you see?'

She saw Johnny with the gun, Sasha moving towards her, mouth open, asking about Bella, holding on to her. Alex tried to explain it to Patterson, but it took a while.

'At the time of shooting, Ms Greggs was moving towards you, blocking your vision of what happened?'

'That's correct.'

'You can't say if Senior Sergeant Kelly shot in self-defence or not.'

'That's correct.'

'But before Ms Greggs obscured your vision, the only person you saw with a gun was Mr Ewart.'

'That's correct.'

'Could Ms Greggs see what was happening?'

In her mind, Alex could see Sasha's terrified eyes staring straight at her. She cleared her throat. 'I don't believe so.'

'Are you aware that Ms Greggs claims she saw Senior Sergeant Kelly shoot first?'

'No,' said Alex. 'I wasn't aware of that.' She closed her eyes and could see Sasha scrambling towards her, flinging her arms out and grabbing at Alex, stumbling, asking who had been arrested. Then came the sound and Alex, sitting on a chair in the police station, flinched with the memory of it.

Patterson pulled out a diagram of the back garden and asked Alex to mark where everyone was standing. Her hand trembled when she picked up the pencil. Patterson smiled, trying to encourage her. He had a comforting solid presence and waited in companionable silence as Alex took her time.

'If Ms Greggs was running towards you, facing you, how would she know who shot first?' he asked.

How indeed?

'You'd have to ask her,' said Alex. 'It all happened so quickly.'

'Senior Sergeant Kelly said Mr Ewart shot first but missed, and he returned fire, killing Mr Ewart.'

Alex shook her head. The same incident was being bent into two different stories and even though she'd been present, she didn't really know which one was true.

'Do you know of any reason why Senior Sergeant Kelly would want to shoot the victim other than in self-defence?'

Patterson knew Kelly was Bella's father, Alex could tell. Sasha must have said that Johnny had taunted him.

'No. I knew they didn't get on, that Kelly had tried to bring charges against him.'

'That would be' – Patterson looked at his notes – 'domestic violence and drug charges. None of which went to court. Did you hear any threats being made towards the victim by Senior Sergeant Kelly?'

That Alex had to think about. Slowly, she shook her head. Abuse yes, but not a specific threat.

'When you heard the shots, who did you think had fired?'

Alex breathed out. 'I thought Johnny had,' she said, because in that moment, Johnny was the only one who was threatening to shoot. Johnny was the only one holding a gun. 'I thought it was Johnny shooting at Sasha, just like he said he would.'

The other officer, the one who had sat in silence through the interview, scratched his cheek and took another biscuit.

When Alex walked out of the police station, she saw Lou Buckley standing out in the car park.

'My bloody mower is missing again, and they graffitied my shed,' he told her. 'I'm putting in another report.'

'Dylan Ferris?' she asked.

'My word, Dylan Ferris – and Curtis Stevens. It was bad enough when Kelly was in charge, but the minute he gets suspended from duty, those little buggers start running riot.' He stopped and stared at her. 'You're looking a bit rough.'

To her surprise, Alex was feeling a little better. Now that the interview was out of the way, she did feel as if a weight had been partially lifted from her shoulders.

'You had a ringside seat to the whole debacle. Reckon if we held that talk at the club now it would be standing room only.'

'That is never going to happen,' Alex said.

Lou patted her on the shoulder. 'Just have a think about it.' He sighed. 'This whole thing has everyone on edge. Had a committee meeting last night, almost ended in a punch-up.'

'What about?'

'Idiots objecting to the fact I put up a rainbow flag on the club flagpole in memory of Maxine. Some of the stick-in-the-muds objected but I just told them to shove it. If it goes, I go, and no one else will want to be president, so that's that.'

'Why a rainbow flag?' asked Alex.

'She was a lesbian. You know: LGBTQ and all the rest of the letters of the alphabet.'

'A lesbian?'

'Don't tell me you're prejudiced?' replied Lou. 'Taking after your grandfather, are you? He had plenty to say about women and their loose morals. Always the woman's fault in his world, which let him and all the rest of us fellas off the hook.'

The more she heard about Jack Walker, the more she hated him.

'No, no, of course not,' said Alex. 'It's just that no one told me, so I guess I assumed . . .'

She remembered Silver talking about Maxine having IVF with a former partner; she had jumped to the wrong conclusion.

'That's a heteronormative assumption, that is. Maxine was pretty keen about calling that out in committee meetings.'

'I'll take that on board,' said Alex. 'See you, Lou.'

Lou tipped his hat and then, squaring his shoulders, walked up the stairs to the station.

Alex headed down to the bay, trying to work out the implications of what Lou had just told her. As far as she could see, it merely confirmed that she didn't know Maxine, and if she didn't know Maxine, there had never been any hope of working out what she had discovered about Bella's death. All her efforts had been for nothing.

She watched the waves roll in. The wind was crisp and cold. She recognised Dirk Gardiner's trawler coming back into harbour and wondered if his boat was full of Quirke salmon.

The rural fire truck went past. A rather glum-looking Tayla, sitting in the back, gave her a wave. On their way to another fire drill, Alex supposed.

She began walking along the quay, watching Dirk as he moored and moved around his boat. He noticed her and held up a hand like he wanted to get her attention. She was about to head over when a car horn beeped behind her.

It was Theo in Prue's car.

He rolled down the window. 'Hello,' he called.

Alex walked over. 'Hi.'

'I've been waiting for you. Prue said you had your police interview today. How did it go?'

She made a so-so gesture with her hand. Theo got out of the car and came around to stand next to her on the path.

'It must feel good to have got it out of the way.'

'Yeah.' Alex didn't feel like rehashing it. She groped in her mind for something else to talk about. 'I saw Tayla in the fire truck before. She didn't look too happy.'

'Heading up to the Eyrie with the crew. Curtis and Dylan quit, so Tayla will be on wash-down afterwards.'

'The Eyrie again?'

'They claim they didn't get through the full drill last time. I suspect they're just being nosy.'

'Shouldn't you be up there supervising?'

He ran a hand through his hair and then shook his head. 'I quit this morning. I couldn't keep working for Nic, not after what the police found.'

Alex stared at him. 'That's a big decision. What are you going to do?'

He gave her a half-smile but it looked uncertain. 'Who knows? I'm trying to tell myself that there's opportunity in disruption, but right now it's hard to see it.' He shrugged. 'Anyway, I've got to pick up Tayla later, but until then I've got a clear afternoon, so I thought I'd see if you were free. There's something I want to show you.'

Above them, the clouds were breaking up, the sun finally deciding to show itself. The ocean responded, a rippling stained glass of blues and greens. Alex could taste salt on her tongue, felt it settle on her skin. Denny was with Prue and wouldn't miss her for a few more hours. She would just think that the interview was running longer than expected. Prue had talked about packing up the house, a job that Alex was finding difficult to muster any enthusiasm for. Anything that took her away from the messiness of her life for even a short while seemed attractive.

'The lighthouse?' she asked.

Theo's smile broadened, a proper one this time, more confident. 'We can do that too, if you want, but this is even more special.'

'What?'

'It's a surprise.'

'I'm not exactly dressed for surprises,' she said, looking down at her jacket and pants. At least her shoes were flat.

'You'll do.'

'And it won't take too long?'

'I'll have you back in a couple of hours, on my honour.' Theo made a Boy Scout kind of gesture with two fingers.

Glancing over her shoulder, she could see Dirk Gardiner walking up the jetty towards the car park. An old dilapidated jalopy of a car was sitting there. Alex could imagine it stinking of fish and petrol, much like his boat. He turned back to look at her, then cupped his hands over his mouth to call out something, but the wind tossed his words away. Maybe she would come past tomorrow and see if he was around. Whatever he had to tell her could surely wait.

Chapter 24

Theo turned the car around, indicated and pulled out onto the main road. As they drove past the museum, Alex caught sight of the closed sign in the window and a pile of wilting flowers dropping petals on the doormat. She quickly looked away.

They turned onto the highway towards Durrell.

'I promise to take this trip a little easier than the last time,' Theo said.

'I'd appreciate that.'

The sunshine warmed the air, her face, the seat. She took a deep breath. It felt like the first time she had breathed properly since Johnny was shot.

'Did the police say anything about Nic?' Theo asked. 'You're in contact with that detective, aren't you? Vandenburg. The one investigating it all.'

Alex nodded slowly.

'He's going to be charged, right? The media keeps saying he's assisting with inquiries, but they don't say anything else.'

'Is this why you came to find me?' she asked.

He turned his head briefly and shot her a rueful grin. 'It wasn't the only reason, promise.'

She should have expected this. Of course Theo wanted to know what was going on. The whole town did, and she couldn't blame them.

'They'll take their time to get it right,' Alex said, trying to sound more confident than she felt. 'He'll have a whole legal team ready to fight any charges.'

Nic Quirke would have the best lawyers money could buy. Even if the police did have the balls to charge him – which seemed unlikely going by her conversation with Vandenburg – Quirke would be prepared to spend millions on his defence and money could slow the wheels of justice considerably. Any barrister who got that gig would earn enough to buy a house, a big one, by the end of it.

Theo kept his eyes on the road. 'He *is* going to be charged, though?'

'I don't know.'

They continued in silence as Theo turned off to head towards Eden Point. Alex gazed out of the window at the bush; there were no houses this far from town.

As if guessing her thoughts, Theo said, 'It was my dream to see this place developed appropriately in an eco-friendly way. Close to the beach, respectful of the landscape. The Bird Boxes would have worked perfectly here.'

'With a recently renovated lighthouse as a near neighbour,' added Alex. 'It would have been a drawcard.'

'That was the idea,' said Theo. 'But if Nic pulls out now, everyone might lose their investment.'

'Who's everyone?'

'Lots of people in town. Alby Sadler has probably put the most in. That's the reason he came back to Merritt – he wanted to know why there had been so many delays on the project. Poor bugger, he's going to be working forever. Perhaps we can find another backer to pick it up, and this time I can be a proper partner and not just an employee.'

This seemed overly optimistic, but Alex didn't want to discourage Theo's wishful thinking.

They drove up the hill towards the lighthouse. Alex caught glimpses of the top of it, like the tip of a spear, as they moved upwards. The trees seemed to change shape as well. Unlike the tall straight trees of the Wyld and the Eyrie, which looked like they could grow forever if only they were left alone, these were twisted, bound together, salted by the sea, bent and tangled by the wind.

Finally, the trees receded enough for her to see the top section of the lighthouse.

'There,' said Theo. 'Built over a hundred and thirty years ago, and one day we'll get her working again.'

From a distance, the lighthouse was an impenetrable fortress, but up close it was discoloured and seemed more vulnerable. A Cyclops queen standing alone like she was the last piece left on the chessboard.

Theo revved the engine to climb the last steep section then parked in front of a small brick bungalow with a tin roof and picket fence out the front.

'Home sweet home,' said Theo. 'This was the deputy keeper's house. That's why it was built further down the hill, almost a kilometre away from the lighthouse. The head keeper's house was much closer, but it was also more exposed. It got wrecked in a storm in the eighties, so they had to pull it down.'

Alex heard the sound of a dog barking.

'That's Luna,' said Theo. 'She's not that fond of strangers. Give me a minute and I'll tie her up.'

Alex stayed by the car, while Theo went through the gate. A large German shepherd, all teeth and tongue, brandishing a thick scimitar tail with a life of its own, came bounding up to Theo who started baby-talking – 'Who's a good girl? Who's a good girl?' – as he knelt down to her level and buried his face in her coat, before grabbing the collar and walking her around the back of the house.

The soundscape of this world was different. Beneath Luna's barks, she could hear the rumble of the ocean. In a strange way, this seemed a more isolated place than the Wyld or the Eyrie. It was a world that had been preserved and hardened, an almost island. From where she was standing, not quite at the top of the point, she could see a sea of leaves, an army of dark green, leading up to the now clear blue sky. From this perspective, they seemed endless.

The wind picked up and the green around her began to ripple. The trees whispered to one another, their leaves undulating.

Theo returned. 'Come on,' he said. 'I want to show you something.'

'Not the lighthouse?'

He shook his head.

'This way.'

They moved through the gate and around the house. Luna was straining on her chain and growling.

'Quiet, Luna,' called Theo.

They walked slowly under the shade of the trees. These were different from the ones she had seen on the drive up. Even though they were wild and unkempt, there was an order and symmetry to them. It was the memory of an orchard, with the trees spaced out evenly in rows, and she guessed that they had been planted by some industrious deputy lighthouse keeper long before. She wondered how fruit trees fared so close to the sea.

In time they came to a clearing with one enormous giant of a tree standing alone in the centre. Its bark was muted browns and reds, with a deep understorey of ferns at its base. There were multiple thick-girthed trunks, stretched out at all angles like many arms, each furred with moss.

The tree was shining.

On the bark was a haphazard collection of tin rectangles that had been attached to each limb. They were like Christmas decorations catching the light. Moving closer, Alex saw they were metal plates, dozens of them, with words engraved on each one. Some were roughly scratched, as if whoever did it was in a hurry, only a name visible with dates underneath. Others were more elaborate, carved with elegant square letters spelling out a sentence.

She bent down to read the nearest one, a plaque at the base, half hidden in dried leaves. Brown rust bloomed through the metal. *Patchett, Tony and Mary. 28 March 1963–16 April 1965.*

Alex turned back to Theo. 'What is this?'

'This is my secret. I've shown Tayla, of course. People in town don't know or they've forgotten, but it was tradition for each keeper to add a nameplate at the end of their service.'

She stared up at the tree, trying to take it all in. 'It's like a living memorial.'

'The human side of the lighthouse,' Theo said. 'The bit the government ignored when they decided to shut it down. But you can't bury the past. If I get the lighthouse operational again, I reckon I will have earnt the right to put my name here. Go on, read them. You'll recognise a few of the surnames. Some of them couldn't bear to leave the lighthouse completely so they just retired to Merritt. Their descendants are still around.'

'There are so many,' marvelled Alex.

Theo found a sunny spot and flopped down on the grass to watch as she wandered around the tree, calling out what she could see: Blackwell, Banks, Roberts, Ferris – the latter related to Dylan, she supposed. Most included a few words or a quotation. A few referenced the Bible. Some were unreadable, the tin torn, the words worn away by the elements. Theo told her what he knew about each one. Between the two of them, they were summoning old memories, calling up ghosts into the clearing.

'This one's over a hundred years old,' she exclaimed. 'Another Blackwell. Lighthouse-keeping must be an intergenerational occupation.'

Theo waved his arms as though presenting himself as living confirmation of her hypothesis.

There were no patterns to the squares. Older ones sat beside more recent ones. Some had fallen off the tree altogether. The highest was way above their heads and Alex imagined a determined keeper shinning up into the branches with a collection of nails in his mouth and a hammer in hand, wanting to claim the top spot. Then she noticed the name Walter Rushall and called it out.

'That's my grandfather, Walter Theodore Rushall,' Theo said. 'The last lighthouse keeper. It broke his heart when they shut it down.'

Rushall. She kept her eyes fixed on the plaque. There was a chance, a tiny chance, that this might be her grandfather as well. Was that why Theo had brought her here? Was this a way of saying that they were family? She thought about Walter and tried to imagine the effort it must have taken to run a lighthouse back in the days before mechanisation, to be in constant service to it. The relentless checking of the light, the continual weather observations, the never-ending repair work, the lack of sleep and, most of all, the isolation. What sort of person was drawn to that life?

Next to Walter's, there was a series of plaques nestled together, made of darker metal, sitting on a smooth-skinned branch, attached by two screws. The words were made up of small, punctured holes, painstakingly pressed into the tin with a nail and hammer. The Campion family – six names, each in different writing. The last seemed to have been done by a young child. Husband, wife and four children, she assumed. Trying to decipher each name, she struggled with the last one, but eventually worked out it was 'Elizabeth'. She glanced over to Theo for confirmation. He had rolled onto his side, his face resting on his arm, eyes half closed against the sun.

'I should take a photo of you and send it to Tayla,' she said with a laugh.

'She'll really appreciate it when she's having to wash out the equipment. Because it's at the Eyrie, it will take twice as long as usual.'

Alex pulled out her phone and moved over to him. 'Why twice as long?' She opened the camera app and snapped a picture.

'The swimming pool is ocean water,' he explained. 'Nic's allergic to chlorine and he had some theory about ocean water being most therapeutic, so she has to spend time flushing it all out so that salt doesn't corrode the inside.'

Alex attached the photo to a message. *Up at the lighthouse with Theo*, she typed. *He's hard at work.* She pressed send then peered at the screen. 'It's not going through,' she said.

'It won't from here. Really pisses Tayla off when I don't respond to her texts. Signal quality's better at the lighthouse.'

The photo suddenly seemed quite a private image. Theo lying there, eyes closed, face softened, vulnerable, like he was in bed. His top had bunched up, revealing skin, a trail of hair on his belly leading down into his jeans, the waistband of his underwear exposed. It was a photo that a lover might take, and perhaps could be misinterpreted. Maybe she shouldn't send it to Tayla. She was about to delete it, her thumb hovering on the trash button, when she saw the mark. She zoomed in on it. A tattoo just above his right hipbone.

'You've got a tattoo,' she said.

'The old fishhook,' said Theo, rolling over and then squinting up at her. 'It was the symbol of Dad's mussel business.' He hesitated for a moment and Alex thought he was about to say something more about Ted, but all he said was, 'I might resurrect it again for my own company.'

The image of the fishhook snagged something in her mind, a flicker, but it had escaped again. What was it? She had the feeling she had seen it before, but that was impossible. Closing her eyes for a moment, she found she could conjure it up in her head, except that it wasn't a photo she saw. It was a drawing.

'Is it all right if I take some photos of the plaques?' she asked.

'Sure. Take your time.' Theo yawned. 'We're in no hurry.'

Walking around to the far side of the tree, she kept one eye on Theo, who lay contented in the grass. Opening her photos, she scrolled through her camera roll until she found it among the drawings from Maxine's diary.

There was Theo; it was obvious now she had made the connection. She could tell from the shape of the body, the way he held his arm, the dashed pencil marks that caught the angles of his face and, above all, the quick sketch of his tattoo, the scrawled J. But that wasn't all she recognised from the picture. He was lying on Bella's bed. That was the wrought-iron bedhead from Bella's bedroom.

When she had first seen the image, Alex had mistakenly thought that this was Maxine's lover, but now she knew that wasn't possible. So what was a half-naked Theo doing in Maxine's diary? She flicked through the pictures that had surrounded it: the black wings; parts of Bruegel's painting. The first two parts of the triptych . . . Suddenly it clicked: this must be the third part of *The Accusation*.

Maxine must have copied Bella's original. Of course she would have done that. That was exactly the type of thing she would do.

In that instant, three more ghosts appeared in the clearing.

Theo was still talking, describing the effort that had gone into building the swimming pool, and how only a rich fool would have decided to have an ocean water pool so far from the sea.

Once the first domino falls, others follow.

Bella's death had a knot at its core, the one fact that had been kept from the public. What killed Icarus wasn't plunging from the air but drowning in the ocean. Bella had drowned in salt water, which Alex had thought meant the ocean. Now, she realised that was wrong.

She leant against the tree, finding it hard to breathe. Like the men of Maxine's painting, she had been looking in the wrong direction all along. It was like a magician's trick revealed, so obvious once you know. She had been distracted by the wings, Kelly's misguided behaviour, Johnny's thuggery, Nic's money. Sasha had told her she had been sure it was a boy from school that Bella was sleeping with.

What if it was a boy who had been at school but had then left?

Instantly, she thought of everything Theo had found out about the police investigation. She had told him so many things. Maxine keeping paintings at Nic's place, for starters. She had even warned him about the police search, giving him time to go back to the Eyrie and plant the naked photo of Bella and probably the child porn as well as an extra bonus. Theo was trying to frame Nic for what he had done.

'Everything all right?' asked Theo. 'You've stopped calling them out.'

She quickly found the next one. 'Declan Walker, January 1910–August 1920.' Her voice sounded shaky to her ears and tears clogged her throat, because underneath his name were the words *Light in the Darkness*.

Theo must have brought Bella to see this tree.

'That's the one I wanted you to find,' Theo called. 'That's your great-grandfather.'

'I never knew,' was all she said aloud, though her mind was racing.

'He was in charge during the war, then the Rushalls took over. That's the reason your grandfather hated your mum dating my dad. He had dragged the Walkers up a notch, being the town's doctor, and didn't want to remind people of his wickie roots. People thought keepers were mad. Your mum said as much at dinner that time.'

His voice was getting closer to her. 'Boo!' Theo's face appeared around the tree from her. Alex jumped backwards, biting down a natural inclination to scream.

'Sorry,' he said, his face puzzled. 'Didn't mean to frighten you.'

'Think I'm just getting caught up in the atmosphere of the place.'

'I knew you'd like it. Tayla reckons it's spooky, like having graves in your backyard. Ready to go look at the lighthouse now?'

Alex looked at his smiling face and bright eyes. Could it be true? Had this man murdered three women? Already she was assessing him as a threat. He was much bigger than she was, stronger, and this was his home turf. In an instant he had changed from family to foe. She just had to stop him from realising that.

'Could I use your bathroom before we go?'

'Sure,' he said. 'If you go in the back door, it's the first on the right.'

'Thanks.' She turned away from him, fighting the urge to run, forcing herself to walk like everything was completely normal and she wasn't surrounded by trip-wires.

The weight of his eyes on her back made her feel like a target.

Chapter 25

Alex locked the bathroom door then sat on the edge of the bath, trying to tell herself that she'd got it wrong, that her imagination was running away with her like it had about Kiran, but looking again at the photo of Theo and then the drawing, she knew she was right. Other thoughts followed almost immediately. Theo had said he barely knew Bella and yet she must have been at his house to have seen the tree – a place he said hardly anyone knew about other than him. Maybe that could be explained, but right now she couldn't think how. A girl he barely knew and yet she had spent time making an artwork for his lighthouse fundraiser. Even today, he had been pressing Alex for information about the police investigation into the murders, wanting to know when Nic would be charged.

If she rang triple zero, they would only ring the local station and get Julie. Eden Point was too far away for any other police to arrive in time and she had no idea if the detectives were still in Merritt today. She couldn't put this on Prue or Tayla. Would they even believe her? It would take too long to explain. In the end she settled on Kiran. *Help. At lighthouse keeper's cottage. Think Theo killed Bella. Call police.* She tried to send the message but there was still no signal. What should she do now? Spend a couple of hours pretending everything was fine and send it from the lighthouse when she could? Her hands were trembling so hard she almost dropped her phone on the tiles. Alex didn't have the nerve to pull that off. After Johnny's death, her composure was the thinnest of bubbles; it would burst at the lightest touch.

You look petrified, she told her reflection in the bathroom mirror. *Pull yourself together.*

First, she needed to find something to protect herself with, and then she needed to make an excuse to leave. She would tell Theo she wasn't feeling well and had to go back to town.

She flushed the toilet and ran the tap. Then, opening the bathroom door, she moved further into the house. It was small. The kitchen, up the hall from the bathroom, opened into a living room, and beyond that was the front door.

She tried the kitchen first. Lino floor, table with a couple of chairs, wooden cupboards painted a mint green. There was a dirty cereal bowl in the sink with a half-drunk cup of coffee next to it and, on the counter, a knife block. Alex grabbed the biggest knife and put it into her bag. Was there anything else here she could use? She was just opening a drawer when she heard a voice behind her.

'What are you doing?'

Theo didn't sound so friendly now.

'Sorry,' she said, moving to the other side of the table. 'It's a bit embarrassing.'

'What is?'

'I got my period and didn't have tampons in my bag. I was just looking for some.' It was, a small part of Alex's brain thought, a pretty good lie. Men were never comfortable talking about periods.

'Tampons? In my house?'

'Maybe Tayla had some here? I already checked the bathroom. But just some kitchen paper will do.'

Theo was staring at her.

'Actually, I'm not feeling that well. I might head back into town, drop by the pharmacy.'

'You don't want to go to the lighthouse?'

The more Theo stared at her, the more panicked Alex felt. She could feel herself starting to gabble. 'We can do this another time. I'll walk back. It's not so far.' It was like her mouth had run out of control.

'It's okay, I can drive you,' Theo said, but everything had changed. There was an electricity to him now, a spark of violence. Alex recognised it because she had felt it before, with Johnny Ewart and also Kelly, so by the time Theo lunged at her, she was already running through the living room, knocking over chairs to block his path, to the front door. She wrenched it open and kept running, faster than she would have thought possible.

She ran across the road and into the forest on the other side. There was no path that she could see, so she plunged into the cover of the trees, scrambling up the hill. Taking a quick, desperate glance back, she could see that Theo had stopped.

He was standing in front of his house, watching her. Alex found a tree to hide behind and crouched down, legs burning, arms scratched, lungs on fire, and tried to work out what he was doing.

Birds called in staccato trills from the trees around her. Shut up, she thought.

Theo stood there motionless. It was like an elaborate game of bluff, as they waited to see which of them would make the next move. The world around them seemed to slow.

Clinging to the trunk to steady herself, heart galloping in her chest, Alex stayed frozen.

Then Theo turned and walked back towards the house.

The excited sounds of barking reached her ears.

He was going to hunt her down with his dog.

Instinctively, Alex knew she would never make it to town before he caught her. Her only hope was to get to the lighthouse and ring the police. Theo wouldn't guess that she would run that way, but then he had a dog who would. Getting a message out was important. He couldn't get away with it. She would call triple zero and say who the murderer was and how she'd discovered it. The record of the call could be used as evidence against him. Even if he killed her, there would still be a record. A wave of fierce determination forced her into action.

The red blouse she was wearing would have to go; it was too conspicuous against the green. Quickly, she pulled off her bag and jacket and ripped the shirt off, goosebumps appearing in response to the air. It was cold in the shade of the trees with the chill of the sea breeze. She stuffed the shirt into some nearby ferns, in the hope that it might fool Theo into thinking she was hiding there and buy her a few more precious minutes.

She checked her phone as she resumed her climb up the hill, but there was still no signal.

Alex tried to move where the trees were thickest, to keep herself hidden from the road. Almost straight away, she had to slow down, grabbing at the nearby branches for assistance as she clambered upwards. Within minutes she was panting with exertion. At times she was almost completely hemmed in by the trees, the branches and leaves packed together in a dense thicket, like they were trying to block her way. She squeezed through them, cobwebs and worse sticking to her. The strap of her bag snagged on a sapling, pulling her backwards and almost off her feet. A violent heave and she wrenched it free, slipping on the mud, losing traction and falling forward. Pulling herself to standing, she kept moving. Her shoes, meant for a police interview that now felt like so long ago, were only a liability in this environment. Taking them off, she threw each one in a different direction, hoping to confuse the dog.

Surrounded by bush, it was hard to work out how much further she had to go to reach the top. The trees seemed endless. If Theo had guessed her likely direction, he could easily run up the road ahead of her and be there waiting. She pushed that idea from her mind and kept moving.

Another dog bark. It echoed all around her, seeming louder now. It sounded like there wasn't just one dog but rather a pack chasing her.

Glancing behind, she could see nothing, but then she tripped over a tree root and fell again, badly this time. A sharp jolt of pain as her knees and chest smacked into the ground. Gritting her teeth to keep from making a noise, Alex forced herself to get up. Her breath was splintering now. She couldn't get enough air down into her lungs, her heart almost exploding in her chest.

A gunshot rang out.

A warning.

He was getting nearer.

Things always sounded closer in the bush, Alex told herself.

She pulled out her phone again. Still no signal. But the way wasn't as steep here. Surely she must be getting close to the summit and the lighthouse. The problem was the trees. Soon she would need to break cover.

Looking ahead, she caught glimpses of white amid the green, separate pieces of the lighthouse appearing as if it were a giant jigsaw puzzle that she needed to assemble. Then, almost before she realised it, Alex was at the edge of the bush at the top of the hill and there it was, complete and whole.

Blotches of corrosion marred its white surface. There was a door at the bottom with windows directly above it, all in a line like buttons on a snowman. A dirty bathtub rim of orange rust bloomed just below the balcony. For a moment she contemplated running into it and trying to barricade the door against Theo, making the lighthouse her fortress, but there was a thick padlock dangling from a chain that had been threaded through the door handles.

Desperately she tried her phone again. All she needed was a few seconds of reception to send her message, but there was a scrabbling behind her, and Luna bounded into the clearing. Instantly, the dog was in front of Alex, snarling, open-mouthed. Alex cowered, covering her face with her arms. She moved backwards until she was pinned against a tree.

Theo appeared, cradling his rifle in two hands, Alex's red silk shirt draped over his shoulder. 'Good girl, Luna,' he said.

The dog barked once more and then ran over to her owner, whimpering now for attention. Theo reached out a hand and patted Luna's head, all the time watching Alex.

'I've already called the police,' she said. 'They'll be here any moment.'

He started to laugh.

'I have called them,' she repeated, summoning her last ounce of bravado. 'Don't make this any worse for yourself.'

'You are such a bad liar,' Theo said. 'When I told you there was reception at the lighthouse, I meant it. But you can only get it up on the balcony.'

She swallowed hard.

'I'm curious,' he said. 'What gave it away?'

Theo wanted to make sure it didn't happen again. Alex had backed up the images from Maxine's diary onto her computer. There was still a chance that someone else might stumble across them as she had and recognise Theo in Bella's bed. Perhaps Farinacci; she didn't have much faith in Vandenburg.

'It was the pool,' Alex said. 'Bella drowned in salt water.'

Theo shook his head. 'Good. I'll drain it, change the water over. Nic won't even realise.'

'But why did you do it? Why did you kill Bella?' Alex asked. She was trying to buy time, but also she needed to know, to hear the words that would explain what had happened. Would he talk? She had seen it in clients again and again: given the opportunity, most people were almost eager to confess. It was if they'd just been waiting for someone to ask them.

'It wasn't my fault,' said Theo.

It never is, thought Alex.

'It started when Bella offered to paint a picture for the fundraiser. It was only supposed to be a one-night stand. I mean, she knew I was with Tayla. Then it turned into this casual thing. I'd drop around to her house after having dinner at Tayla's when Sasha was working nights, and sometimes she'd pretend she was visiting friends and we'd come here. Bella knew it was never going to be more than that.'

'You took those nude photos of her with her camera.'

'Yeah, and then next thing I knew she'd painted this picture of herself naked for me. That's when I knew I was going to have to end it.'

Alex thought of that beautiful, playful portrait of Bella, full of life and love. Maxine saw it as an artistic masterpiece, for Sasha it was an embodiment of her daughter, but Theo had only seen it as a threat.

'Next thing I know, I'm at the Eyrie working one day, when she turns up wearing those stupid fucking wings. She had fought with Sasha and wanted to move in with me. She said if I didn't let her stay she was going to tell Nic about us, say that I'd ruined her life.' He shook his head in angry disbelief. 'There weren't even supposed to be any unauthorised visitors to the Eyrie. If I lost my job, I would have lost everything. People like me don't get second chances.'

'So you drowned her?'

'Bella fought hard, I'll give her that. She was stronger than she looked.'

Alex almost wanted to tell him to stop talking, but she knew that she couldn't turn away now. Bella deserved for at least one person to know the whole truth. 'Then what did you do?' Her voice was no louder than a whisper.

'I knew she had walked through the Wyld on her way over and people might have seen her there already, so I decided to dump the body beside the river with the wings. Everyone knew her stepfather was a dealer. Let people think she had overdosed, or suicided or something. See, even I forgot about the salt water.' He shook his head. 'Stupid of me.'

Still, it had been enough in the heat of the moment to fool a father dumbstruck with grief, who had in turn ruined the entire investigation.

'I panicked when I heard there was a homicide detective in town, but then it all seemed to go away, and life just went on. Everything would have been fine if it wasn't for that bitch Maxine. She showed me this drawing she'd found of me lying on Bella's bed. Since when is a stupid drawing evidence of anything?'

Theo was working himself up, still angry at the unfairness of it. But Alex knew Maxine, more than anyone, would have understood how to read the picture. She didn't need words to glean the truth. For her it was evidence, though not the conventional kind of evidence the police would believe.

'At the start she was only puzzled by it. I tried to tell her that Bella had a crush on me, that it didn't mean anything. I thought she had believed me, but then Silver told me how weird Maxine was acting, how she got that feather tattoo for Bella, that there were these secret artworks and she was going to make a big announcement at the exhibition opening – and I knew what that would be. So I bided my time, followed her to the boatshed and then . . .' Theo made a violent clubbing gesture. He could have been describing a golf swing or how to use a baseball bat. 'It was easy. All I had to do after that was find that bloody drawing of me and destroy it, but I couldn't find it anywhere.'

So many things came to Alex in a rush. Things she should have noticed earlier. The fact Theo had taken flowers around to Maxine's gallery and had stayed during the police interview; how he had walked through Robyn's forced adoption exhibition and been so helpful. He had always been one step ahead of Alex, and she hadn't even noticed.

'Until I told you where to find it.'

Theo nodded. 'I hadn't been working up at the Eyrie much so I didn't realise Maxine had been painting up there. But when you told me, I knew there was only one place that could be. I went to the Nest first thing that morning and put a match to the drawing. I had thought to do the same with the other painting, but then I saw the one with Nic right in the middle of it and thought it was the perfect diversion. A dumb picture had nearly derailed everything for me, so what would it do for Nic, the guy who always thought he was the smartest person in the room?'

'What happened to Nic the visionary? The person who you learnt so much from? You told me he was the best thing that ever happened to Merritt.' Alex couldn't help herself.

'Nic, whose salmon farm wrecked my family's mussel business but then expected me to turn around and use that knowledge to make him more money? Yeah, I learnt a lot from him. Always look after yourself and get rid of anyone who gets in your way.'

Theo looked at her and his meaning was more than clear.

Alex was going to have to play every card she had.

'What about family?' she asked. 'You don't want to lose the only family you've got. Together, we can work this out, you know. I can help you legally, get you a good defence attorney.'

'Alex, I could never hurt anyone who is family.' He took a step back, moved the shotgun to one side and held out a hand to help her up. His defences were lowering.

Alex sprang forward, intending to dart around him and disappear back into the bush, but the dog growled and leapt at her, causing her to hesitate. There was a crunch to the side of her head, the sound so loud it drowned out the world, as the rifle butt met her skull, knocking her to the ground. Pain followed in a rush. Alex was overwhelmed by the red hotness of it. She lay sprawled on the ground, the iron taste of blood thick on her tongue, the blow still vibrating in her head.

Theo grabbed a fistful of her hair and the strap of her bag and pulled her to her feet. Alex heard a terrible animal whimpering noise and realised that it was coming from her own mouth.

The dog howled in protest.

'We might be genetically related,' he snarled, 'but you're not family,' and he kicked out viciously. The force of it knocked all the breath out of her. Something cracked deep inside. 'The number of drunken stories I had to endure about Denny Walker over the years. How she left no note. No nothing. My father never got over her leaving, but he was too weak to do anything about it. Whatever I decide to do with you, I hope your mother never gets over it.'

He dragged her towards the lighthouse door. 'You can stay here while I plan my next move. I've got to head back to town before too long to pick up Tayla.'

Alex lay on the ground as he unlocked the padlock on the door. Her phone, she realised. He had forgotten about it. She began to move the hand that was still holding it towards her body to shove it down her pants, but Theo caught the movement, turned, and put a heavy boot on her wrist. He reached down and wrenched the phone out of her hand and Alex realised she was going to die.

'Move again and I'll shoot you.'

But Alex couldn't even contemplate moving, not now. She lay in the dirt and watched as Theo removed the padlock, letting the chain slither to the ground. He pulled back the thick iron bolt on the lighthouse door. It made an ugly scraping sound, like nails down a blackboard, but the door opened easily enough when he pushed it, exposing a dank stone floor with puddles of water.

She made one last futile attempt to crawl away, but Theo grabbed her around the middle, her body tangled up with the strap of her bag. He pulled her up.

'The balcony's railing is almost rusted through, so don't think about stepping out onto it to draw attention to yourself.'

When we fall, was all Alex could think as Theo threw her inside and her world turned dark. Unconsciousness beckoned as the door slammed shut, the bolt screeched back into place and the padlock clicked.

Chapter 26

Alex could smell blood, sweat, dampness and piss as she lay crumpled on the wet floor. It was hard to know if it was her own. She squeezed her eyes shut and then opened them again. There was almost no difference. The darkness was so complete, it had the texture of night and the taste of despair.

All remnants of the rage and anger that had sustained her dissolved now, and all she was left with was a helpless terror so strong it suffocated all other emotions. Curled up on the floor, she began to sob, making no effort to control her tears. It was only when her eyes began to adjust to the darkness that she noticed something which made her pause. There was a faint rim of light outlining an internal door.

Alex came to a hiccuping stop. She wasn't in the tower of the lighthouse, but an entrance hallway masquerading as a tomb. There must be a second door behind her. An airlock, perhaps.

Putting her hand out, she found a wall and used it to pull herself slowly, very slowly, to her knees, feeling the hot raw pain of open wounds. Finally, she was standing, almost vomiting with the effort. After a few breaths to steady herself, she stepped forward, stumbling over her bag. She felt a burst of sudden energy as she remembered the knife she'd stashed inside it, and with desperate hands she grabbed for it. The knife's tip pricked her thumb, which started to bleed. Wincing, she rubbed the open cut against the roughness of the old bricks, smearing the wall to mark the place. If the police ever got this far, she wanted them to know that she had been here, that this was where it had happened. Fuck Theo.

Then, hands out in front of her, walking almost blindly, she moved towards the internal door. Her hands felt wood, damp, soft to touch, as though she could push a hole right through it. She found a handle, round, cold, and turned it. Swinging back on its hinges, it revealed a gloomy but dusk-lit space, empty except for some metal shelving and a staircase spiralling upwards.

Alex shivered so hard she thought she might never stop. This whole place was a trap. There was only one way in or out, but at least there was a promise of light and fresh air above. Holding on to the banister with one hand, she gave it a shake. Reassuringly, it didn't move, and she began to climb. The sound of her footsteps reverberated and coiled around her.

Pausing at the first window, a small square of glass in a thick frame, she was breathing hard. The pain came in dizzying waves and she had to lean against the wall for support. So much of her hurt. Alex tried to look out, but a combination of grime and salt made it almost impossible to distinguish anything, so she kept moving in the joyless grey gloom.

At the next landing, the stone steps changed to a black metal grid, and her legs began to tremble. She sat down to rest for a while and tried to listen, but all she could hear was her thumping heart.

She resumed her climb, half crawling now, though the pressure on her cut and bloody hands made her gasp, but the light was stronger and that gave her comfort. The building was changing from a prison into a refuge. Finally, after what felt like hours, she came to the watch room. A beautiful, latticed late afternoon light, gold, red-tinged, streamed down from the lantern room's massive glass window, patterning the white walls. She lay on the floor, exhausted, and gazed up at it. It was like being inside a kaleidoscope. Brass fittings studded the circular wall, round with flower petal cut-outs. Some sort of air vents, she guessed. A ladder was built into the wall leading up to the small lantern room. Looking up through the metal grid of the lantern room's floor, she could see segments of the giant glass globe.

A door cut into the wall led to the balcony. Pulling herself to standing, she turned the handle, pushed it open, and let the cold wind come rushing in. Alex stepped over the doorframe lip to the outside. The wind was gusting hard, making mournful laments inside the tower. There was the metal railing, thick with rust, so Alex kept hold of the frame with one hand and tried to keep her back to the wall. Far-off birds soared across the sky, their wings sharp blades. They seemed miraculous, gliding in air. Greek myths brought to life.

What wouldn't she give for a pair of Icarus's wings now?

But then she imagined Icarus plunging into the sea. Bella by the river. Maxine's leg. Death was never far away.

The sun cast a golden haze across the water. The ground was a vertigo-inducing distance below. She shuffled a little to her right to try to get a better view of the road leading down the hill towards the keeper's cottage. She could just make out its darkly stained corrugated-iron roof among the trees. There was no sign of Theo.

Hugging the wall, she started to move back the other way, towards the ocean. Maybe there would be a boat she could wave to? She saw the edge of the cliffs, the tops of trees and then, looking down, the sea, wrinkled with waves like a worried forehead.

Shapes moved among the rocks, and her heart began to beat faster until she realised they were only seals.

She traced the shape of the coastline to the next bay and then Merritt, a town full of people but no one close enough.

There was a roar.

At first she thought it was the sea, but then she heard an engine labouring, caught between gears.

Was it Theo leaving to pick up Tayla? She shrank back against the wall, the instinct to hide from him almost overwhelming. But then she caught sight of the car driving down the hill. It was old, dusty and battered. The same car she had seen Dirk Gardiner walking towards down at the marina. She stepped away from the wall, not caring now if she did fall, waving her arms, screaming – not words, but something more primitive. If only Dirk heard her, this nightmare could be over. She would be freed. She screamed so hard that she could taste blood in her mouth. But it was already too late. The car was driving away, exhaust belching black smoke. It moved down the hill and was soon out of sight. The noise of the engine faded and all that was left was the sound of the ocean and the seagulls crying to each other on the wind. She cried too, but they paid her no heed.

Collapsing to the floor, Alex gave up. It was hopeless. She was going to die. Numb, she watched as the sun travelled across the sky and started to sink. Clouds chased behind it. There would be no moon tonight. Theo must be waiting until it was dark before he came back. Sasha's voice came into her head. *How many more dead women is the truth worth?* Alex had been so desperate to find out what had happened that she had never once considered the possibility that she would be one of those women.

She thought of Bella, Maxine and Robyn. Their deaths had been sudden and violent. Each of them must have been taken by surprise, even Maxine. Alex's death wasn't going to be like that. She knew exactly what she was facing. Theo had time to make sure he covered up her death properly – but, then, time cut both ways. Unlike the other three women, she had time as well. Even now there was still a choice. She could fall apart, had almost already done so, or she could pull herself together and keep fighting. She heaved herself up to sit with her back against the wall of the lighthouse. She thought of her great-grandfather working here.

Light in the Darkness.

The light was not going to save her now. She was going to have to embrace the dark.

It was a long time after sunset when she heard the sound of the door at the bottom of the lighthouse open. From the top of the lighthouse it was more of a wail. The metal door to the balcony clanged loudly in reply and the wind hustled into the lantern room. Alex could hear nothing over the sound of it until there was a measured tread of footsteps on the stairs coming closer.

Theo was not rushing. He probably thought that there was no need. Last time he'd seen her, she was barely able to move.

Alex tried to keep her breathing silent and waited.

Next to her was a dome of rippling glass made up of countless prisms, each enormous panel a series of concentric circles frozen in place and designed to shoot out shafts of light in every direction. It was like standing inside a solid chandelier with closed eyes, hoping that no one turned it on. She was lucky it hadn't been fixed yet. By hiding in the lantern room, at the very top of the lighthouse, Alex was trying to be invisible in a chamber whose sole purpose was to be seen for miles.

She saw the torch beam come bobbing into the watch room first, the dark shadow of Theo behind it, and closed her eyes. She needed them to stay adjusted to the dark.

When she opened them again, he stood directly below her. Only a metal grate separated these levels. Alex held her breath and tried to turn herself into smoke. If he shone the torch upwards, she was done for.

Theo stood in the room and looked about him. She could reach a finger through the grate and almost touch the hair on his head. How did he intend to kill her? Would he try to make it look like an accident?

The wind caught the door to the balcony and smacked it impatiently against the frame, the sound like the gong of a bell. Alex had been listening to that sound for what felt like hours. She had deliberately left it unlatched, hoping that Theo would be distracted by it. She watched from above as his head jerked around at the noise and then he walked over to it.

Theo stuck his head out of the door and then took a step out onto the balcony. Alex edged towards the ladder. She needed to be down that ladder and into the watch room by the time he got outside or else he might see her through the window.

Theo swore, his voice coming through the open door. He called her name and took another step away from the door. Standing on the ladder, she could just make out the dark shape of him through the glass, and she ducked out of view.

Alex clambered down the last couple of rungs, landed awkwardly and felt burning pain. No time for that now. Her sole focus was pulling that door shut. She could see the sky through the door. The clouds shifted and all at once stars dotted the darkness. Cold white pinpoints, pure. She had been wrong. There was never complete darkness; there would always be some light. Peering through the door to the balcony, she saw that Theo was no longer there. He was making his way quietly around to the other side of the lighthouse, looking for her.

She grabbed the doorhandle and pulled but the door didn't move. He must have attached it to the hook outside. Stepping out, feet and hands clumsy with cold and fear, wind pushing her hair into her eyes, she fumbled for the latch in the dark and then unhooked it.

A shout of anger.

Theo came from the other direction and charged at her.

Alex dived behind the door, using it as a shield. Back in the watch room, she pulled hard. Theo was gripping the door edge, trying to peel it towards him. He was so much stronger, she was already damaged and weak and felt it slipping from her grasp, but desperation gave her strength.

She saw animal eyes in the gloom. Theo was unrecognisable, no longer human but pure fury.

Screaming, she braced her foot against the rim of the doorframe and pulled, but he pushed an arm into the crack, wedging it between the wall and the door so she couldn't shut it completely. His hand was a claw, trying to grab at her.

Leaning back, trying to keep out of reach, Alex readied herself for the next move.

Another desperate lunge of his hand and he grabbed a fistful of her hair. With a triumphant yell, he yanked hard. Reaching behind her, Alex grabbed the knife from her waistband and slashed at his hand, aiming for the fingers. She wanted him alive.

Howling in anger and pain, he jerked back. Alex felt hot blood splatter across her face.

A final furious wrench and the door clanged shut. Dropping the knife on the ground, she locked it and started down the stairs to a soundtrack of furious banging and screams.

Panting, she stumbled out of the lighthouse.

To her amazement, a pair of headlights was switched on, catching her in their beam.

Sobbing, she ran towards them. Alex ran to the passenger side, pulled open the door and collapsed onto the seat. Dirk Gardiner was behind the wheel of his car. His eyes widened as he took in the state of her.

Looking up, she could see a dark figure standing on the balcony, hunched over. She imagined him cradling his hand, but he was too far away to be sure.

'Can he get out?' Gardiner asked.

She shook her head. 'I locked the door,' she croaked.

'He had Maxine's kayak,' Gardiner told her, as he passed her a blanket from the back seat. 'Hid in my cabin when I saw his truck pull up at the quay. Just about to unload a full boat of salmon and didn't want awkward questions. Saw him carrying it. Didn't think much of it at the time. Could have been doing that girl a favour for all I knew. Could have been borrowing it. None of my business.' He leant over and opened the glove box, pulling out a hipflask. 'Afterwards, thought he might have found it at sea, raised the alarm she was missing. Then you told me that her kayak was still gone and I figured out that he was putting it on his boat, not taking it off. He needed to get rid of it. Still, I couldn't prove anything, and who would believe me over him?'

Alex was too tired to know if that was right or not.

He shoved the flask into her hand. 'Have a nip of that.'

She did as she was told. It made her cough but warmed her up as well.

'Saw you getting into the car with him and I thought I didn't want to be fishing more dead women out of the ocean. Came up here earlier, made up some bullshit excuse about how I saw someone mucking around on Quirke's boat. Told me he had quit and acted like he was up here all alone. I pretended to head off, but I drove back along the fire trail, turned off my headlights and waited in the bush outside his house. Thought you might be in there. When I saw him coming up to the lighthouse, I knew he was up to something.'

Prue had told Alex that finding Maxine's body made her involved. It seemed that didn't apply just to Alex but also to

Dirk Gardiner. Somehow him being here now was right. Another person who couldn't look the other way.

'We need to get the police,' she said.

There were still questions that remained unanswered, but she couldn't think of them now.

As Gardiner swung the car around, the headlights washing over the lighthouse, Alex caught a flicker of movement out of the corner of her eye. A body plummeting, and then the sound, wet, heavy, as it met the ground.

Whether it was an accident – Theo grabbing hold of a piece of railing that had rusted through – or deliberate, she would never know.

Chapter 27

Alex caught sight of her own reflection. There was a graze that ran from forehead to chin, with puffy bruising under her left eye that felt like overripe fruit when she touched it. Her body ached. Two ribs had been cracked. Physically she would heal, but right now she felt sick. The last time she had sat at this table, Theo had been sitting opposite.

She had made a pact with herself that she would tell the story once to the police and then never speak about it again to anyone ever, and yet here she was two days later.

Tayla sat across the table from her. Prue was still fussing around in the kitchen, asking people how they took their tea, information she knew already, but it was a way to fill the silence. Denny didn't sit at the table but instead chose an armchair by the window, as if she really wasn't involved at all. Prue had insisted that she should be present, that she had played her own part in this mess, and Alex had not had the energy to argue.

It was a colourless Tayla who looked across at Alex, as if she had been drained of life. No fluorescent nails today or sarcastic asides. Instead, she sat there mute, a statue, waiting for this to be over.

Alex knew her words would be inadequate and for the first time she appreciated why Maxine had painted a picture instead. Sometimes the truth was too awful to be spoken aloud. Art was a way to make the ugly beautiful and therefore bearable.

'Now then,' said Prue, bringing over the tray. 'There you go, love.' She placed a cup in front of Tayla, who didn't acknowledge it. 'And you, Alex.'

Alex tried to smile, but her face hurt so much it turned into a grimace.

'Now you're sure you don't want anything to eat?'

A shake of the head, which Alex immediately regretted. A dull ache had set up a temporary home in the back of her skull and it objected to any sudden movement.

'Let's get started,' Prue said, sitting down.

And so Alex began, stumbling at first, with long pauses as she tried to collect her thoughts. As the recollection gathered speed, she could feel herself splitting in two, with one part of her watching the other part talk as if it was another person entirely. It was this second Alex who noticed how Tayla reacted when Alex described how she'd realised that Theo had shown Bella the special tree. The girl physically shuddered as though the implication of the words rippled right across her skin. She screwed her eyes shut and Alex almost expected her to put her hands to her ears to block out what was to come. Alex considered stopping, but in the next moment Tayla's eyes were open, sharp little pebbles, so she kept going.

On it went. The tattoo. The bathroom. The dog. The lighthouse. For a moment she imagined she was back up there sitting on the balcony, watching the sunset.

Waiting in the darkness. The banging door. The knife. And then. And then.

Prue appeared weighed down, drooping shoulders, back curved. She looked as if she had barely slept in the last few days. She kept her hands locked around her mug as if trying to keep warm, though the day wasn't cold. Periodically, fingers would venture out to pat Tayla's shoulder only to creep back when Tayla ignored them.

Only Denny seemed unaffected. Perhaps she wasn't even listening as she gazed out of the window at the garden. The hammock was still out there, empty, and Alex wondered if her mother could still remember the day – it felt like so long ago – when she had found a leg on the beach.

Eventually, Alex finished her recount. There was silence for a moment, then: 'Show me the photo,' said Tayla.

'What photo?' Prue asked, momentarily confused, but Alex understood. Tayla wanted to look at the photo Alex had taken of Theo resting, stretched out on the ground. She wanted to see the moment before everyone's world fell apart.

'Sorry,' Alex said. 'I can't. The police still have my phone. It's evidence.'

Tayla made a noise of disgust – or was it disbelief? It was hard to tell.

Prue shook her head in response.

'Do you remember,' Tayla said, addressing Alex, 'how we sat here that day and I said I wish I knew what had happened to Bella so I could claim the million dollars?'

Alex nodded. The pain in her head sloshed around in response.

'Now I'd pay a billion dollars to have never heard any of this.' Her composure was in tatters now as she slammed her palms down on the table and scraped her chair back as if she couldn't bear to look at Alex anymore.

'I'm sorry,' Alex said again. She rested a finger on the bruise beneath her eye and pressed it. She wanted to feel pain.

Tayla stood up and walked from the room.

'No,' said Prue, her voice sharp. 'Don't be sorry. She had to hear it. It is always better to know the truth. Do you hear me? It is always better.'

And it seemed to Alex that Prue was speaking to Denny as much as anyone else.

A fortnight later, Alex sat on a park bench just near where Theo had picked her up, telling her he had something to show her. It was a challenge she set herself most mornings. Some days it felt like this spot was nothing special, on others she only had to catch sight of it and mentally she would shatter into pieces. The external cuts were healing, the bruising had disappeared; it was the damage inside that would take longer to recover from. Theo was a murderer. She could be certain of that. Was he also her half-brother? Alex wasn't sure she ever wanted that question answered.

Today she was early enough that Merritt hadn't quite woken up yet. Only utes and the occasional truck ran along the main street, mostly tradies heading out to work with surfboards in the back, hopeful of an early knock-off. Alex turned her gaze to the water to see if she could see Dirk Gardiner's trawler, but he was still out fishing. Glancing over to the pier, she spied a lone fisherman casting a line out, a bright blue esky beside him. He was hunched against the cold, head down, concentrating.

Alex recognised him twice over.

It was Kingsley Kelly, but it was also the fisherman in Maxine's painting. He wore the same light grey overcoat and bright red beanie. The fisherman: the last of the three figures condemned by Maxine for not saving Bella. Each of the men who'd refused to witness what was going on had played a part in her death. She should have guessed.

Alex had been told by the investigating officer that under no circumstances was she to talk to Kelly or accept any contact from him or any intermediary acting on his behalf, but she had already provided her statement in relation to Johnny's shooting and had no intention of deviating from it.

She still couldn't work out who'd fired first, but she didn't think it was Kelly. You can be an average policeman and a terrible father, but that doesn't make you a murderer. She wasn't sure if Sasha was lying deliberately to get her revenge on Kelly or if she had just convinced herself that it had really happened as she described. If Kelly had wanted to kill Johnny, he could have done it years ago. He might have stuffed up a murder investigation, but he had done it with the best of misguided intentions. Alex could understand how that happened because she had almost done the same thing herself, inadvertently alerting Theo to where Maxine kept her paintings, warning him that the police would raid the Eyrie.

Kelly landed a small fish, dropping it next to an earlier catch. The little fish, slate-grey back, snow-white belly, thrashed about. Moving his rod behind him, Kelly got out a pair of long-nose pliers and, wrapping one large hand around the fish, took the hook out like a dentist extracting a tooth. The fish's mouth kept opening, gills moving like a beating heart. Kelly appeared so absorbed in his task that Alex presumed he wasn't aware of her watching until he said without looking up, 'You're running late this morning.'

'What?'

'Been waiting for you for over an hour. Luckily, dawn's the best time for pier fishing. No one around to tangle up your line.'

'You were in Maxine's painting,' she said. '*The Accusation.* Did you know that?'

A nod. 'She sketched me fishing years ago, back when we were on speaking terms.'

Another fisherman came past, younger, in a big khaki over-coat, black skinny jeans, a scarf wrapped around the lower half of his face. He nodded at Kelly, grunted a hello, and then took up his position a little further away.

'What did you want?' asked Alex.

Kelly was looking older now and more vulnerable out of his uniform, like a snail without a shell. He considered the fish in his hand for a moment, then threw it back into the sea.

The difference between life and death.

'Think this is over?' he asked.

'I guess so.'

'I'm not so sure.'

'What?' Alex could feel a blind kind of fury begin to bubble up inside her.

'Theo killed Bella and Maxine all right, but what about Robyn?'

Alex stared at him.

'Why did Theo need to kill Robyn?' asked Kelly.

'I presume because she had worked out what happened with Bella and Maxine, like I did. She certainly wanted to.'

'I knew Robyn most of my life. Not a week went by that she didn't call me complaining about one thing or another. Maxine would never have come to me but Robyn was entirely different. If she had evidence of something, I'd have known. So, I got her phone records pulled.'

The old dog's teeth might have worn down, but Kelly still had plenty of bite.

'Aren't you technically on leave?'

Kelly's days as a policeman were over. If by some miracle he got through the investigation into the shooting of Johnny Ewart, then there was still the issue of the wings. Kelly would never be back in uniform again. Instead, he would be indistinguishable from his mates in the front bar of the Sail. Probably drink his way to an early grave. She knew of other coppers and lawyers who'd done it before. You take away the job and there was almost nothing left.

'Are you interested or not?'

'Go on.'

'Robyn had been pretty busy on the phone the day before she was murdered. She tried phoning the landline at your house several times.'

'Vandenburg told me. It's not that surprising. It was the day of Mum's accident. I was barely at home.'

'But why phone the landline? She had your mobile number. It was in her phone.'

'So? Who do you think she was trying to call then?'

'She did talk to Denny, I understand. Called her at Prue's house and spoke to her there.'

That was true. Prue had told her about that.

'Leave that for the moment and let's focus on another phone call. One she made straight afterwards.'

'Who was that to?'

'The Australian Medical Board. She talked to someone about how to make a complaint against a doctor.'

Alex felt exhausted. First Johnny, then Theo and it still wasn't finished. Would there ever be an end to this?

Kelly looked along the pier, back towards the road. A car had pulled up and a man got out.

'He got here quickly. I called him when I saw you run up. He's the key to this.'

Alex watched as the man walked slowly towards them. He pulled up his jacket collar and shoved his hands in his pockets to keep out the cold wind.

'Hello, Alex,' Kiran said.

Chapter 28

Alex parked in the driveway of her grandparents' house, gripping the steering wheel so tightly her knuckles whitened. Kiran had offered to come with her, but he had a waiting room full of patients and, besides, she wanted the time alone to think.

Prue's car wasn't parked on the street. She had been dividing her time between the Walker house and her own of late. Tayla wasn't eating enough was all she had told Alex.

Alex walked up the front steps, stopping for a moment to look in the window. Denny was sitting on the couch in the living room. Why had Denny moved back here? Was it some sort of victory over her parents? To show that in the end she had prevailed, after leaving so many years before? Or was her childhood home a refuge from an increasingly bewildering world? All Alex knew was that this place was poison.

She unlocked the front door and stood in the hallway. Denny was watching daytime television, some sort of game show. It was all she seemed to do these days, other than sleep. She glanced up as Alex entered the room.

'I saw what's-her-name. You know. Wears too much make-up.'

Amazingly, Alex did. It was always surprising which bits of information seemed to sink into her mother's mind, only to resurface unexpectedly.

'Tom's fiancée, Shantelle.'

'I pity her,' said Denny.

Alex lowered herself gingerly into the armchair. Catching sight of the old photos up on the mantelpiece, she felt choked by her grandfather's presence. She wanted to sweep them off in one great clatter onto the floor, but she couldn't do that – not yet, anyway.

Denny protested when Alex picked up the remote and switched off the television. The game show host's Cheshire cat smile seemed to linger as the screen went dark.

'I was watching that!' Denny fussed with her dressing-gown, pulling the sash tighter as Alex began to talk. As she began to comprehend what was going on, Denny stopped moving. A single tear rolled down her face as Alex explained what she had been told that morning and what had to happen next.

When she had finished speaking, Alex leant back in her chair, pulled a crumpled tissue from her pocket and handed it to her mother. Denny was so frail, but there was one question that had to be asked. For a moment, Alex almost hoped that Denny would give one of her blank stares and not answer, but instead her mother gave her a small, hard nod.

'Then we need to do this,' she said to Denny. 'We owe it to Robyn and we owe it to those women.'

Denny, who had shown more courage than Alex had realised, closed her eyes.

'I'm going to ring him now,' Alex said, and her mother did not stop her. Instead, Denny sat there hunched, a tiny bird in a storm, as Alex picked up the phone and told one lie after another.

The doorbell rang. Alby Sadler stood on the doorstep, dressed formally in a jacket and tie, carrying an old, battered doctor's bag in one hand.

'Alex,' he said, 'I came as quickly as I could.'

'Thanks, I appreciate it.'

'Where is she?'

'In the living room on the couch. Please do come in.'

Alby moved forward, taking what was no doubt a path familiar from those long-ago Sundays when he would come for lunch. He hesitated on the threshold of the room, and Alex almost walked into the back of him. Did memories hold him there? Or did he have a sense of what was coming?

Greeting Denny, he shuffled forward, his footsteps making no sound on the threadbare floral carpet. Alex looked over his shoulder, catching the expression on Denny's face. With her green eyes open wide, it was easy to imagine her mother as a frightened nineteen-year-old who had found herself in trouble.

'Take the armchair,' said Alex. It was her grandfather's chair. Alby would know that.

He nodded and sat down, placing his doctor's bag beside him. Looking at these two people, a stranger might guess they were the same age. If anything, Denny seemed older. It wasn't hard to believe that she would need a home visit, that she was too sickly to go to the surgery.

'And how are you today, Denny?' Alby asked, his glasses perched on his nose. 'Alex tells me that you are still feeling out of sorts.'

He was the perfect doctor, with his kindly manner and open face, all his attention fixed on the patient. There was such authority in his voice. Here was a trusted person who was practised in delivering good news and bad. A person who had changed people's lives. A person who would make sure your baby was taken care of.

'That bag belonged to my father,' said Denny.

Alby smiled. 'You recognised it after all these years. Looking its age, I'm afraid, much like myself. I've had it reconditioned so many times. Jack gave it to me when he retired. I intend to keep using it when I start working again at our old clinic.'

'Plenty of people in the town still remember my grandfather,' Alex said. 'Former patients of his.'

Alby moved forward in his seat. 'Yes, I expect they do. Though they must have been quite young when Jack treated them.'

'I'm thinking of young women in particular. Pregnant women.'

Alby gave her a sideways glance, almost a glare, but it was quickly smoothed over. 'I'm glad to see you looking so well, Alex. I heard about the terrible ordeal you went through. I'm glad that you can put it all behind you. Now, Denny, what seems to be the matter?'

'Actually, it's not quite over,' interrupted Alex. 'There are still some loose ends in relation to Robyn Edgeley's death.'

Alby turned towards her. 'Oh really?'

'Telephone records show that Robyn phoned my mother before she was murdered.'

Alby said nothing, but he took his glasses off and began to polish them with his tie. Some people looked blind without their glasses, unable to see the world in focus, but Alby seemed more alert, as if he took them off to see them both more clearly.

'And Denny remembers this conversation?' asked Alby. 'My apologies' – he nodded at Denny – 'but I did notice that you can get a little befuddled. Quite common for dementia patients, of course. You'll find I mentioned that to Kiran. As her treating physician I thought he should know. Also, I made sure it was documented in her file.'

'Robyn was very concerned about past events in this town. She wanted to do something about them but she needed more evidence. That's what she was talking to Denny about.'

Alby blinked and shook his head. One hand tugged at his earlobe. 'As interesting as all this is, I'm afraid I will have to cut this consultation short, especially as there doesn't seem to be a patient here who needs treating.' He made a great show of looking at his wristwatch, the links scuffed and scratched with age. Had that belonged to her grandfather as well?

'It won't take long,' said Alex. 'I just want to know about the forced adoptions that you and my grandfather organised.'

It was Kiran who had explained it to her. Robyn's husband had found a draft letter on their computer and had taken it to the surgery to show it to him. Kiran had contacted Kelly. Robyn had heard fragments of stories from different women who had come into the exhibition. The same names had been repeated over and over again. One woman's story would be easy to dismiss with a hot cup of tea, but after the fourth one, Robyn had wanted to do something about it. She wasn't sure there would be enough evidence for any criminal case, but surely someone could put in a complaint to the medical board and have Alby struck off. Kelly didn't know for sure how Alby had discovered Robyn's plans, but he had a theory.

'Illegal adoption?' Alby said now, more in sorrow than in anger. 'I can assure you there was nothing like that. Our practice always prided itself in assisting young women and their infants, and the women were very grateful for the help.'

'I said forced, not illegal – though I suspect there was both.'

'Denny,' Alby said, turning to the older woman, 'how can you just sit here and listen to your daughter's accusations? You know it isn't true. You know how I helped you.'

Hard knots lay under the surface of his words.

But Denny said nothing.

'I'm asking the questions,' said Alex.

'It was so long ago.' Alby's voice was much colder now. 'A different time. In the city there would have been options for termination. There was nothing available to the girls of Merritt that wasn't dangerous and illegal. They kept their condition hidden from their families, and begged us for help.' He slammed his hand down on his knee to emphasise the point. 'Suitable homes were found for those children with good Christian people. Perhaps at times it was done informally, I grant you, not every form filled in, but it was by far the best outcome for all those concerned, especially the children. I have nothing to reprove myself for.'

Here was a different side to Alby.

'It must have been quite a shock when Robyn confronted you about it all these years later. Did she tell you that she was planning to go to the medical board and demand they revoke your licence?'

'I doubt there isn't a person in this town who hasn't been at the end of one of Robyn Edgeley's pointless vendettas. No one would take anything she said seriously.'

'The council did,' said Alex. 'That's how she succeeded in delaying the Eden Point development.'

'And what has that got to do with it?'

'You would lose a lot of money if that project folded. Isn't that why you needed your old job back?'

'This is preposterous . . .'

'So, when you heard that Robyn was interfering yet again, planning on making a complaint against you, wanting to take away your medical licence, you just couldn't risk it.'

'I had no idea what nonsense Robyn was cooking up, and if I had no idea of it, then none of your absurd story makes sense.'

'I told you,' said Denny. 'I told you that Robyn had rung asking if I knew about those women's babies being taken. I warned you.'

Alex thought of all the Sunday lunches that Denny must have had to sit through. Alby and her grandfather talking about their work. Had they talked openly about those women and their babies? Or was it just something that was always understood in this house, that single women could never be good mothers?

The sunlight streamed in from the window, catching the top of Denny's hair, turning it white-gold. Her hands were clenched. Alex could imagine Denny's nails making little crescent moon indentations in her palms. She hadn't been sure if her mother would have the strength to tell the truth, but she should never have doubted her. Both the old people in this room had been affected by Jack Walker's rigid puritanical view of the world, but only one of them had shown the strength of character to fight it.

Alby did not try to deny any of this, as Alex thought he might. Perhaps he would later on, but somehow, he couldn't lie directly to Denny. Not today.

'They were fanciful allegations,' he blustered. 'Supposed to have taken place decades ago. I told Robyn to her face that the authorities weren't going to waste their time on old gossip with no proof.'

'When did you tell her that?' Alex spoke calmly, but her mind was racing.

Alby hesitated, sensing that he had made a mistake. 'I don't quite remember.'

'Where did you tell her then? You must know that at least.'

Alby shook his head. He was getting agitated now.

'There can't have been many opportunities. You only recently returned from overseas. Let me help you. It was at the museum, wasn't it?'

He said nothing.

'Robyn was instrumental in delaying the Eden Point project you had invested in and now she was trying to wreck the only thing that mattered to you: your ability to practise medicine. You must have been very angry. Perhaps you only intended to reason with her, but when she refused to budge, you lost control and lashed out with what was nearby? I can see how that could happen.'

'This is all speculation!'

'Or perhaps it was premeditated, because immediately afterwards you went to the library to ensure that when the body was discovered, you could insist on examining her so that there would be an explanation if your DNA or fingerprints were found.'

Alby gave an involuntary gulp, like he was struggling to breathe. Alex had seen this reaction in court before. It was when someone was forced to confront publicly what they had done. The shock of a secret being exposed.

For the tape, could the accused please answer the question? Alex thought. How do you plead, guilty or not guilty?

Alby gave a dry cough, visibly attempting to pull himself together. 'According to the front page of my newspaper, poor Robyn was murdered by a young psychopath called Theo Rushall, who had killed two other women previously and very nearly killed you. In my professional opinion, that experience has affected you more than you think, Alex. I would encourage you to seek help for these disturbing fantasies.'

'I will give your professional opinion all the respect it deserves,' Alex said.

His face was changing now, anger distorting it. The kindly old man facade had been abandoned. Standing up, he looked at Denny. 'Are you going to say nothing? After all I did for you. You should have been the one here taking care of your parents. *I* was the one who kept the practice ticking over when Jack got too old. *I* was the one who helped care for your mother when she was ill. And yet you are the one sitting in this house today.' Swept up in a flood of rage, he seemed almost helpless to stop himself talking. He turned back to Alex, gesturing with his hands. 'You think you're so smart with all your questions, just like Robyn. Your mother came to see me, asked for my assistance. She was pregnant and I helped her. Got her a job away from Merritt, encouraged her to study, even gave her some money. Instead of attacking me, you should be on your knees thanking me. I shouldn't have lifted a finger.'

Alex quickly positioned herself in front of her mother to try to protect her from this attack. 'You want to change the one good thing you did,' she said to Alby, 'rather than all the things you did wrong.'

Alby leant down and opened his bag, fumbling through the contents. There was the gleam of something silver in his hand – a scalpel. Alex screamed.

Vandenburg and Nathan burst into the room and overpowered him. She heard the clang of something falling onto the coffee table and then to the floor.

The pair had been sitting in Alex's bedroom with recording equipment, listening to the exchange. Nathan, the officer in charge of Merritt Police Station since Kelly had been suspended, began to speak: 'Alby Sadler, I am arresting you . . .'

Alex wasn't listening. Instead, instinctively, she flung her arms around her mother, thankful it was over.

Denny didn't react.

Alby stood there, staring at the two of them. 'If it wasn't for me,' he said, 'you would have been adopted out as well. Your own grandfather would have seen to that. He could see what you were from the moment he lay eyes on you. Your mother's a slut and you're a bastard.'

Alex recoiled at the ugliness of this, felt the echoes of the past. She had heard that word before in this house, but from another mouth.

'Jack was right all along,' Alby sneered. 'No family stability, little money, no moral upbringing. What sort of life could you hope to have?'

Alex looked him in the eye. Her mother was not an easy woman to have as a parent but she had tried her best, which was more than could be said for Denny's own parents. 'A good life,' she told him.

Chapter 29

Denny refused to get out of the car.

'It's your last chance to go inside,' said Prue. 'Final look around.'

Alex watched her mother shake her head and then stare out the window in the opposite direction. The day had been beautiful and sunny, as if to show them that this part of the world was capable of producing such weather but usually chose not to.

'There they are,' said Alex.

The two men who had been sitting on the front step of the house clambered to their feet.

A hatchback sped up the street and pulled in behind Alex's car. The real estate agent stepped out of it, phone glued to her ear. Tayla emerged from the passenger side.

Alex glanced at her aunt.

'She knew you'd be here,' Prue reassured her, then added, 'Your grandfather will be rolling in his grave right now.'

'That,' said Alex, 'is exactly the point. You getting out?'

'No,' said Denny.

'I will,' said Prue.

'Hello,' called Paolo, one of the men, giving them a friendly wave. During an earlier inspection he had been very enthusiastic about having a large backyard for a veggie patch and chickens.

'Sorry we're late,' said Prue. 'Came the back way from Durrell and got stuck behind a tractor.'

Alex handed two sets of keys to Paolo.

'Are you all settled into your new place?' asked Dan, his partner.

'Everything is still in boxes, but we're getting there,' said Alex. 'I hope you haven't been waiting too long.'

'We've been sitting here working out our renovation plans,' said Paolo.

'We'll give the old lady a bit of care and attention to restore her former glory,' explained Dan.

Alex looked up the stairs to the front door. It had never been a proper home for Denny; hopefully it could become one for Paolo and Dan.

'You do whatever you like to it,' said Alex. 'Nothing can stay the same forever.'

'Tell me,' said Dan, 'it doesn't rain here every day, does it? Seriously, this is the first time I've seen the sun.'

Prue began a detailed description of Merritt's weather as Alex turned to Tayla. She had lost a lot of weight. Underneath the mask of make-up, she seemed brittle.

'How's the new job going?' Alex asked.

'I've decided to get my real estate licence,' said Tayla.

'That's great.'

'Mum says you've got a new job as well.'

'Durrell Community Legal Service,' answered Alex. 'Getting a regular pay cheque every fortnight will be a welcome change.'

Tayla gave a distant smile and then looked the other way. There was an awkward pause as Alex groped for something else to say, but fortunately Prue had turned her attention to them. 'Did Tayla tell you that her band is playing on Thursday night at the Sail? You and Denny should come along.'

'It was Silver's idea,' said Tayla.

The real estate agent click-clacked her way over to them, wearing an expensive smile and holding a cheap bottle of sparkling wine.

'Congratulations!' she said to Paolo and Dan. 'I hope you two know you got a real bargain.' She waggled her finger at the men. 'We could have got a higher offer at auction, but Alex was determined to sell to you. Now, come on, Tayla, or we'll be late for that house opening.'

The two of them headed back to their car, and it was only as Tayla held up her hand in farewell that Alex noticed her nails were painted a bright pink.

'Would you all like to come in and have a glass of this' – Paolo looked at the bottle's label and tried not to grimace – 'cheeky little number?' He worked in hospitality and had plans to open a restaurant in Merritt, while Dan, who did something in finance, was going to work remotely.

'Well, I won't say no,' said Prue. 'You can tell me all about these plans of yours. What about you, Alex?'

Alex glanced back at the car. 'Mum's a bit tired today. We might leave you to it.'

'Promise me you'll come back for a meal when the restaurant opens,' said Paolo.

'You can go there with Kiran,' Prue said enthusiastically. 'He told me you had dinner plans when I ran into him at the supermarket.'

Alex had talked to Kiran several times in the last few weeks about Denny's care and he had helped Alex to find a new doctor for her in Durrell. Slowly, she had managed to get over her embarrassment at ever thinking he could have anything to do with Robyn's death, and when he had asked her out again, she had accepted.

'Hard to keep things secret around here,' she said to her aunt.

'Depends on the secret,' Prue said, and in that moment she looked shattered, and Alex guessed she was thinking about Theo.

'How are you finding Durrell, Alex?' interrupted Dan. 'I've heard such interesting things about it from the locals.'

'Merritt has lost the footy grand final to Durrell four years running,' said Alex. 'I wouldn't believe everything they tell you.'

'Any time you want to come back for a visit, just knock,' said Paolo.

Alex promised she would, then returned to the car. 'Time to head home?' she asked Denny. Home was now a modern townhouse in a place neither had lived before. Alex was trying her best to be optimistic about the move. Denny hadn't complained as much as she had expected. Her mother was getting stronger, had put on a little weight and was at least eating regularly.

'Let's watch the sunset at Beacon,' Denny answered.

It was the first time she'd suggested an outing since the move. Alex thought about all the reasons why she could say no to this and then said yes instead.

The sand was still warm from the day's sun as the two women walked through the hills and hollows of the dunes to the sea. The light had a gauzy quality; almost like a mist. There were a few other walkers on the beach, some with dogs trotting beside them. Seagulls sat content on the shore like ducks on water, beaks as dark as tar. One hopped up and opened its wings to test the breeze but then thought better of it and nestled down again. Alex wandered along the water's edge, Denny content to walk beside her. There was no marching off today.

A single bird's feather had been stuck into the wet sand like a marker of some kind. Black and white it stood upright, jaunty like a boat's sail. It was the type of feather Alex could imagine Bella collected to use for her wings. She watched as it disappeared under the whitewash of the next wave and then reappeared as the tide went out. Alex had toyed with the idea of getting a tattoo of a feather as a way to remember the three dead women, some sort of permanent mark that she could choose for herself rather than the scars that had been inflicted, but in the end she had decided against it. The feather was their story, not hers.

'If you had to get a tattoo,' she asked her mother, 'what would it be?'

'Don't be ridiculous,' said Denny.

In the distance was the lighthouse, a silent witness to the world moving around it. It remained a brilliant white as the shadows slowly climbed across the beach, until suddenly a ray of the setting sun hit and for a moment it flickered gold, as though on fire, but then it dulled and faded, swallowed by the creeping darkness.

Other lights came on instead.

Around the rocks, Alex could just make out kayakers moving through the black water on their boats, little dots of LED bobbing up and down like hovering fireflies. As the boats came closer, she could hear snatches of their conversation on the breeze. She recognised Lou Buckley's laugh.

The wind picked up; it was getting colder. Time to head back to the car. Alex held out a hand, a hurry-up gesture that pre-empted her words, but to her surprise, Denny caught hold of it and gently squeezed her fingers. 'The tide is turning,' she said.

Alex breathed out as she waited. The world began to slow and it felt as if the receding waves were taking away what was terrible, leaving behind the hope of something kinder and more generous. Her mother stood there, fingers linked through hers, anchoring Alex to the moment. In time, it would be Denny who needed mooring to the world, and Alex knew she would be there, holding her hand. As the boats disappeared into the inky blackness, their comforting lights fading with them, stars appeared, scattered across the sky.

Acknowledgements

Even though what I write is fiction, some of the events I describe have a real-world counterpart. The exhibition referred to in this book was based on the National Archive's exhibition *Without Consent: Australia's past adoption practices*, which I visited at the National Wool Museum in Geelong. It was a deeply moving and thought-provoking experience and I commend the curators and applaud the bravery of the survivors who shared their stories. Thanks to my friend Leanne Hunter-Knight who encouraged me to go to it. My lighthouse and keeper's tree strongly resemble the equivalents on Maatsuyker Island, which I discovered via Paul Richardson and Amanda Walker's *Maatsuyker through our eyes – Caretaking on Tasmania's wild and remote Maatsuyker Island.* Whenever lockdown got too hard and the four walls were closing in, this was the book I picked up. Bella's black wings and environmental activism were inspired by

Anna Beltran and her sculptural performance piece, The Weld Angel, which was part of The Weld Valley Old Grown Forest blockade in Tasmania.

A pandemic does make writing an even more insular experience than usual, but I was so lucky to have experts be prepared to make time to answer my questions over the phone or via email. Dr Sarah Healy gave me advice about GPs and dementia patients and Melissa Lowe once again put my characters on the couch and gave wisdom and insight. I discussed sea kayaks with Wayde Margetts and retired Commissioner Sandra Nicholson talked to me about policing and rewards. Prue Walker won a Love Your Bookshop Day raffle and got a character named after her. She hoped for the villain, but writing is a strange business.

This book would not have been written without the support and advice of my agent, Clare Forster. This is a better book because of you Clare (and also a finished one!). Thanks also to Benjamin Paz and Curtis Brown. Tania Chandler and Tom Bromley cast expert eyes over my manuscript and their thoughts were invaluable. Luckily, my mother-in-law Glenys Harris's eagle eye and encyclopaedic knowledge of grammar is hereditary, and I thank her and my daughter Genevieve for critiquing. Good writing pals are hard to find but I got lucky with Ruth Cooper and Carolyn Tetaz.

This book found its home at Ultimo Press and I couldn't be more delighted. I feel honoured to be part of their first dozen books and excited as a reader about what else they are publishing. It has been one of my best writing experiences of my career to be edited by Alex Craig. Thanks also to Ali Lavau (Sword Girl lives!), James Kellow, Brigid Mullane, Pamela Dunn, Julia Kumschick,

Emily Cook, Katherine Rajwar and Simon Paterson (Bookhouse). The beautiful cover was designed by Josh Durham. It has been wonderful to work with you all.

Thanks to colleagues and customers alike at Fairfield Books who make going to work such a highlight of my week. The Bread Engineers, Marg Tregurtha, Jackie Quang and Yen Wong, who remotely helped to make weekends, lockdown or not, fun and tasty. It's impossible to be grumpy with friends like these and fresh bread in the house. Even when times were toughest, and 2020 was, Kerry Ruiz coped with it all with grace and kindness and I'm just thankful she's my friend and lives within my five kilometres. Thanks also to the Cliffords, big and small, who are just as funny on zoom as they are in real life. I can't think of a better bunch to play (and win) Lockdown Trivia with.

To Richard, Aidan, Genevieve and Evangeline who were my constant lockdown companions during writing this book. Thank you for everything. I love you.

Finally, to the city of Melbourne, which has been through so much in these last two years. There is no other place I would want to live.